Love Finds You™

IN

FollyBeach
SOUTH CAROLINA

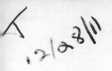

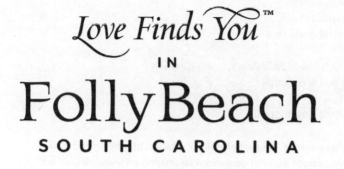

Love Finds You™

I N

Folly Beach

SOUTH CAROLINA

FIC
LOUGH
2011

LOREE LOUGH

summerside
PRESS™

Summerside Press™
Minneapolis 55438
summersidepress.com

Love Finds You in Folly Beach, South Carolina
© 2011 by Loree Lough

ISBN 978-1-60936-214-0

The town depicted in this book is a real place, but all characters are
fictional. Any resemblances to actual people or events are purely
coincidental.

Cover Design by Lookout Design | www.lookoutdesign.com

Interior design by Müllerhaus Publishing Group | www.mullerhaus.net

Back cover and interior photos of Folly Beach provided by Loree Lough.

*Summerside Press™ is an inspirational publisher offering fresh,
irresistible books to uplift the heart and engage the mind.*

Printed in USA.

Dedication

....

To Larry, whose steadfastness taught me what lasting love is all about. To my daughters and grandchildren, whose understanding makes it possible for me to "live my dream." To friends and relatives, for patiently enduring my never-ending chatter about Folly Beach and the characters who brought it to life. And most of all, to my Lord and Savior, for infusing me with the desire to deliver Your Word through the pages of Christ-inspired fiction.

Acknowledgments

....

My heartfelt gratitude goes out to all the wonderful people at the Folly Beach Chamber of Commerce, the Folly Beach Turtle Watch Program, and the Save the Light (Morris Island) organization for providing a slew of past-and-present information about your projects and your lovely town.

Thanks to Ann, who, despite caring for dozens of hungry patrons at The Crab Shack, graciously took the time to tell me about "all the nifty Folly places you just can't miss!"

And a great big thank-you to Jim Taylor, for pretending you didn't mind that all the big ones got away when I interrupted your peaceful fishing at Folly's fishing pier with nonstop questions about your hometown.

I pray that I've done y'all proud. And, God willing, the US Postal Service will help me put those copies of *Love Finds You in Folly Beach, South Carolina*, I promised into your oh-so-helpful hands!

If you, dear reader, would like to learn more about the
Save the Light and Turtle Watch programs,
visit www.savethelight.org and www.follyturtles.com.
I think you'll find the information fascinating and educational!

Folly Beach, South Carolina

JUST SOUTH OF HISTORIC CHARLESTON LIES THE BARRIER ISLAND Folly Beach, one of the East Coast's best surfing destinations. Whether vacationers crave a lively holiday spot or a haven from life's hassles, this stunning seaside town delivers.

Translated from old English, *folly* means "area of dense foliage," so it isn't surprising that it seemed the ideal location for harried ship captains to abandon cholera-infected passengers…who dubbed it "Coffin Island." In no time, this sandy slice of heaven healed and prospered and earned a new moniker: "The Edge of America."

Folly Beach legends boast of pirates and buccaneers, while history books list Civil War officers who plotted battle strategy on the island that eventually became a Union stronghold. Three hundred feet offshore stands the old Morris Island lighthouse, a defiant sentinel and ghostly reminder of the days when its beacon guided vessels into port. And did you know that, while vacationing in Folly Beach in 1934, Ira Gershwin wrote the opera *Porgy and Bess*? These days, any visitor can claim "writing fame" by adding a message to the hundreds layered onto the hull of "The Boat," washed ashore during Hurricane Hugo.

So grab your fishing poles and prepare to snag a big 'un from the Folly Beach Fishing Pier. Bring your camera and capture the dazzling dawn on film. If you're patient (and a little bit lucky), you might catch the infamous "green flash" glowing on the horizon at sunset. But even if you miss it, your time in Folly Beach will be dazzling and memorable!

Loree Lough

Chapter One
....

Holly steered the sporty convertible onto Center Street, where the houses glowed with summery pastel hues and vibrant awnings shaded outdoor cafés and sidewalk sales. Everything about the charming South Carolina town whispered "Welcome," from the soft hiss of waves that lapped the sand to the briny sea-scent of the air. With every puff of the balmy breeze, palmetto palms swayed in syncopated rhythm—like tall dancers on a stage of concrete and cobblestone. Gulls soared overhead, shrieking as they swooped in to grab a discarded french fry or cookie crumb.

A sense of belonging enveloped her, inspiring a quick and heartfelt prayer of thanks that she'd finally arrived. Folly Beach seemed like a perfect name for the town, considering all the foolishness she'd endured to get here. So much for her father's step-by-step directions and the loan of his GPS. If anyone back in Baltimore knew how far out of the way she'd driven—or how many times she'd been lost—Holly would never live it down.

At least the weather had cooperated.

Just outside of Richmond, where she'd stopped to top off the gas tank and get directions back onto the highway, she'd put down the convertible top. The sun on her face felt so wonderful that Holly almost forgot about the crazy detours.

Almost.

Yawning, she slowed for a traffic light. Tucking windblown curls behind her ears, she pulled down the visor mirror. "Rats," she told her reflection, "more freckles." As if she didn't already look more like a high-school kid than a nearly thirtysomething scientist...

Well, there wasn't a thing she could do about that now. The time for action had been at five thirty this morning, when she'd been so preoccupied with packing shoes to match every outfit that she'd completely forgotten to apply sunblock.

Stifling another yawn, she tapped the steering wheel in time with "The Beat Goes On." Hopefully the song's lively tempo would keep her awake until she settled into her room at Coastal Cottage Bed and Breakfast. For the past ten miles, she'd thought of little else but the home-squeezed lemonade and fresh-baked brownies pictured in the colorful brochure. And a hot shower sure would feel nice right about—

The blare of a horn startled her enough to produce a quiet yelp. With one hand over her hammering heart, she stared into the rear-view mirror.

"Light's green!" the driver bellowed, pointing up.

She started to say "Sorry," but he never gave her the chance. Instead, he sped by on her left, glowering. "Well, I never," she huffed, taking her foot off the brake. "Aren't *you* just the welcome-wagon poster boy?"

Instantly, guilt washed over her. For all she knew, the guy had a perfectly good excuse for behaving like an impatient boor. What if his wife was in labor? Maybe he was a doctor, rushing to perform emergency surgery—or a firefighter, on his way to help douse a three-alarm blaze. She said a little prayer for him and got on her way.

At the next corner, a white-haired man stepped off the curb, and Holly slowed to let him pass. He tipped his hat and mouthed "Thank you" as he walked in front of her car. *Now that's what I call Southern hospitality.* She nearly giggled out loud at her next thought: *Maybe if Mr. Baseball Cap loosened his hatband a notch or two, his mood would improve.*

Bless him, Lord, she prayed, *and fill him with the same peace that I'm feeling right now.*

"Amen," she whispered, as a familiar green-and-orange convenience store sign came into view. Magazines, snacks, and bottled water would help to pass the hours as she pored over her notes at the end of every day. And what better way to meet a few locals? Maybe they'd know something about the man who'd hired her to help write the chapter about sea turtles for his book about the Morris Island lighthouse.

One quick turn aligned her car with two big pickup trucks beside it. Then, hoisting her big faux-alligator purse onto one shoulder, she aimed for the double glass doors, where colorful, bigger-than-life photos of donuts, ice cream, and hot dogs made her mouth water. "Decision time, Hol," she whispered, stepping inside, "something to eat and then a nap, or the other way around?"

She got the answer to her question in the form of a smiling young mother, who led her ice cream–eating toddler from the store, oblivious to the strawberry-pink trail that led from the cashier's counter to the door.

* * * * *

Of all the days to get stuck behind a dizzy blond, why today, when his patience had all but reached its snapping point?

Stifling a groan, Parker drove toward Coastal Cottage and tried not to think about his hectic day. As he left the early-morning Save the Light meeting for his charter fishing boat, his first mate had called to say he'd picked up a stomach bug. Parker had made three calls to replace Joe, all with no success. He considered canceling the trip until he remembered that his client, Sam, enjoyed baiting his own hooks and setting his own lines. But even with Sam's help, he'd be forced to troll—a colossal waste of fuel and time—and rarely as successful as dropping anchor when his sonar screen told him they'd found a hot spot. Then, to further complicate things, Kate Sullivan's whining thoroughly tested his "customer is always right" principle:

The motor's vapors were "stinky" and the engine itself was too noisy. The wind mussed her blond hair—but when the wind stopped, she whimpered that the heat and humidity were sure to smother her. In response to her complaint that the deck was too hot for bare feet, Parker suggested shoes, inviting a scowl rivaled only by the stuffed barracuda in the window at Temple's Taxidermy.

"If you don't quit acting like a two-year-old," Sam had scolded, "I'm gonna toss you overboard."

For a minute there, it looked like Kate's moping might just succeed in pulling an apology from her husband. Instead, Sam provided the only enjoyable moment of Parker's day by saying, "On second thought, that seems like cruel and unusual punishment... for the fish."

Chuckling at the memory, Parker tugged at the bill of the Orioles cap that had belonged to a fallen comrade who'd been born and bred in Baltimore. *Poor Sam,* he thought—because, by now, Kate had probably doled out some form of pouty payback for her long-suffering husband's wisecrack. If Parker lived to be a hundred, he'd never understand why every man he knew tried so hard to please their wives and girlfriends. Every last one of them was his age or older, so why hadn't they figured out that it was an exercise in futility? He wanted a home and children as much as the next guy, but to have them, he'd first need a wife. The irony might have been comical if he hadn't just spent four grueling hours with Kate Sullivan.

"Better get hold of yourself, Brant," he grumbled. He would arrive at his mother's cottage any second, and the last thing he wanted was for his rotten mood to foul up her evening too. When it got a little tough to balance the demands of his charter-boat business, a book deadline, and helping out while his mom recuperated from surgery, he just reminded himself that for every night of sleep he'd lost these past weeks, Maude had devoted a year of her life to him.

The list of things that needed his attention at the cottage his mom had shared with her grandparents was as long as his anchor. He needed to get up onto the roof and straighten a crooked lightning rod, for one thing, and while he was up there, he might as well replace those slate shingles that had cracked during the last storm. The shutters on the turret needed a fresh coat of paint, and so did the turret itself. And when he got it all done, there were a dozen similar chores waiting for him at his own house, just up the road.

As he pulled into the driveway of Maude's cottage, the old quote "Man plans, and God laughs" came to mind, inspiring a gruff chuckle. Now if Parker could depict *that* concept on canvas, maybe he'd finally sell another painting!

He threw the gearshift into PARK. A glance at the cloudless blue sky was enough to encourage the decision to leave the windows down; it wouldn't take long to change Maude's bandages, fix her something to eat, and make sure her medications and a thermos of lemonade were within easy reach.

With any luck, it would still be light enough to check the progress of his vegetable garden and then catch the Orioles game when he got home. Parker stooped to pluck a weed from between two flagstones in the walk. No way he'd have the time or the freedom for either with a wife and kids. *An uncomplicated life is a happy life,* he thought, climbing the porch steps. And maybe if he said it often enough, he'd come to believe that someday.

Without warning, the blond at the traffic light popped into his mind, the one who'd been so busy fussing with her hair and earrings that she hadn't even noticed the light change from red to green. Though younger and cuter than Sam's wife—way cuter, from the little he'd seen of her—it seemed pretty clear that, like Kate, she made a habit of putting her own needs ahead of others'. Parker couldn't say which made him wince, the sudden high-pitched squeal of the screen door or the notion that self-centeredness must be a "blond thing."

"That you, son?"

"Yeah, Ma." He hung his baseball cap on a hook behind the front door and made a mental note to oil those hinges first thing tomorrow. He found his mother at the tile-topped table, both feet propped on the cushion of a nearby chair. A dewy glass of iced tea sat beside an issue of *Greatest Gardens* magazine.

"Henry stopped by earlier," she said, pointing to the towel-covered pies on the counter.

Why does she persist in calling him that, Parker wondered, *when the man has said time and again that he prefers "Hank"?*

"He said his daughter baked too many pies for him to eat alone, so he brought those over for us. Even popped them into the oven so they'd be nice and warm when you got home."

Home.

The word only served to remind him how little like home his house felt. Parker hid a scowl and forced his attention to the desserts. He'd known Hank's daughter almost as long as he'd known the retired FBI agent himself. Nice enough girl, but even on her best day, she couldn't have worked her way through a recipe for buttered toast without setting off the smoke alarm. How like Hank to pick up the sweet treats on his way over and give her the credit.

"They almost look good enough to eat."

"Help yourself, and help me to a slice while you're at it!"

Parker stepped up to the counter and slid two dessert plates from the cupboard. "Apple or cherry?"

"Surprise me."

Maude had never made a secret of the fact that cherry was her favorite, and although Parker preferred apple, he grabbed a knife from the drainboard and sliced the pie with the big *C* carved into its crust.

Too bad he couldn't express gratitude for the pies—for all the considerate things Hank did for Maude every day. For everything he'd done for Parker too, like filling in as first mate and helping repair that leak in the porch roof. Would've made a great fill-in father too, if not for Maude's stubborn refusal to remarry.

By the ripe old age of ten, Parker had figured out that admitting he liked her latest beau was a surefire guarantee that she'd kick them to the curb with no explanation and no invitation to return. The only way to keep the ones he liked, at least for a little while, was to pretend that he *didn't* like them.

"Henry said that if you leave a can of oil where he can find it, he'll fix that squeak in the front screen door when he stops by tomorrow."

"What a gem."

If Maude had heard the sarcasm in his voice now, it didn't show. They were the very words *she'd* used more than a decade ago—the final time he'd asked about his father. "I couldn't compete with the exciting life of an Air Force test pilot," she'd said, "and neither could you." A sucker punch would have hurt less, he'd thought, and he decided then and there never to expose himself to that kind of pain again. Someday he'd find out, all on his own, if his father had left by choice or if Maude had sent him packing before the fighter jet he'd been testing exploded over the Atlantic. Not that it mattered. Gone was gone. What good would wondering and whining do? Still, if God ever saw fit to bless Parker with a son, no one—not even the child's mother—had better try and keep him from—

"Help yourself to some iced tea, son. Henry made it fresh just a little while ago."

He topped off her glass then poured some for himself.

"Mmm, this pie is delicious, isn't it?"

It was tasty enough—for store-bought. But even if Hank had rolled the crust and baked it himself, Parker wouldn't have admitted it. The man had been a Coastal Cottage fixture for the past six years. More important than that, he'd become a trusted friend. At this stage of his life—and Hank's—it wasn't likely that Maude's feelings would change the friendship that had developed between them, but why risk it?

"...and Neapolitan ice cream too," Maude was saying, "because Henry knows you like it on warm pie."

Good old Hank, always thinking of others. But memory of the two blonds who'd rained on his day made it easy to put a hard edge on his voice. "God bless Henry Donovan."

She clucked her tongue and then said, "He offered to change my bandages too."

"Yep, he's a real prince, all right."

He watched her take a long, slow sip of tea. Odd how uncomfortable she seemed to be with his attitude, especially considering that she was part of the reason for it.

"Henry made me a roast beef sandwich and chicken noodle soup for lunch."

Parker sat across from her, waiting for her to add that Hank had baked the roast and cooked the soup from scratch. He was mildly surprised when, instead, she announced that a guest would be checking in tonight.

"What?" he said around a bite of pie. "But didn't you say this morning that every room was booked?"

"I did, and we are. Dr. Leonard was the last person to reserve a room."

"Dr. Leonard?"

She nodded.

"Not Dr. *Hollace* Leonard?"

"Yes." She frowned slightly. "Why?"

In her last e-mail, the good doctor hadn't said a word about renting a room at Coastal Cottage. Not that she owed Parker any explanations. She'd promised to pay her own way while in Folly Beach if he'd give her a tour of nearby Charleston. Not his favorite way to spend a day, but a penny saved and all that.

"I get it," Maude said. "You must have read the guest registry. That's how you know her name."

Since his mother's surgery, he *had* been checking the book daily, to make sure that every room was in tip-top shape before the guests checked in. But with his early-morning meeting and the Sullivans' excursion—and the mate's cancellation—he hadn't had time today. "Dr. Leonard is the woman who's coming to town to help me with the book, remember?"

"Oh, yes. Yes, of course."

She was wearing that "I know something you don't know" expression, but Parker wasn't in the mood to play "Guess What?" He speared a cherry and popped it into his mouth.

"She told me that, God willing, she'd arrive by three. You know, to give herself plenty of time to settle in and rest up."

Makes sense, he thought, *given her age.* Dr. Leonard had racked up a long list of credentials in her lifetime. Apparently she wasn't married, based on the fact that she could pick up and spend the entire summer in Folly Beach all by herself. A grandmotherly widow, perhaps. Hopefully one with both orthopedic shoes planted solidly on terra firma. He couldn't have chosen a better partner to get his notes into publishable shape if he'd ordered her from a catalog.

Maude glanced at the clock above the door. "She's late."

Only by three hours, Parker thought as his wristwatch beeped. "What do you bet that our dear Dr. Leonard is *blond.*" *Or used to be, before her hair turned gray.*

Chuckling, Maude waved his comment away. Just as well, because he didn't much feel like reliving the crazy day that included Kate Sullivan and the inattentive driver of the little red convertible.

"I'm putting her in the Captain's room."

Maude's favorite movie was *The Ghost and Mrs. Muir,* and the only thing stopping her from calling the B&B Gull Cottage was the five-foot wooden medallion her grandfather had carved and hung beneath the scrolled eaves. She'd done the next best thing, though, by naming every guest room after its characters. Despite the fact that the "Captain Dan" suite cost twice as much to rent as the other rooms, it had always been a guest favorite. In addition to the best view of the back gardens and the beach, the space included a kitchenette, a bright and airy bathroom, and French doors leading to a covered balcony. Under the right conditions, the good doctor might even catch a glimpse of the loggerheads from up there.

"Good choice," he said, slicing into the apple pie. He'd naturally assumed that Dr. Leonard would rent a room at one of the name-brand hotels farther up the beach. Without even trying hard, Parker could name a half-dozen perks of having his writing partner so near.

Partner. If he had any writing talent at all, Parker wouldn't have needed the help of someone like Dr. Leonard. Oh, he'd played around with a blog that described his charter services and the turtles and lighthouse projects, and though "Sea Maverick" had earned a respectable following, it had only inspired a couple hundred comments by the time a New York editor contacted him. Write a book about Folly Beach, she'd said, and the company would split the profits between his two pet projects. Hank had calmed his "What have I done to myself?" fears by suggesting that he hire a pro to help with the writing. An Internet search led Parker to Dr. Hollace Leonard, whose fee was more than reasonable, despite her proviso that he show her around Charleston.

He shoved their pie plates and silverware into the dishwasher. "Has Dr. Leonard called, at least, to explain *why* she's so late?"

As if on cue the phone rang, startling Maude so badly that she nearly upended her ice-filled glass. "Goodness, I need to lower the volume on that ringer!"

He picked up the magazine she'd dropped. "Can't do that, because then you'd never hear it from the parlor or the—" He silenced the second ring by grabbing the receiver. "Coastal Cottage..."

"Um, hello? I'm, ah, my name is Dr. Leonard, and I, um..."

She sure didn't *sound* like any grandma he'd ever met.

"...I'm afraid I got a little lost. Well, actually, *very* lost, to be truthful. Three times." Her voice brightened a degree when she added, "But I'm here in Folly Beach, finally, thank the good Lord, at a convenience store on Center Street."

She sounded surprisingly upbeat for a woman her age, especially after having driven all the way from Baltimore. It was looking more and more like he'd made the right decision, hiring her. "Just hang a left out of the parking lot," he told her, "then make the next left and follow the road to the last house on the block. There's a sign out front. You can't miss it. I'll wait for you on the porch so I can help you with your bags."

"Oh, wow, you're the best," she all but sang. "See you soon!"

Parker hung up and headed for the door. "Soon as we get her settled in," he told his mom, "I'll change your bandages."

"You're a good son."

"If I am, it's because you're the best mom on bandaged feet." Smiling, he grabbed his cap and headed outside, where he paced the length of the porch and wondered if God counted half truths as full-blown lies. But that wasn't fair, and he knew it. Maude had done her best, given the circumstances, scrimping and saving to buy the cottage from her grandparents and then putting in all sorts of odd hours so she'd never miss one of his football or baseball games. What sort of self-centered jerk had he become, that her hard work and sacrifices were still shadowed by his belief that she'd driven his father away?

A Swainson's hawk shrieked overhead, and Parker stopped pacing long enough to follow its flight path. As it disappeared into a thicket, Parker couldn't help but pity the rabbit or chipmunk that had lured the stunning bird from its roost. Sometimes he envied anything with wings—how incredible would it be to float up there, above it all?

Shrugging, Parker leaned on a support post as a blue sedan slowed and made a U-turn. Thirty minutes later, a white box truck teetered and ground its gears in the driveway before aiming its big, square nose in the opposite direction. His patience frayed, Parker stomped inside. "Of all the rude, inconsiderate—" Did Dr. Leonard think her time was worth more than his simply because she had a string of fancy initials behind her name? If so, it was going to be a long, hard summer. He grabbed the shoe box of bandages and ointments that his mother kept in the powder-room linen closet and then took a moment to gather his self-control.

"Ready for your cleanup?" he asked, scrubbing his hands before kneeling at her feet. Maude's grateful smile warmed his heart, and when she pressed a palm to his cheek, he turned his face and gently kissed it.

"I take it Dr. Leonard didn't show up?"

"No," he all but growled. Gentling his voice, Parker added, "No sense in making you wait for the self-centered old bat."

"Now, now. Maybe she has a good excuse for being late."

"And maybe you're too sweet and forgiving for your own good."

But that was hardly a fair statement, and he knew it. A wide gullible streak was one of her more lovable flaws, and since he'd inherited most of her flaws, how could he help but forgive them?

Chapter Two

....

If it wouldn't break her father's heart, Holly might just change her last name to Murphy, because then, at least, she could blame Murphy's Law when things like this happened.

Already three hours late, she certainly hadn't needed a flat in the convenience-store parking lot. Not that changing a tire scared her, with the numerous opportunities her bad luck had provided. Like the day she'd backed over a soda bottle, and the afternoon she'd rammed a curb to avoid hitting a squirrel. And what about the time a belt buckle had become wedged in the treads, when her dad had stood, hands in his pockets and muttering, as he tried to figure out how she'd managed such a feat.

No, the prospect of getting the old tire off and the spare in its place didn't faze her. The impression she'd make on her boss-for-the-summer, showing up with grease-stained hands *and* three and a half hours late? *That* fazed her, big-time! Surely God had a lesson in mind in all this, but at the moment, Holly had no idea what it might be.

Wiping grimy palms on a towel from the car's trunk, she remembered a recent sermon: "Patience is earned through testing, by trial and tribulation," Pastor Clemens had teased the congregants, "so it makes more sense to pray for endurance!" *Okay, Lord, so help me endure the rest of this day,* she prayed, grinning as she added, *without another awkward event!*

The COASTAL COTTAGE sign came into view, and she read it as an answered prayer. She scanned the porch, looking for the man she'd talked with on the phone. He wasn't there to help with her bags, but that didn't surprise Holly. Nearly an hour had passed since he'd made the generous offer. Surely he had better and more important ways to spend his time than waiting for her.

She got out of the car slowly, taking in the cottage and its grounds. The fragrances from the red and yellow larkspur and the dancing spikes of yucca plants sailed to her on the late May breeze. Pale yellow-green with white trim, the tidy house boasted a two-story turret and a wide, covered front porch. She could almost picture herself in one of the big white rockers on the second-floor balcony, sipping her morning coffee and watching the birds soar overhead. Would the cottage have a matching porch out back, with a view of the ocean too?

"Careful, Hol," she warned, "or you'll end up changing your address. Again."

After selling her Ocean City condo to move back to her hometown, she'd promised her mom she'd stay put for a while. Packing for her temporary assignment in South Carolina made move number six in a span of three years. So she couldn't allow herself to fall in love with Folly Beach, because that would mean yet another move, this time to a house or apartment, and Holly didn't think her mom's pink-and-blue address book could survive another big *X* across Holly's contact information!

Holding her breath, she climbed the steps and rapped on the wooden screen door. Maybe this place and everything about it only *seemed* like paradise. That sure would make it easier to go home in August.

When no one answered, she opened the door and cringed when it creaked. "Hello? Hellooo…"

In the hushed foyer, the blades of a ceiling fan whirled slowly overhead, and above the half-moon mahogany table pressed against sea-green wallpaper, a baseball cap hung from a row of matching pegs. Down the hall, the glow of a bright yellow kitchen beckoned, and Holly followed the braided rug.

"This shouldn't take long," said a hearty, masculine voice.

"I'm in no hurry," a woman replied. "It isn't as if I'm going anywhere in this condition."

The condition, Holly noticed as she stepped into the arched doorway, was two white-bandaged feet, now propped upon the lap of a broad-shouldered man who knelt in front of her chair. As Holly opened her mouth to say hello, the woman shook her head and pressed a finger to her lips. Then, winking, she said, "Well, I'm sure Dr. Leonard will be here soon."

His back was still to Holly when he gently rested the woman's heels on the cushion of a nearby chair then stood to gather rolls of gauze and white tape. She noted that he had to duck to keep from bumping his head on the ceiling fan's light fixture.

Stuffing the supplies into a black shoe box, he said, "Lucky for her, you taught me to respect the elderly, or she'd get a piece of my mind when she gets here."

Holly met the woman's eyes then pointed to herself and mouthed, "Elderly? Who, *me*?"

Grinning, the woman nodded.

"Better watch out," Holly said, leaving the doorway. "Giving away pieces of your mind can be costly."

Facing her, his dark eyes flashed as recognition dawned. And then she recognized him as Mr. Baseball Cap.

"*You!*" they said in unison.

The other woman looked from the handsome young man to Holly and back again. "You two have met?"

"Not exactly," they said together.

"Well, seems to me you're pretty like-minded…for strangers."

For the next unbearable moment, the only sound in the room was the ticking tail of the black cat clock above the sink. "My apologies for arriving so late," Holly said, breaking the silence. "I hope it didn't inconvenience you in any way."

"Not at all," the woman said. "Sorry to hear you got lost, though. I hate being lost."

"Oh, this was actually a really good trip. I only got lost three times." She laughed and, extending a hand, added, "Hollace Leonard, but I hope you'll call me Holly."

"I'm Maude," she said, shaking Holly's hand, "and this is my son, Parker."

He held out his hand, and as she shook it, Holly said, "Oh, brother. Talk about your weird coincidences, huh?"

A crooked smile brightened his handsome face. "Pleased to meet you too."

If this wasn't Murphy's Law at work—again—she didn't know what was.

This time Maude broke the silence. "Parker, would you mind showing the doctor to her room?"

He blinked several times before releasing her hand and then fixing his brown-eyed stare on the box of first-aid supplies still tucked under his arm.

"I can do it myself. There's no need to go to all that bother," Holly said. "I've already inconvenienced you more than enough. If you'll just point me in the right direction, I'm sure I can find—"

"It's no bother," he interrupted. "Give me a sec to put this stuff away, and I'll meet you out front." Before Holly could thank him, he disappeared around the corner and then poked his head back into the room. "You won't get lost, will you?"

Recalling the "more flies with honey" adage, she chose to ignore his sarcasm. She had only herself to blame for it, after all.

"Don't worry," Maude said once he was out of earshot, "he doesn't always behave like a big ol' grizzly."

"That's nice to know. But just to be safe, I'd better get moving." Grinning, Holly held out her right arm and showed Maude the long, thin scar that ran from wrist to elbow. "Because I learned the hard way, while volunteering at the zoo, that even cute little cubs can draw blood...."

* * * * *

Great, Parker thought, shoving the shoe box onto its shelf, *just great.* A long, hot summer working side by side with a self-interested, hare-brained woman. He wondered how anyone that silly had earned a college degree, let alone a doctorate. Maybe her dad had alumni connections...or her mom's relatives had donated big bucks to build a wing at her alma mater.

And maybe he wasn't being fair. She *had* sounded sincere, apologizing for her late arrival and any trouble it might have caused. And those articles she'd written had been insightful and informative without being the least bit highfalutin. It wouldn't kill him to give her the benefit of the doubt, because even he'd sat daydreaming behind the wheel a time or two. Distracted enough not to notice a red light turn green—for that long? Not that he could recall, but then, the doctor *was* blond.

Speaking of which, he'd never seen hair of that particular shade before. It wasn't quite goldenrod, certainly not cadmium.... The color of her too-big-for-her-face eyes wasn't easily described, either. He'd added bluebells and cornflowers to a few of his landscapes, but neither cerulean nor phthalo described her eyes. He had a feeling this would become one of those ridiculous and annoying things that would bug him until he got home, where he could check his assortment of acrylics and watercolors. And what about those Bambi-like eyelashes of hers? Were they the glue-on kind, or—

Get a grip, he warned. This was exactly the way things had started with Stephanie. He'd be better off finding the nearest lemming community and following them to the closest cliff than going through *that* again.

On his way outside, Parker dropped fresh ice cubes into Maude's glass. "Soon as I get Little Miss Holly Folly settled in, I'll help you into the parlor and set you up with a movie and some snacks."

"Holly Folly?" Maude laughed. "Don't let *her* hear you call her that. I can rent the 'Captain Dan' suite to the next tourist who needs a room, but if you lose your writing partner, you're in big trouble."

Good point, he thought—but there was no way he intended to admit it out loud.

"Go easy on her, sweetie. Anybody can have a bad day."

Another good point, but based on what he knew about the good doctor, he figured she'd survived more than her fair share of bad days. Ill-timed luck, he wondered, or the product of her own clumsiness?

He got his answer the minute his deck shoes hit the porch floor, for there sat Holly in the middle of a huge, foot-deep muddy puddle in the front yard. Yesterday's rain had filled the rut carved into the lawn by a utility truck last week. One glance at the exasperated expression on her gorgeous face made him wish he'd found the time to fill in the hole.

He held out a hand. "Anything hurt?"

"Only my pride," she said as he wrapped his fingers around hers.

How had she managed to *find* the puddle, let alone fall into it, Parker wondered, with her car all the way on the other side of the yard? When he tried to gauge the distance, he noticed the little spare where her right rear tire should have been. "How long have you been driving around on *that*?"

Wiping her palms on her skirt, she followed his pointer finger. "Oh. That." She shot him a sheepish grin. "Not long, thankfully. I was backing out of the parking lot at the convenience store. To head over here. And, well…" She shrugged. "Y'know."

No, he didn't know. Partly because he was too busy watching the muck squish between her pink-painted toes as muddy water dripped from the ruffled hem of her gauzy, now-muddy, white skirt.

"I sure hope your mom has one of those nifty beach showers,

'cause I'd sure hate to track this mess all over her spick-and-span house. I'd tidy up after myself, of course, if I did make a mess, but what if a prospective guest came in while I was fetching the cleaning supplies? Imagine the first impression they'd get!"

"Yeah," he said, thinking that maybe instead of *Holly Folly*, he ought to call her *Chip*. Or *Dale*. Because Parker had never met anyone who did a better impression of the chattering cartoon rodents. His gaze traveled from the flowered flip-flops to her damp, curly hair. He jerked a thumb over his shoulder. "The, ah, the shower's out back."

"Excellent! Just let me grab a few things from my suitcase," she said, backpedaling toward her car, "so I can change out of this mess and into something presentable once I've washed off your mom's front yard." Holly blinked up at him and smiled. "And then maybe we can start over. So I can prove to you that I'm really not always so...you know."

A day like this would've instigated a full-fledged hissy fit from any other woman he'd known. At the very least, it would've brought them to tears. He walked beside her, hands out and nodding, ready to catch her in case she tripped over something, walking backward that way. There weren't any more puddles for her to fall into, but he wouldn't put it past her to find a clump of grass or a tree root and maybe twist an ankle.

Thankfully, she was still upright and in one piece when she popped the trunk. With her pinkies in the air, she used muddied thumbs and forefingers to unzip her suitcase. "Could I impose upon you to grab an outfit for me?" She showed him both still-grimy hands. "Please?"

The last thing Parker wanted was to paw through that tidy, multi-colored stack of feminine clothing, but how could he say no, with her standing there looking so helpless and…and sweet?

"I packed all the blouses and shirts on the right side of the suit-case, and I put the matching skirts and pants on the left. So how about if I point and tell you what to grab?"

It took a couple of tries, but in no time, Parker found himself draping a navy-and-white striped shirt atop cropped red pants over one forearm as a pair of white sandals dangled from his fingertips. "Give me your keys," he said, extending his free hand, "and while you're hosing off, I'll take your bags upstairs. Your room is at the end of the hall, first door on your right."

While she searched for the keys in her seemingly bottomless purse, he added, "Mom's in no condition to show you around, so whenever you're ready, I'll give you the nickel tour of the place. Oh. She couldn't get to the store, either, so she put me in charge of buying things for the bathrooms. Shampoo, conditioner, soap, candles…" He groaned inwardly, remembering what a pain it had been—and how long it had taken—to decide among all the brands and scents on the drugstore shelf. "Not in my usual job description, so if I've forgotten anything, just holler."

Holly closed her purse and looked up at him. "Thanks, Parker."

Teachers, neighbors, ex-girlfriends…how many times had he heard a woman say his name? Hundreds? Thousands? So why, he wondered, did hearing *Holly* say it make his ears feel hot and his heart beat double time? The reaction stunned him, and he stood taller and cleared his throat to hide it. *What are you, fourteen again?*

She dropped the keys into his hand. "I sure hope you're not one of those guys who judges people by first impressions, because if you are, I'm in biiig trouble!"

He'd been hurt and humiliated three times by ex-girlfriends, so if anything, the exact opposite was true. But rather than admit, Parker said, "While you're settling in, I'll see about patching your tire."

Holly gasped then groaned and hid her face behind her hands.

That was a weird reaction to his offer. "What's wrong?"

"The tire, that's what." She smacked herself in the forehead. "It's in the parking lot. Down at the convenience store. Right beside my tire iron. And the towel I keep in the trunk for cleaning up after..." Eyes shut tight, she tilted her face to the sky. "Arrggh! I'm such a *ditz*!"

Cute *and* self-deprecating? "Aw, don't be so hard on yourself. After getting lost as many times as you did today, something like that could've happened to anybody." It wasn't like him to fib, not even to spare a person's feelings. But there wasn't time to puzzle out why he chose to do so now, especially not with her standing there looking like a cross between a lost puppy and a deer in the headlights. "I'll toss your bags upstairs and ride on up to the store." Wasn't like him to repeat himself, either. "Folly's an honest town, so I'd stake my reputation on your stuff being right where you left it." Parker wished she'd quit gawking up at him with those beautiful blue eyes, because if she kept it up, he was bound to say something *really* stupid. "I, ah, I've got some tire patches over at my place. If they're not the right size, I'll get some at Casey's Garage."

She took a step closer and laid a warm hand on his forearm, putting herself close enough to kiss.

Kiss? He'd known her all of fifteen minutes. Where had *that* crazy notion come from?

"Be sure to keep the receipt," she said, giving his arm a gentle squeeze, "so I can reimburse you."

Parker nodded, feeling like one of those back-of-the-car doggies. Her sweet, grateful gaze would melt him for sure if he didn't get a move-on. *Right now.*

"Let's follow this flagstone walkway here," he said, pointing. *Safer than the lawn, where she could very well find something to stumble over.* "It'll lead straight to the outdoor shower. There should be soap and shampoo in there, and a towel…" The second he realized she had to half run to keep up with his long strides, Parker slowed his pace. And *that's* when he noticed that the top of her curly-haired head barely reached his bicep.

He jerked open the shower door. "Let me check it for spiders," he said, stepping inside. She didn't impress him as the type who'd get all squeally at the sight of a bug. Clumsy as she was, maybe he ought to be more concerned for the welfare of the critters. Grinning, he gave the all-clear sign. "Give 'er a few minutes to warm up. Takes a while for the hot water to make it this far from the basement water heater."

"Cool showers are better for human skin, anyway."

He handed her the outfit she'd chosen. As a former soldier, he'd always been partial to the Old Glory color scheme. The picture of her, all cleaned up and wearing it, made his mouth go dry. "I put a shelf in there," he said, swallowing, "and hooks too, for your towel and the stuff you're wearing and…" She could figure all that out on her own, if he'd just stop talking and let her get started.

"Thanks," she said.

And then she winked, making Parker hope that his tan from hours of hard work under the Atlantic sun was deep enough to hide yet another blush. "So, okay, then," he said, walking backward now himself, "while you're in there, I'll stow your bags." He jangled her keys. "Upstairs. In your room. Top of the stairs. First—"

"—first door on the right, end of the hall."

"Right." Parker jogged back down the sidewalk. "And for the luvva Pete," he said over one shoulder, "be careful, will ya? If you fall in there, no one will hear you, and it could be ten, fifteen minutes before I get back."

He hadn't meant it as a slur, but the slanted grin and disappointed glint in her eyes told Parker that's exactly how she'd heard it. And unless he was mistaken, she'd heard it before. Plenty of times. In the few minutes since they'd met, he'd felt confused, amused, guilty, and now surprised. Because it took all the strength he could muster to tamp down his desire to protect her from herself forever.

Chapter Three

....

On Holly's first night at Coastal Cottage, she felt like a movie star vacationing at a private luxury resort. Following a light evening snack of cucumber sandwiches, cherry pie, and mint tea, she retired to her suite to enjoy the sea view from the balcony. Leaning back in a comfy Adirondack chair, bare feet propped on a matching footstool, Holly inhaled the perfume of the rose hedge surrounding the flag-stone terrace below. How did her hosts expect her to concentrate on the leather bound volume of *A Tale of Two Cities* she'd found on the well-stocked bookshelf in their parlor with all this to distract her?

Before she knew it, darkness settled around the cottage, and Holly headed inside for a relaxing soak in the claw-foot tub. She'd left the French doors ajar so the sound of the waves could entertain her as mounds of rainbow-sparkling bubbles tickled her chin. When at last she snuggled into the big canopied bed, she luxuriated among eiderdown pillows, Egyptian cotton sheets—hand embroidered by Maude's grandmother—and colorful quilts.

Maude had thought of everything to make her guest feel welcome and right at home, from the scented candles on the dresser to an old-fashioned double-belled alarm clock on the nightstand. As she snuggled in, Holly pictured Parker—her boss and partner for the next three months—and wondered what event from his past had made a man his age seem so stodgy and serious.

Well, she thought, burrowing deeper into the pillows, *maybe by the time my work here is complete, I'll have the answers to those questions...and hundreds of others that are bound to crop up as the summer slides by.*

When the clock clanged at five thirty, Holly at up, stretching and yawning, and remembered that twice last night, her dreams had taken her to those warm moments out on the front lawn, alone with Parker. She'd never gone for the stereotypically tall, dark, and handsome type, but, she supposed, there was a first time for everything. Besides, after losing her precious Jimmy, and then the humiliating breakup with Ethan, she'd sworn off men forever. If Parker's finer qualities were more than purely physical, what did it matter?

"We'll make better use of our time in Charleston," he'd told her last night, "if we leave here by seven." And then he'd donned the orange-billed baseball cap—a larger version of the one she'd tucked into her suitcase—and left her alone in Maude's parlor to contemplate the weird blend of anticipation and loneliness swirling inside her. Maybe later she'd ask him why a deep-fried Southern boy seemed to be a die-hard Baltimore fan.

For the time being she focused on the question at hand. "But Maude's brochure says that breakfast is served between seven and nine." If she had it to do over, Holly would have zipped her lip instead of adding, "How on earth will your mom get a full meal on the table—for eight guests—in her condition?"

The moon had slid behind the clouds, so she couldn't see him or his truck, which was parked near the end of Maude's drive. His voice slid through the dark, though, and eased into her ears like vel-vet. "Don't you worry your pretty little head about it," he'd drawled, "I've got it covered."

She'd taken him at his word, and although the first night in a strange bed usually found her tossing and turning, Holly had slept soundly. Feeling rested and refreshed, she all but bounced down the stairs and followed the scent of fresh-brewed coffee straight into the kitchen. The clatter of stoneware lured her into the dining room, where she found Parker neatly positioning hefty ironstone place settings on crisp white tablecloths.

"You're up early," he said without looking up.

It was six fifteen, if the clock on the white-marble mantel was correct. She watched him stuff an accordion-folded napkin into a juice glass. "Well, you said you wanted to hit the road by seven, and, well, I guess I'm a bit overeager to get started here in Folly Beach." Stepping up to the table, she added, "And...and I thought maybe Maude could use some help." She glanced around. "Where is she, anyway?"

"Maude," he echoed, one brow high on his forehead, "is sleeping in." He jabbed a thumb into his chest. "Doctor's orders."

She couldn't be sure, but Holly thought maybe he'd grinned. Just a little bit. She spied a row of thick mugs stacked pyramid-style on the sideboard across the way. Hanging two from each forefinger, she carried them from table to table, placing one beside each plate. He was watching her—closely. *He probably thinks you're going to drop them and make a mess all over the carpet.* And why wouldn't he, after the way she'd behaved yesterday?

"Will her friend Henry stay with her while we're in Charleston today?"

"Nah." Parker shook his head. "And Henry prefers *Hank*, by the way. He works weekdays. Desk clerk at—"

"Really? Wow. Your mom showed me a picture of the two of them. Just goes to show you, I guess."

"Show you what?"

"That you can't judge a book by its cover. I would've guessed that when he retired from the FBI, he really *retired*."

Shrugging, Parker said, "If we're not back by five, he'll stop by to relieve Maude's cousin." He chuckled. "Knowing Hank, he'll stop by anyway."

"Goodness. All that schedule rearranging, just so you can give me a tour of Charleston?" Holly sighed. "That's just as silly as silly can be."

"Silly?"

And there it was again, the frown that etched the number eleven between his eyebrows.

"It's just, well, we have all summer to see the city. We don't have to go today."

"The longer we wait, the hotter it'll get. And the more tourists we'll have to deal with. To tell you the truth, I'd just as soon get it over with."

Almost immediately, he winced. Did he regret the words—or just his curt delivery? Holly glanced at the mantel clock. "So, you're serving breakfast, then?"

"Once I set up the buffet, I'll roll Maude's wheelchair in here, so she can do the hostess thing while her cousin does the rest." He got onto all fours to plug in the coffee urn. "Opal has worked here part-time since her husband died, so she knows the routine almost as well as Maude does."

"Oh my. A widow? I'm so sorry."

"Don't be. Amos was a bum. A drunken skunk. Cheated on Opal every chance he got." He slammed a salt-and-pepper shaker onto the center of the table with enough force to rattle the flatware. "She's better off without him."

He faced the wall to arrange sweet rolls on a paper doily–lined tray. And a good thing, too. "Every thought in your head," her mom loved to say, "is written all over your face." Holly didn't think she wanted Parker reading her mind just then, because she might have to tell him about who *she* was better off without, and…

And she'd rather not dwell on that episode from her past, let alone talk about it. "So, what can I do next?"

"You've already done enough," he said, sliding each mug she'd set out an inch to the right. "Guests don't work at Coastal Cot—"

"I'll be here all summer, so I'm not a guest in the traditional sense of the word." She paused and, smiling, added, "Don't you abide by the 'customer is always right' rule?"

Parker rewarded her with one of those rare, striking smiles, and her heart responded by counting out an extra beat.

"Have it your way, then," he said, nodding toward the kitchen. "I've got biscuits in the oven. Maybe you could see how many minutes are left on the timer."

Even before she took a step toward the heavy swinging door, his expression changed from sunny to cloudy again. "And for the luvva Pete, don't burn yourself or anything, okay?"

Holly pretended she hadn't heard him and focused on the quiet beeps emanating from the timer. She scanned the room in search of oven mitts and, seeing none, opened and closed doors and drawers until she found a pair. It wasn't until she slid the baking sheet from its rack that she realized Parker hadn't left an inch of counter space free. It didn't take long for the 450-degree heat to seep through the pot holders; if she didn't find a spot soon…

"Yikes!" she said through clenched teeth, dropping the tray onto a cutting board. There just had to be a Murphy in her lineage. How else could she explain that she'd grabbed the only pair of oven mitts with a threadbare thumb? She shook her hand, sending the mitt flying into the suds-filled sink, and glared at the ugly red blister already forming on her skin. Oh, she'd be a big help to Parker now. Her very first thought was to cancel the trip to Charleston, because only the good Lord knew what crazy, clumsy, klutzy thing she might do next!

What choice would he have but to question his judgment in hiring her? And who would blame him?

"So how are those biscuits coming alo—"

The sight of her at the sink, running cold water over her hand, cut his question short.

"Good grief, what have you gone and done to yourself *this* time?"

As he sidled up to her, Holly matched his frown with one of her own. "You sound just like my dad. And trust me, that isn't a good thing."

Gently, he turned her hand over to get a better look at her injury. Grimacing, he shook his head. "No wonder I smelled meat cooking."

She saw the teasing glint in his chocolate eyes and smiled too. "Am I hearing things, or can Mr. Serious crack a joke after all?"

For an instant, she thought her question might change his

mood back to no-nonsense. "Yeah, Miss Accident-Prone, Mr. Serious *is* capable of humor."

Well, at least he hadn't called her *Holly Folly*.

Yet.

She put her hand back under the cool stream of water. "So when do folks start coming down for breakfast?"

"Neatly sidestepped," he said, making his way to the hall. "You stay right there while I fetch some salve and gauze."

"Fetch some salve and gauze"? He reminded her of the grizzled old fellow who played Doc in that 1960s TV Western. She was still grinning at the image of him in a long white lab coat with a stethoscope draped around his neck, when he returned, carrying the black shoe box of first aid supplies.

"The water can't feel *that* good," he said, grabbing a clean towel from the drawer beside her. "You're grinning like the cat that swallowed the canary."

He had no way of knowing it, of course, but Parker had just proved her mother's theory. "So what's in the box?" she asked. "Running shoes, so you can hightail it far, far from my klutzy self?"

He turned off the water and lightly dabbed her palm with the towel. "Don't worry. No way a germ could survive one of Maude's bleach and boiling-hot water launderings."

She wasn't worried, and as she opened her mouth to admit it, he squeezed a dollop of antibiotic ointment onto the burn. "You're pretty handy with this stuff," she observed, as he blanketed it with a thick sterile pad.

"Practice makes perfect," he droned.

She'd seen him yesterday while he changed the dressings on

Maude's feet. If he'd felt any aversion to the task, it certainly hadn't shown in his voice or on his face. So why the sour tone now? And why did he constantly refer to his mother as *Maude*?

"If I'm not being too nosy, what happened to your mom's feet?"

Parker put everything back into the shoe box. "Surgery," he said, "to correct…I don't know…a bunch of long-standing problems."

"Such as…?"

"I guess decades of on-your-feet work is tough on the *sole*."

Three jokes right in a row? Holly didn't dare comment for fear he'd go back to behaving like a grumpy old man.

She'd tried hard not to let her thoughts show on her face. Not hard enough, as evidenced by the deep furrow reappearing between his eyebrows. "Thanks for this," she said, holding up her white-padded hand. "Feels much better, by the way."

Tucking the box under one arm, he turned off the oven. "Don't mention it. To anyone."

Then he winked. *Winked!*

"Can't have folks thinkin' I'm some kind of marshmallow nurse-maid, now can I?"

No sooner had he disappeared from sight than a plump, rosy-cheeked woman blustered through the back door. "Hello!" she said, plopping an overstuffed faux leopard tote bag onto the table. "I'm Opal. Opal Miller. Maude's first cousin on her mother's side." Squinting one eye, she pumped Holly's unbandaged hand as if expecting water to trickle from the fingertips. "Guess you must be that hotshot doctor from Baltimore. The one who's come to town to help Parker write his book?"

Laughing, Holly said, "Must be true, what they say…"

Opal opened her mouth to respond, but Parker spoke first. "That bad news travels like wildfire?"

Surprised by his sudden reappearance, Holly winced. He'd probably been teasing, but if she saw so much as a glimpse of mean-spiritedness today, she'd run straight to her room and pack... one-handed.

"Well, doggies," Opal scolded, "you sure do know how to dazzle the girls, don't you, ya big galoot?"

Both brows lifted as his mouth formed a silent O. "Hey. Wow. Man," he said, taking a step closer to Holly. "Aw, I was... I never... I didn't..." Slapping a hand to his forehead, he said, "I was just pullin' your leg. You know that, right?"

And though she wasn't at all sure his remark *had* been a joke, Holly waved it away. "Of course."

"Honeypot, don't you dare come to this gorilla's rescue," Opal told her. "Let the big oaf squirm. How is he ever gonna learn the proper way to treat a lady if no one ever calls him to the carpet for behaving like an inconsiderate ape?"

Parker sighed and met Holly's eyes. "I hate to admit it, but she's right. I *am* an oaf. Sometimes."

Opal grabbed the apron draped over a chair back. "'Sometimes'?" she quoted. To Holly, she said, "I'll have you know, this boy has had three fiancées." She let a moment pass, as if to let the words sink in. "*Three!*" Clucking her tongue, Opal tied the apron strings behind her back. "And he wonders *why.*"

Holly's "defend the underdog" nature kicked into high gear. Parker might've been partly responsible for the demise of one of the relationships, but all three? Impossible. Especially considering the way he'd looked out for her yesterday, tended her burn just now, and affectionately taken care of his mom last evening…

"I'm taking Holly to Charleston today," he said, changing the subject, "so she can see the sights before we get to work." He held up a hand, traffic-cop style. "Just part of our work arrangement, so don't get any romantic notions."

"Hmpf," said Opal.

"I saw to it that everything's under control until lunchtime, but you and Mom are on your own for supper. Hank said he'd be here by five, but if you need to leave before that, Cousin Pearl says to give her a call."

"Pearl," Opal huffed. "You're kidding, right?"

"She said—"

"Why, that woman's about as nurturing as a hyena." Then she reached out and gave each of Parker's cheeks a pinch. "Now, don't you worry none, darlin'. The way you work? Why, I can't name a body who needs a day off more'n you do. You two have fun…*sightseeing*." She winked and then fixed her steady, dark-eyed gaze on Holly. "If he can't sweep you off your feet in a city like Charleston, well then, I don't believe it can be done at all."

Holly didn't know what to make of the wink…or the comment, for that matter.

"Ready?"

At first she thought he'd addressed the question to Opal. But when she met his gaze and saw that humorless lift of his left eyebrow, Holly knew better. "I'll just be a minute. I need to run upstairs to grab my purse. And a sweater. And an umbrella, in case—"

"My truck's out front," he said, using his chin as a pointer. "Meet you there in two minutes."

Holly was halfway up the stairs when she heard Opal say, "Oh me, oh my. I have a good feeling about this one, Parker darlin'."

There was no rational explanation for the hurt and disappointment Holly felt when she heard him say, "Let's hope you're wrong, 'cause look where I ended up the last time you said that."

Chapter Four

. . . .

"Oh, wow. Look at this!" She glanced over at him. "How thoughtful of you to pack breakfast for me." Holly poked around in the tiny cooler. "Sandwich, fruit, napkins, juice... Why, it looks like you've put everything in here but the tuxedoed butler to serve it."

"It's the least I could do, since it was my timetable that cheated you out of a full-fledged Maude Brant breakfast."

"But...you're the one who did all the work this morning."

"Yeah, using her recipes."

She handed him a sandwich then unwrapped her own. He could use this time to tell her that he and Opal shared a long-standing "dumped" gag—one she enjoyed far more than he did, because that last breakup made the score Opal 2, Parker 3.

Or not.

Explaining the joke would involve the story about how the last breakup had left him at the altar, a full-regalia groom version of the proverbial jilted bride, and he'd just as soon not revisit that fragment of his life. Besides, what did it matter *what* Holly thought? She was here for the summer to work on his book, period. When the end of summer rolled around, she'd head north, to everything and every-body she cared about. For all he knew, she had a fiancé of her own back in Baltimore—though he didn't know how any man in his right mind could let a woman like her out of his sight for three long months.

A woman like her...

He blamed the twin fudge pops he'd devoured before hitting the hay for the crazy thoughts looping in his mind, and he made a mental note to do a better job of of abiding by the "don't judge a book by its cover" rule.

"Why so quiet?" she asked around a crunchy bite of apple.

He shot her a quick glance then stared straight ahead and smirked. "*My* mother taught me never to talk with my mouth full."

Holly went into hiding behind her bandaged hand. "Mine did too. Oops."

Did she have a clue how *cute* she was? Not likely, because if she knew, she wouldn't seem nearly as adorable.

Cute? And *adorable*? What in blue blazes was happening to his vocabulary? Parker could count on one hand the number of times he'd used either word and have fingers left over. So why had both pinged in his head at least a dozen times since she rode into town in that teeny red convertible?

"*Teeny*"? Parker groaned inwardly then shook his head. *Better get a grip, pal, before you turn into one of those poetry-spewing dudes who picks bouquets of roadside flowers for his best girl.* He pictured the rows of paint tubes and brushes in his so-called studio and shrugged. Was it possible he already *was* that dude?

To his credit, Holly *was* different. Despite the detours that put her into town three hours late...and the flat tire...and falling into the mud...and burning her hand, she hadn't uttered a word of complaint. Even more remarkable, she hadn't tried to blame something or somebody else for her bad luck. If she minded riding all the way to Charleston in his battered, un-air-conditioned pickup, she hadn't said so, not even after the wind and humidity restyled her eye-catching hairdo.

Artists tended to be more aware of things like hue and texture and scent. At least that's what he told himself when he noticed that she'd swapped her sporty red, white, and blue outfit for a flouncy pink skirt and matching blouse. Her blond hair bounced into curls, and freckles dotted her cheeks—and some scent between line-dried sheets and lilacs followed her like a sweet shadow.

"I have aspirin in my purse. Of course, you'd have to wash the tablets down with coffee, and I don't know if that's the best idea."

"What?"

"Aspirin. You know, for your headache?"

"Headache?" He didn't dare look over at her. One more peek at those full pink lips, pulled into a concerned pout on his behalf, and he'd be a goner for sure. "What makes you think I have a headache?"

Peripheral vision told him she'd shrugged one pink-sleeved shoulder. He'd known her, what, twelve hours? He'd fallen hard and fast for a pretty face in the past, but this? This was just plain ridiculous!

"Well, when *I* get a headache, I take deep breaths and frown too."

Great. So she wasn't just one of the most stunning girls on sneakered feet, she was also observant. And caring. And thoughtful. *Lord, help me,* he prayed.

"I don't have a headache," he admitted. "Just trying to decide which exit will put us in the best part of Charleston to start your tour, is all."

Holly gathered up their paper napkins and the foil he'd wrapped their sandwiches in, tucking everything back into the cooler. "More coffee?" she asked, holding the thermos in her good hand.

And risk having her spilling it all over her pretty outfit, or worse, burning herself in the process? "I've had my caffeine quota for the day." Then, in case he'd sounded as gruff to her as he had to himself, Parker quickly added, "But thanks."

"You have a terrific smile, you know. You should show it off more often. Lots more often."

His mom, Opal, Pearl, Hank—just about everyone he could name had made similar comments. And his routine retort? *"I'll smile when I have something to smile about."* But he didn't say that now. In fact, he couldn't think of a valid comeback.

"I know, I know," she said, holding up the bandaged hand. "You're right. I tend to speak before I think. My family says it *all* the time. Feel free to tell me to shut up." A nervous giggle punctuated her statement. "And don't worry about hurting my feelings. I've heard stuff like that so often, I'm practically immune to it."

Practically?

The wounded expression on her face earlier, when his "bad news travels like wildfire" joke backfired, hadn't lasted more than a nanosecond. But it glittered in her eyes long enough to prove she was anything *but* immune to "stuff like that."

"No way I'll ever tell you to shut up. I love the sound of your voice." Parker resisted the urge to smack himself in the forehead. Had he actually said that out loud? He stared hard through the windshield and pretended that the big green sign overhead had captured his total attention: CHARLESTON, NEXT TWO EXITS. Maybe she hadn't heard him. *And maybe you ought to shut up.*

From the corners of his eyes, he could see her over there, grinning and blinking those long thick eyelashes. He didn't know if it labeled Holly as one of those females who enjoyed the "Good golly, *me*?" game to stir additional compliments, or if she'd exaggerated when talking about her big, close-knit family.

"So I guess it's okay for me to admit it now...."

He turned the radio off. "Admit what?"

"That right from the get-go, I thought you sounded like a DJ. And that I've always loved a Southern accent."

Not high praise, exactly, so why did it feel so good, hearing it? Feeling playful for the first time in longer than he cared to remember, he lowered his voice half an octave. "Why, thank you, my dear."

The moment of silence that followed made him wish he had the sense God gave a turtle. And then her cell phone rang, rescuing him.

He fiddled with the radio dials again, adjusted the rearview mirror, dropped the sun visor.... Despite his attempts to give her privacy, he could tell that it was her mom on the other end of the phone, and from what he heard, it was clear that Holly had promised—and forgotten—to call home when she arrived yesterday. The mostly one-sided conversation lasted all of two minutes, and when Holly snapped her phone shut, she leaned against the headrest and groaned.

"Sometimes I think that crazy family of mine forgets that I'm thirty. A tad 'up there' in age for scoldings, don't you think?"

The last thing Parker wanted to do was come between Holly and her mother.

"Oh, don't get me wrong, Mom's great, and I love her to pieces—really I do. There are only a handful of things about her that drive me nuts."

Did she expect him to ask what those things were? No way he intended to step into *that* quagmire!

"She's a great mom, but boy oh boy, sometimes, let me tell you, she's like the proverbial mother hen, you know? One who hasn't figured out how to let go of her chick even after she's fully grown and ready to leave the nest!"

He was tempted to say, "Don't you mean 'coop'?" Instead, Parker took his earlier advice, played it safe, and kept his mouth shut. "So what do you think you'd like to see first? The fancy mansions on Battery Row? The French Quarter? The pirates and buccaneers tour?"

"Oh, the pirates, for sure. Anything but those old mansions." She held up one hand. "Don't get me wrong, I'm sure they're all filled to overflowing with history and beautiful furniture and antique tea services, but to be honest? That would simply bore me to tears. I mean, really, how many sterling silver punch bowls and King What's-His-Name settees can a body look at in a lifetime?"

Where have you been all my life? Parker asked silently. He was about to say something akin to "Your wish is my command" when she continued:

"I took a job in Ocean City, Maryland, just over a year ago. Bought myself a really great little condo overlooking the Atlantic. But Mom cried buckets every time I called home, and it was even worse when I'd visit. After a while, guilt got the better of me, and I sold the place and moved back to Ellicott City. Took a beating, financially, what with the shape the real estate market is in, let me tell you! Not that I don't love my hometown, mind you, because it's charming and quaint and—"

Her bandaged hand caught his eye, reminding him how

accident-prone she was. "Maybe she feels you need more protection than her other, ah, chicks."

"I wish my mother had other kids to focus on. I'm an only child. Mothers generally reserve this sort of 'hovering' for the baby of the family, don't they?"

"Wouldn't know. I'm an only child too," he informed her, pointing to himself.

Holly was the proverbial accident waiting to happen. What mom *wouldn't* worry about a kid like that? "Well," he started, choosing his words carefully, "I'm sure your mother means well."

When Holly expelled a sad sigh, he resisted the urge to give her hand a reassuring squeeze. For one thing, the hand closest to him was the one she'd burned. Ironic, he thought, that the fat white bandage was a testament to her need for protection.

Yet again, he found himself fighting his desire to save her from harm forever.

Chapter Five
....

Parker started the tour at the American Military Museum, where he pointed out a tattered uniform and told her that he'd spent five years in the army. The news didn't surprise Holly, given his straight-backed posture and close-cropped hair. That and his "devil's in the details" mind-set.

She'd only known him a few short hours, but already he'd demonstrated skills in multiple areas. As one who'd changed a dozen flat tires and watched nearly as many mechanics perform the same task because she'd cut corners too sharply, Holly couldn't help but marvel at the speed and accuracy of Parker's tire-changing system. She added to the quickly mounting reasons to admire him with the fact that he was tall and broad-shouldered and made transporting her heavy suitcases up two floors to the "Captain Dan" suite look like child's play.

If asked, she would have said that entertaining clients aboard a charter boat was on a par with the skills required of a tour guide—until today. Holly smiled to herself, remembering the stiff-lipped way he'd brought her attention to Charleston's diverse points of interest.

Now, as they stood side by side on an ornate footbridge over-looking the Ashley River, he leaned both forearms on the wood rail and expressed regret for not knowing more about the history of Mepkin Abbey and Gardens. "Never took anyone here before, but since you said you like flowers and stuff…" He ended the apology with a one-shouldered shrug.

"No problem," she said, giving him a playful elbow jab to the ribs. "I saw a computer in your mom's parlor. You can look it up when we get back to her place. That way, the next time you bring someone here, you'll be 'up' on all its history."

On the heels of a dry chuckle, he said, "There are two chances of me bringing anyone else here…slim and none." A harrumph followed, and then, "I have chores to do at *my* place when we get back to Folly Beach."

A swan paddled past, followed closely by a mallard. "He'd better watch himself," Holly said, pointing at the duck. "Swans are as mean as they are beautiful."

"Mean?"

"You bet…with a capital *M*! The reason I know is…" She rested against the rail and said, "Since Baltimore is only a short drive from DC, friends and family from all over the country used our house as free lodging when they wanted to visit the Capitol. Sometimes we'd tag along. The last time I was there, a swan came up and bit me." She held out her hand. "I sported a bruise for nearly a week!"

He frowned then watched the bird's graceful glide across the pond. "Ah, doing the 'bring some bread, attract some birds' tourist thing and didn't let go fast enough, eh?"

"Nope. No bread, not even a crumb. That crazy thing singled me out of the crowd and backed me into a tree, wings flapping like crazy, and grabbed hold of my thumb. Held on tight for what seemed like a full minute." Shivering, she laughed. "I had nightmares about it for *years,* I tell you!"

By now the swan had rounded the bend of the tiny stream that fed the pond. "Is that why it was your last visit to DC?"

She laughed. "No. With school and work, I just never had the time."

"How old were you?" Parker asked, absentmindedly rubbing his knee. "When the swan bit you, I mean."

She glanced at his fingers. An injury sustained while serving in the military? She hoped not, because the thought of him facing an enemy in battle made her cringe. "I was ten. Almost to the day." They'd been walking nearly an hour before stopping here on the bridge. Maybe he could use a short break, to rest his leg. Holly pointed to the many-windowed building across the way. "I sure could go for a cup of coffee. Maybe even a sandwich." She looked up at him. "How 'bout you? Hungry?"

"You're hungry already? After egg biscuits and fruit—*and* coffee? You must have a hollow leg."

Groaning, she hung her head. "Oh, great. Now you sound like my mom. 'You can eat your father under the table,' she says. 'Where do you put it all...in a hollow leg?'"

He checked his watch. "Well, it is after noon." After a quick glance toward the building, Parker said, "There is a luncheonette in there, but I have a better idea." Then he grabbed her hand. "When was the last time you took a carriage ride?"

"Well, I—would you believe I've never been on a carriage ride?" She'd seen horse-drawn carriages in movies, even watched a few trot by while in New York on business, and without exception, it had seemed a charming mode of travel.

"Well, then, it's high time you learned what you've been missing."

As he helped her into a buggy, Holly wondered which of the ex-girlfriends Opal referred to had shared romantic carriage ride moments with Parker. The question rang in her mind even as he rehashed the sights he'd shown her in the French Quarter and at Marion Square. Then he mentioned Sullivan's Island and Patriot's Point. "We won't have time for that today," he was saying as the carriage driver turned on to Anson Street. "But like you said earlier, we have all summer. If you want to see the rest of the city, I'm sure you won't have any trouble talking Maude into going with you. Once her feet are all healed up, of course. She loves it down here. For that matter, so does Opal. The three of you could make a day of it, shopping and...and doing whatever it is that women do when they're together."

Sweet and fun-loving as they were, Holly didn't want to see those things with Maude or Opal. Didn't want to make a day of it with either of them. If she came back to historic Charleston, it would be with Parker or not at all. Which made no sense. No sense at all. What sort of airhead starts falling for a guy she'd only met hours ago?

The same kind who falls for a card-carrying womanizer, that's who. It surprised her that it still hurt this much, remembering how Ethan Jeffreys had so blithely left her without explanation or apology. She'd taken a chance on him—a big chance, considering how long it took her to get over Jimmy's death and—

"Better get your cameras loaded and aimed," said their driver as he led his two-horse team up Concord Street. "I'm sure you've read all about it, my friends: *this* is the world-famous Rainbow Row."

Holly sat up straighter and pretended that it took all her

attention to prepare for a photo op. She'd read about these beautiful old houses while studying for her trip south, and she'd hoped to see them while in South Carolina. Built in the mid-1700s, the neighborhood definitely earned its name.

So why hadn't the colorful neighborhood brightened her mood?

"You're awfully quiet."

She hid behind her camera. "Just trying not to miss anything, that's all."

If anyone had asked her to repeat the back-and-forth banter between Parker and the driver during the rest of their hour-long tour, Holly didn't know how she'd have answered. *Snap out of it, Holly, because what's done is done.*

It was nearly two when Parker slid his pickup into a parking space at Bubba Gump's Shrimp House. "I have two confessions to make."

"Oh?"

He held up a forefinger. "That was my first carriage ride." His middle finger popped up beside it. "I rarely eat out much, and when I do, I avoid chain restaurants." After helping her step down from the truck, he added, "But I think you'll find that this one is an exception."

After asking the hostess to seat them near a window, Parker made a few menu suggestions. They'd barely placed their orders when a blaring baritone turned every head in the place. "Parker, you young rascal, you, come over here and say hello!"

Grinning, he waved at the white-bearded gent across the way. "That's Colonel Boone, my former commander and one of my best charter-boat customers. Would you believe that the old general is a direct descendant of Daniel himself?"

"Daniel, as in *Boone*?"

"One and the same." He winked. "Or so he claims." Parker gave Holly's shoulder a gentle squeeze. "C'mon, I'll introduce you."

"No, no...you go ahead and say hello. I need to powder my nose anyway."

"Okay, I won't be long." He started to walk away and then said, "Don't be surprised if he invites himself to join us."

"I hope he does. He looks like a man with some wonderful tales to tell." *Tales about you*, she thought, smiling.

And then before he'd taken more than a couple of steps, a beautiful blond walked up and took hold of his arm. "Well, as I live and breathe," she said, "if it isn't the handsome and elusive Parker Brant."

Chapter Six

....

Parker had made it halfway to Boone's table when a tall, willowy blond blocked his path.

"Stephanie," he said, looking into that oh-so-familiar face. He prayed she hadn't heard the hitch in his voice. "What are *you* doing here?"

Her smile had often reminded him of the Cheshire cat, but never more than at that moment.

"Well, that's hardly what I'd call a warm welcome." She laughed. "I could ask you the same question, but…"

Her cool green-eyed gaze slid to Holly, who was so busy reading the menu that she didn't seem to have noticed Stephanie's scrutiny.

A waiter stopped beside them and hoisted his food-laden tray onto his shoulder. "Can I help you, sir? Ma'am?"

Blinking, Parker stepped aside. "No. No, the lady was just making her way back to her own table."

The man gave Stephanie a quick once-over and shrugged, as if to say, "Your loss, pal, 'cause she's a looker," before walking away.

Peripheral vision told Parker that the hall leading to the restrooms was only steps away. He might have taken it…if he hadn't noticed Holly, looking from him to Stephanie and back again.

"Well, nice running into you, Steph. Enjoy your lunch," he said, striding purposefully back to his table.

The hint of a smile lifted one corner of Holly's mouth as he slid onto his chair. "Old friend?"

"Hmpf. More like an old—"

Stephanie stepped up beside him and said, with one long-taloned hand on his shoulder, "I can't tell you what a wonderful surprise it was, seeing you after all this time."

Parker heaved a sigh.

"I've missed you so. And who can blame me? You're even more gorgeous now than—"

"Seriously, Steph. Don't do this, okay?"

Uninvited, she sat beside him. Only concern for Holly kept him from giving her a scene to remember.

"To answer your unasked question, Parker, I'm in town for the week on business." She raised one severely plucked eyebrow and added, "Wouldn't it be lovely if we could get together for dinner... or something?"

He started to say "Not on your life," but as usual, she was a beat quicker.

"So tell me, what brings *you* to Charleston? I remember only too well how much you despise the hustle-bustle of the tourists."

He shouldn't have hesitated, because in the instant it took to decide whether or not to admit it wasn't *Charleston* but her demanding *ways* he'd come to despise, Stephanie zeroed in on Holly.

"I'm Stephanie. And you are...?"

"Holly Leonard."

He knew that *look*. If he didn't do something, and fast, Stephanie would find it necessary to point out that they'd been engaged. She might even add that when the preacher got to the part where she was supposed to say "I do," she walked out of the chapel and never looked back. Or that three days later, when she finally answered her door, she'd calmly announced that it hadn't been fair, leading him to believe that she could spend a lifetime in Folly Beach, married to a charter fishing boat captain.

"Aren't you the slightest bit interested to hear what sort of business brings me back to South Carolina?"

He got a quick mental picture of the way her suitcases looked that day, lined up in the foyer where it would be easy for the taxi driver to grab them.

His silence wiped the phony smile from her face, and she fiddled with his napkin. Rearranged the salt and pepper shakers. Tapped the pad of her forefinger against the handle of his butter knife. Next, he knew, her lower lip would poke out and she'd start blinking, one of a half-dozen "bring on the tears" exercises she'd mastered.

Through it all, Holly sat stiff-backed and stiff-upper-lipped. She didn't know anything about his history with Stephanie, and if he had anything to say about it, she never would.

But he didn't want her thinking he was a heartless cad, either, so he said, "Look. Steph. I hope you enjoy the rest of your stay in town. It was…" He swallowed, mostly to buy time as he summoned the nerve to tell her to take a hike. "It was good seeing you, but we need to get back to Folly, so…"

Stephanie rose slowly then stood beside him. "Not a day goes by that I don't regret leaving the way I did. I should have called. To apologize, if nothing else, but—"

"Seriously, Steph," he said again. "It's all water under the bridge."

"Good-bye, Parker. Have a nice life."

And with that, she swaggered toward the door and hopefully *out* of his life.

A minute, perhaps two, passed before Holly said, "I've learned through painful experience never to order crab cakes outside Baltimore city limits." She rolled her eyes. "Oh, the awful things they do to them!" A light laugh punctuated her opinion. "I think I'll try the sampler…a little bit of everything. And tell them to hold the crab."

She met his eyes. "So tell me, Romeo, what're *you* hungry for?"

The answer lay somewhere between the biggest lobster in the tank, a minute in the alley—where he'd give Stephanie a *real* piece of his mind—and a kiss from Holly's still-smiling lips.

On second thought, he didn't really feel much like tearing into a crustacean. Didn't relish the idea of a skirmish with his ex, either. And it was way too soon to think about kissing Holly. One finger aloft, he signaled their waiter and ordered two samplers and then asked if she preferred iced tea or lemonade.

"Water's fine." She looked up at the waiter. "With a slice of lemon, please, if it isn't too much trouble?"

"That sounds good. Make it two." Parker handed the man their menus. "Well," he said, laughing, once they were alone again, "*that* was uncomfortable."

When she fixed those big blue eyes on him, he was powerless to do little more than blink.

"*Now* who's making mountains out of molehills?" she said, grinning. "I'm sure people ask him for lemons dozens of times a day."

When she pursed her lips, he read it as a sign that she didn't want to discuss the scene with Stephanie. Maybe at some point during their summer together, he'd tell her the whole sad story. Or not. For now, he'd stick to small talk. Unfortunately, he'd never been much good at it.

"Not bad," he said, looking around.

He half expected her to agree, by commenting on the nautical decor or the water view on the other side of the window. Instead, she wrapped both hands around the bowl of her water goblet and chased a dewdrop with the pad of her thumb. As she caught it, one corner of her mouth drew back in a slight smile. "Yes. It's a very nice place." Then, "I thought your friend was coming over."

Parker glanced to his left and saw that Colonel Boone had left. Knowing the colonel, he'd seen Stephanie and decided against interrupting. "I've got his number."

"And I'm sure he has yours."

If he had more time—or a lick of sense—he probably could have figured out what she meant by that. So he didn't know what prompted him to say, "I'm sorry as I can be that you had to see all that. But I meant what I said. It's water under the bridge."

"And you're well rid of her, if you want my opinion."

"And if I don't? Want your opinion, that is?"

She grinned good-naturedly. "Guess I had that coming, poking my nose in where it didn't belong."

"Why don't you let me be the judge of that?"

Holly shrugged. "While we're on the subject of noses and where they do and do not belong, when that check gets here, you're to keep your nose *out* of the little black case."

And then she winked. *Winked!* Was she...was she *flirting* with him?

"I never would have agreed to a restaurant meal," she continued, "if I thought for a minute that you intended to pay for it."

Parker started to object, but she stopped him with a quiet "*Sssst!*" Shrugging, he sat back, all set to say fine, he'd pick up the next check. But before he could, the reedy voice of a woman said, "Daniel, look!"

Parker—and everyone within earshot—looked at the elegantly dressed elderly woman.

"Take me over there," she said, pointing at Parker.

The man pushing her wheelchair bent at the waist. "But, Mom, your book club meets in less than an hour," he said near her ear. "Wouldn't want to keep the ladies waiting, now would you?"

Either she hadn't heard him or she chose to ignore his reminder. "He looks like you did twenty years ago, Daniel. *Exactly* like you did." She kept her dark gaze fixed on Parker. "Now take me over there, so I can ask him if—"

"Mom, please." He sent Parker an apologetic smile as they rolled toward the exit. "Let's just get you home, okay?"

Once they were out of sight, Holly leaned in to whisper, "You don't know them?"

"No." And yet, there was *something* about the pair of them....

"Well, that's just plain weird."

"What is?"

"The woman was right. You do favor the man. More than just a little, too, especially around the eyes. I would've bet a double wedge of strawberry cheesecake that you were going to say, 'Hey, there's my grandma and my cousin.'"

"No," he repeated. "No relation."

"Then I guess you must have reminded her of someone she knows. Or of someone from her past." She wiggled her eyebrows. "Her first love, maybe!" Then she flapped her napkin and daintily draped it over her lap. "But that's just crazy talk. Brown is the most common eye color on the planet, right?"

Parker shook his head. "Poor woman. Alzheimer's, maybe. I sure hope Maude never—"

"She won't."

He met her gaze. "She won't?"

"Nope."

Grinning, he said, "You sound awfully sure of yourself."

"Not of myself. Of *God*."

"God?"

"Because I'm going to pray that it never happens to her."

"And that's that."

"Mm-hmm."

She said it so matter-of-factly, he was almost tempted to believe her.

Almost.

God had never done much for the Brant family. Why would He start now?

"So, you were in the army, were you?"

"Um-hmm," he said distractedly. Past tense.

She regarded him from the corners of her eyes. "Something you prefer not to talk about?"

"Not if I can help it."

Holly propped one elbow on the table, then rested her chin in the palm of her hand and leaned closer. In this position, she was close enough to kiss. *Not that nonsense again...* Parker cleared his throat and made a big deal of positioning his own napkin across one knee.

"Something tells me you would have been a career soldier, if..."

He sat back a little farther and grabbed his water goblet. Did she *know* how unnerving that steady, direct gaze of hers could be? And how unsettling it was when she read his mind like that? He didn't think so, because she didn't seem the type who'd consciously make him uncomfortable.

Parker took a big swig of the water as he waited for her to finish her sentence.

"...if not for your mom. You came home because she needed you, didn't you."

A statement, he noticed, not a question. Nodding, he crunched an ice cube.

"That's bad for your teeth, you know."

He stopped chewing.

"Before I decided on marine biology as a major, I thought I might want to become a dentist, like my dad. So I spent a summer working in his office." She wrinkled her nose and cringed. "I developed a whole new respect for him and his assistants and technicians, let me tell you! People do some very unpleasant things while those little paper bibs are clipped under their chins."

If she wasn't aware how unsettling her stare could be, she probably had no idea how gorgeous she was, either.

"...and picked up some cool tips," she was saying, "one of which is—and I quote my dad—'Crunching ice can cause tiny fissures in your tooth enamel, which can eventually lead to cavities.'"

Would he ever outgrow this irrational envy he felt when people talked about their fathers? "Fissures, eh?"

She nodded.

"Duly noted." He returned the goblet to the two o'clock position beside his bread plate.

"I wonder…"

She was staring out the window now, nodding and tapping one finger on the tablecloth. And though he was fairly certain she'd been thinking out loud, he asked, "What do you wonder?"

"Why J-U-L-Y is pronounced *Joo-LIE*, but D-U-L-Y is *DOO-lee*?"

He'd half expected her wondering to lead to questions about what had happened between him and Stephanie or why he hadn't reenlisted, so her remark stirred a surprised chuckle. "I have no idea. The English language is full of words like that." He chuckled again and then said, "Goes a long way to explain why it wasn't my best subject in school."

The waiter chose that moment to deliver their meals, and when he was gone, Holly said, "So what *was*? Your best subject in school, I mean."

"Science." He almost followed it up with, "What are you all of a sudden, the Mistress of Small Talk?" But he didn't. Instead, Parker said, "I gave some serious thought to med school." *Don't go there,* he warned himself. The reasons why he hadn't would only put him in a foul mood, and the day was young.

"How 'bout you? What was your favorite subject?"

"Science. I was pretty much the only girl who didn't get all creeped out about dissecting frogs and grasshoppers and cow eyes and—"

"Cow eyes?"

"Well, yeah," she said as if *he'd* grown a cow eye. "How else were we supposed to learn what was inside our own eyes?"

He thumped the heel of his hand against his forehead. "Well, yeah," he echoed. "Of *course.*" Then it dawned on him that she'd probably learned that in *honors* biology. On a whim, Parker grabbed her hand, turned it palm-up in his own, and slowly inspected every finger, every crease and crevice.

"Looking for evidence that the scalpel slipped and clumsy ol' me carved up my own hand?"

"No." Not the whole truth, but not a lie, either. She tucked in one corner of her mouth. Oh, to have the power, just for a minute, to read that mind of hers!

Holly plucked a curvy shrimp and dipped it into her bowl of cocktail sauce. Parker had no way of knowing what the summer might be like. Good weather or bad, plenty of volunteers for the turtle project or only a handful, one thing was certain: it wouldn't be dull. Not as long as Holly was around.

"So what's your favorite memory of being a soldier?"

"There was this kid…"

"Oh, Parker, he wasn't killed, was he?"

"No, thank God." He told her all about the boy who'd become his miniature shadow and how he'd begged Parker to take him home with him. "When my last tour of duty ended, I couldn't find him. Probably would've been too much red tape involved anyway, but still…I've never quite forgiven myself for letting him down."

Good grief. She wasn't going to cry, was she? Parker didn't know what he'd do if she did. "Hey, don't feel sorry for me," he quoted her, grinning.

"I don't."

"Then what's with the long face?"

"Well, okay. Maybe I do feel sorry for you. But only a little."

Smiling, he said, "Hmpf."

"It couldn't have been easy, walking way from an innocent child you'd come to think of as family."

She'd hit the nail square on the head, and it made him uneasy. If she'd figured out that much about him after only a few hours together, what would she know when the summer ended? "Pass the salt, will you?"

She wrapped her hand around the shaker and held it like a hostage. "You're kidding, right?"

Did that mean his meal was already salty enough, in her opinion, or that *she* knew she'd hit the nail square on the head?

"It isn't pity I feel, Parker; it's gratitude." She sent him a sweet, lopsided smile. "I've never known a real-life hero before." She slid the salt closer to his plate. "Thank you, Parker."

Now, really, how was a guy supposed to react to a statement like that? He picked up the shaker and tilted it left and right, watching as the contents shifted like sand in an hourglass. "You're probably right."

One side of her mouth lifted in a comic grin. "Um, I'm right? About what?"

"The food's plenty salty enough."

"Nice to know that you're reasonable and health-conscious. Not so nice to know you're a mind reader too."

Too? He didn't trust himself to ask what *that* meant.

Yes, the summer would be a lot of things, all right, but boring would *not* be one of them.

Chapter Seven
....

Parker took Route 17 home, describing points of interest as they crossed the Ashley River Bridge. As soon as she'd accepted the assignment, Holly had read up on Charleston and its rich history, so it wasn't difficult to feign interest in each landmark. Holly's *real* interests, however, were the questions swirling in her head. Because who was this guy, anyway? She'd read up on him too, and in the hours since they'd met, she'd added "attentive son" and "affable tour guide" to what she'd learned. But his reaction to the woman in the wheelchair? *Way too cool and collected,* she told herself.

He reminded her a lot of her cousin, who'd served two tours in Afghanistan. Though he seemed to enjoy talking about the ways he and his pals passed time between attacks, Aaron got a far-off look in his eyes if conversation veered too near his memories of combat.

Just like Parker.

Unlike Parker, Aaron had come home unharmed—physically, anyway—to the loving, welcoming arms of his wife and kids and enormous extended family. He went right back to work and church, and except for occasional nightmares (which he was seeing a doctor about), his life was pretty much what it had been before the army.

She had a feeling none of that was true for Parker.

Holly looked over at him, relaxed and content as he maneuvered his old pickup through the streets of Folly Beach, talking about how much Charleston had changed over the years, and not necessarily all for the better.

Nodding, Holly agreed. "But clogged highways and smog and noise and, yes, even crime…that's the price of progress for every city and town, don't you think?"

"Maybe," he said, thumping the steering wheel, "but that doesn't make it right. Or easier to live with. Take the Morris Island lighthouse, for example." He drew her attention to its silhouette visible on the horizon. "It stood out there offshore for centuries, yet most folks would be content to let the sea swallow it up."

"But didn't I read someplace that since it was added to the National Register of Historic Places, it belongs to the good people of South Carolina? Wouldn't that qualify it for state assistance?"

"Yeah, but the amount of work that needs doing is way out of balance with what the government can do." He shot her a half grin. "I'm impressed with the thoroughness of your research skills."

"I might be a klutz out there," she said, pointing through the windshield, "but I take my work very seriously. I think you'll find I manage a modicum of decorum and grace when I'm on the job."

"No need to 'sell' me. You had me at 'Will pay for my own room and board.'"

"How involved are you with the lighthouse project?"

"Not very."

"Ahh, so he's modest, too…."

He chuckled. "'Too?'"

Well, if he expected her to say "Modest, intelligent, brave, and gorgeous too," he had another think coming. "Didn't I read some-place that you're on the Save the Light board?"

"Yeah…"

"And that you offer excursions on your boat in the silent auctions that raise funds for the project?"

And there it was again, that arresting grin. "Wow. I'm almost afraid to ask what else you know about me!"

She knew that he was willing to fight for things he believed in and people he cared about. It explained why he wanted to see the lighthouse out there on the horizon last for centuries more. So how could a guy with that much *caring* in his makeup so quickly forget the woman in the wheelchair?

Parker maneuvered onto East Ashley. "So that woman and her son," Holly said, laughing, "wasn't that the weirdest thing?"

Brows high on his forehead, he made a tiny *O* of his mouth. "Strictly a case of mistaken identity."

Three minutes, tops, she guessed, before they arrived at Coastal Cottage.

"Not a half-bad English accent, boss!" She laughed, even as she wondered if he'd stay awhile or hurry off to his own place farther up the beach. "So how far is your house from the B&B?"

"I could throw a stone from my place and it'd land on Maude's roof." He shrugged. "If I had a better arm, that is, and any aim at all." Parker chuckled. "With my luck, I'd break a window." He looked over at her. "You want to see it?"

"Well, sure, if there's time."

"Why wouldn't there be? Ain't like I have a wife and kids waiting for me there."

Was that an edge of regret she heard in his voice, or wishful thinking? "I thought maybe you'd need to change your mom's bandages or something."

"Nope. She oughta be good to go until she sees her surgeon next week. Unless she lets that goofy habit of hers mess things up. Again."

"Goofy habit?" she asked as he passed the cottage.

"We could call her Cricket, if we wanted to, the way she rubs her feet together when she's asleep. Never would have known that little tidbit if she hadn't decided to get both feet operated on at the same time."

"So it was an option? She could have done one foot and then the other?"

"Yeah, but she was afraid she might never have the other one done after the first surgery. And to be honest, I can see her point."

"Because of your leg, you mean."

"And my thigh, and my shoulder, and—" His truck wheels crunched over the pulverized shells that paved his driveway. "Home sweet home," he said, nodding toward the house. "C'mon. I'll show you around."

The house wasn't anything like the others she'd seen since coming to town. The simple white two-story boasted black shutters and a brick walk and porch, reminding her more of a simple Midwestern farmhouse than a pastel-and-gingerbread island cottage. "It's beautiful," she said, meaning it.

"Should've seen it when I bought it." He opened the wide oak door and led Holly into a sunny foyer. "It sat empty for about fifteen years, so the gulls and spiders were none too happy to be evicted. Would you believe I even found evidence that a horse had been in here?"

"Hard to believe it was once a wildlife habitat." She followed him into the kitchen, where the cabinets glowed with a gleaming coat of white enamel. "You've done an amazing job."

Parker opened the French doors and stepped onto a screened-in porch.

Holly crossed the painted-wood floor. "There was a screen door exactly like this at my grandmother's house." She plucked the spring that kept it from slamming then tapped the hook that dangled across from its matching eye. "Oh, the memories it conjures! In and out, out and in, with the spring squealing and the door slamming..." Laughing, she added, leaning on the jamb, "I daresay that door was responsible for half my scoldings as a kid."

"Careful there," he said. "If you take a tumble down the steps you'll land in sand, but you'll still have taken a tumble down the steps."

Holly turned to see which steps he was referring to...

...and lost her balance.

If not for Parker's quick reaction, she'd have found out firsthand what a tumble down the steps felt like.

"You okay?" he said, one hand gripping her upper arm and the other pressed to the small of her waist.

"Yeah," she said, nodding. "Thanks."

"I declare, I think I'm gonna start calling you T.M."

"For 'Trips Much'?"

"Trouble Magnet."

Holly might have laughed—if she hadn't noticed him wince as he stepped back. Had he pulled a muscle, lurching forward that way to catch her? "Are *you* all right?"

Frowning, he harrumphed. "I'm fine."

Why did she get the feeling he wanted to tack on "...no thanks to *you*..."?

"Let me show you my pride and joy," he said instead. Brushing past her, he held the door open, and once she'd planted both feet in the soft white sand, he wasted no time turning the corner of the house. "The beginnings of my garden," he added when she caught up to him.

Nodding, she stood on the ocean side of the knee-high fence he'd installed around it. *Stay where you are, you klutz, before you trample all his seedlings.* She pointed at the colorful markers that stood at the head of every tidy row. "Did you paint all those signs yourself?"

He nodded too and poked the one that said ZUCCHINI with the toe of his shoe. "Serves as my artistic release."

"Oh?"

"Let me take you to my studio," he said in a terrible French accent, "where I will show you my etchings."

Laughing, she fell into step beside him. "How long before you're picking beans and tomatoes?"

"Oh, months for that stuff, but the spring onions and leaf lettuce will be ripe for the pickin' soon." He opened the porch door again and, as she climbed the steps, said, "Maybe I'll have you over one evening for steaks on the grill and a big ol' salad."

"Sounds lovely." *But why the maybe?* she wondered as this time he led her past the front parlor.

"This is my sunroom-slash-studio," he said, stepping inside.

The right and left walls were made up of floor-to-ceiling shelves, while dead center, straight ahead, were two sets of French doors that led out to a stone terrace.

"If I could, this is where I'd spend all my spare time."

Holly did a slow half turn, taking in leather-bound books, faded seashells, and tarnished brass ships' clocks that decorated the shelves. She liked the simple Shaker furnishings that stood on a slate-blue braided rug. Liked the stone fireplace too. "Does it work?"

"Sure does."

As she completed her turn, Holly noticed three easels holding canvases of varying sizes and stages of completion. Bending at the waist, she read the signature in the lower right-hand corner of the biggest one. "You did these?"

"Uh-huh."

"They're beautiful. Why, at first glance, they almost look like photographs." She commented on all the detail in the sea grasses and the waves, in the feathers on the gulls' backs and the clouds in the sky. "You could sell these!" She shook her head and started counting on her fingers. "Carpentry, gardening, painting...is there anything you *aren't* good at?"

"I'm not too good at responding to compliments." Then, with a nod, he indicated the paintings. "There are thousands just like them all up and down the East Coast. Thousands more on the West Coast, I'd bet." He shrugged.

"I disagree. I lived in Ocean City, Maryland, remember, so I saw things like this all up and down the boardwalk. Some were really beautiful, but I have to be honest," she said, tracing the contours of a dune, "none were anywhere near as beautiful as these."

She received another shrug, and then he said, "So I guess I should get you back to Maude's place. Opal has probably talked her ears off by now. And anyway, it's almost suppertime."

Holly wanted to see the rest, wanted to drink in every rug and knickknack and all the polished floors in between. But he'd already made it to the front porch, where he stood waiting for her to catch up.

"Your mom's guests are on their own for everything but breakfast, though, right?"

"What's that," he said, grinning as she slid into the front seat of the pickup, "a 'buy me supper' hint?"

"No! Of course not! I was just thinking that, maybe on the way to the cottage, we could stop and get subs...or a pizza."

His laughter filled the cab as he fired up the truck's engine. "I guess you didn't notice on the way over here that the only thing between here and Maude's place is sand. And reeds. And more sand."

"I didn't mean *literally* on the way. I just meant, you know, we could—"

"Holly..."

"What?"

"Do you make a habit of that?"

"Of what?"

"Of defending yourself. Of explaining everything."

"Do I do that?"

"A lot."

"Gosh. I had no idea."

He only shrugged.

"Well," she said on the heels of a sigh, "I guess when you're as clumsy as I am, explaining and defending sort of becomes second nature."

"There's no need to explain. It's a good idea. And I know just the place."

A moment of silence passed between them as he slid into traffic.

"And by the way...you aren't clumsy."

"So I can add 'comedian' to the list of your talents?"

"Comedian...?"

"I'm not clumsy? Ha. Ha-ha! What would you call it, then?"

Parker tilted his head slightly. "Hmm," he said, before pulling into a sub shop parking lot. Turning the key in the ignition, he faced her and draped one arm across the seat back. "You're smart. Maybe too smart for your own good, and your poor little body can't keep up with that goes-a-mile-a-minute mind of yours." He gave her shoulder an affectionate squeeze. "Might be interesting to see how your life changed if you slowed down just a hair."

As if on cue, he tucked her hair behind her ear.

"But just a hair, mind you. Because you know what?"

His big fingers were surprisingly warm and gentle, and she fought the temptation to press her cheek against them. "What?" she whispered.

"Because I like you just the way you are...."

With that, he climbed out of the truck, raced around to her side, and opened the passenger door. As she hopped to the ground, he tucked her hair behind her other ear and added, "...bumps and bruises, broken fingernails, and all."

Wow, she thought, grinning at her hardworking, neglected hands, *this has to be a first.* She followed behind him like a happy pup and never saw the curb until she tripped over it and landed face-first against his big, hard chest.

* * * * *

The ships' clocks were sounding the eleven o'clock hour when Parker walked through his front door, and for the first time, he gave a little credit to the "time flies when you're having fun" expression.

He couldn't remember a time when Maude had laughed harder. It was good to hear. Good to see too, because working forty hours a week while fulfilling her duties as full-time mother and father to him hadn't left much time for her to cut loose and enjoy life. Maybe that explained why none of her relationships with men had ever worked out….

Maude got real serious real fast, though, when Holly told her about the elderly woman in the restaurant, and for a reason that made no sense to him, his mom's laugh-rosy cheeks went pale as Holly described the man pushing the wheelchair. The reaction made him sorry that he hadn't acted on his impulse to follow them and find out *why* the poor old thing had mistaken him for someone else.

"What's done is done." He sagged into his recliner and massaged his right thigh, which strained the right shoulder, also shredded by the IED. The doctors would have prescribed muscle relaxants and painkillers—if he'd asked for them. But the discomfort served as a reminder that he'd survived the attack, unlike three of his men. If he'd been made of sturdier stuff, he wouldn't have been unconscious when he was airlifted to Germany, and would have been able to tell them about the boy....

Holly had called him a hero. "Hero, my foot," he muttered, grabbing the remote. Behnam, orphaned by sniper fire before Parker arrived in Afghanistan, had learned to survive by wits and charm, inspiring soldiers of every rank and gender to contribute to his daily food supply. Since none could provide Ben a proper home, Parker took it upon himself to build him a hut from cast-off lumber and corrugated tin. After caulking every crack and crevice, he fashioned a door from thick Plexiglas and bolted it in place with hinges borrowed from the tailgate of a defunct truck. He traded a penknife for a blanket and sunglasses for a pillow and taught Ben how a fat candle, standing in a sand-filled coffee can, could provide heat and light.

Unless Parker was leading a mission, the two were inseparable. Soon Ben could speak broken English and taught Parker some Arabic. While Ben dreamed aloud of going to school and living in a proper house, Parker secretly planned for the day when he'd go home...and bring Ben with him.

The boy's big-eyed, trusting face flashed in his mind. Groaning with regret and concern, Parker heaved himself out of the recliner, limped over to his desk, and fired up the computer. Maybe this would be the day he'd find a reply in his e-mail in-box, telling him that the State Department had found Ben and that the paperwork granting him permission to adopt the skinny eight-year-old was in the works. He'd been patiently working toward that goal since arriving home from overseas.

Ten minutes and twenty-seven messages later—spam, mostly, promising a free credit check or a meeting with the girl of his dreams—he shut the computer down. He felt like a moron admitting it, but he'd already found the girl of his dreams. He'd never admit it to *her*, of course—how selfish would that be?—because Holly had way too much going for her to get saddled down with a has-been half-crippled ex-soldier whose main ambition in life was fulfilling a promise to a curly-haired boy.

A ruckus outside brought Parker's pity party to a close. "High time," he said, wincing as he rose from the desk chair. "Spend another minute feeling sorry for yourself," he mumbled, flipping on the back porch light, "and you're likely to get—"

There, in the halo of the yellow bug bulb, was the biggest, orangeest tomcat he'd ever seen. It had overturned a clay pot, which had rolled into the railing. He half expected the cat to bolt. Instead, it sat on its haunches, squinting and licking its chops. He knew better than to feed a feral cat. Why, that was as good as handing it an engraved invitation to come back, day after day, for more of the same. But it looked hungry. And tired. And lonesome. And its eyes were the same shade of pale brown as Ben's. "Don't go anywhere," he said through the screen. "I've got some bologna in the fridge with your name on it."

As he peeled off a slice, Parker shook his head. "Should I, or shouldn't I?"

A sorrowful meow was all it took to answer that question.

Easing open the door, Parker stepped onto the porch, crouched, and tore the lunchmeat into thin strips. "Now don't go making a pig of yourself," he said when the cat wolfed down the first ribbon. "Hard to tell when you last had a meal. You're likely to give yourself a bellyache."

When the animal finished its meal, it flopped onto its side and proceeded to groom itself. "Feeling pretty much at home, are you?"

It stopped licking its paws to look at Parker, as if to say, "Well, *yeah*. And why wouldn't I, Bologna Man?"

"I don't see a collar...."

This time, the cat's wide-eyed stare put him in mind of the woman in the restaurant, who'd scanned Parker's face as if looking for some telltale proof that she knew him. Yet again he wished he'd gone after her and the guy pushing the wheelchair. "Probably would've turned out to be nothing anyway," he said. "But at least you'd have known, one way or the other."

Then, calm as you please, the cat sauntered across the porch and hopped up onto Parker's favorite chair, where it curled into a ball on the plaid cushion and promptly went to sleep.

If the cat was still there in the morning, he'd take it to a vet. With a clean bill of health, it could become the cottage cat Maude could advertise in her next B&B brochure. "And maybe I'll just keep you myself." Might be nice to have someone to talk to besides himself for a change.

The cat raised its striped head and chirruped something that sounded an awful lot like "Hero."

"Been talkin' to Holly, have you?"

The tabby only blinked.

"Well, once you get to know me, you'll realize I'm anything *but*."

When the cat yawned, Parker shrugged. "Yeah, self-pity is an ugly emotion, isn't it?" Self-depreciation had never been part of his makeup before. So why was it now?

Maybe because he did feel sorry for himself—a little, anyway.

Because despite two years of phone calls and e-mails and paper-work, he hadn't been able to find Ben. He'd been unsuccessful in keeping Stephanie from descending on their table. And when the old woman insisted that Parker looked like a younger version of the man pushing her wheelchair, he'd failed to get to the bottom of it. According to Maude, Parker's father had been an only child and, near as she could recall, his parents had died before he'd enlisted in the Air Force.

But what if she'd been mistaken? What if Parker had a grand-mother or an aunt, an uncle or a cousin, out there that Maude didn't know about? Is *that* why he'd pretended the woman's words hadn't affected him, that he hadn't noticed the resemblance between him and the man—especially around the eyes—because he was afraid of learning the truth?

As he trudged up the stairs, Parker shook his head. If he did have family out there, he hoped they were happy and healthy. Hoped the same thing for Ben, though he was helpless to know for sure. It dawned on him as he stood brushing his teeth that adopting the cat might take the edge off his feelings of power-lessness. With a pet, he'd have some control. Selfish? Possibly. But at least the cat would benefit from his conscience-easing exercise.

In bed now, on his side, Parker stared into the darkness and pictured Holly. Clumsy, cute, caring Holly, who seemed to have sensed how badly Stephanie's appearance had rattled him. Parker punched his pillow. If he didn't get a handle on his emotions, fast, he'd need a shrink—not a cat to talk to.

Rolling onto his back, he slapped a hand over his eyes. How

much simpler things would be if Holly had been the grandmotherly matron he'd imagined, instead of the pretty, sweet-tempered young woman who'd stumbled into his life!

"Yep," he groaned into the dark, "it's gonna be a long summer, all right."

And unless he pulled himself together, a long and *heartbreaking* summer.

Chapter Eight

....

"Well, good mornin', sunshine."

Startled by the sudden, happy voice, Holly nearly sloshed hot coffee on her hand. "Good morning, yourself," she said, smiling over her shoulder. "My, but it's quiet around here today."

Maude wheeled herself into the kitchen and parked beside the table. "Midweek is usually slow. Except at the height of the season." She pointed at the percolator. "Mind pouring me a cup?"

Holly was only too happy to oblige. "Last time I saw one of these was at my grandmother's house." She delivered a mug, cream and sugar, and a spoon to her host.

"That one belonged to my sainted mama." Maude stirred sugar into her cup then added a dollop of milk. "I've tried those new-fangled coffeemakers, but you can't beat this one for consistency." With a wink, she added, "Besides, I love every lid-rattling bubble that jumps up the tube."

"I was just about to pour myself a bowl of cereal. What can I get for you?"

"Cereal's fine. Cornflakes, if there are any left." She shook her head. "That son of mine is just about addicted to them."

"Speaking of that son of yours," Holly said, sprinkling flakes into a bowl, "where is he this morning? I thought he'd be here at first light. He said we'd get an early start today."

"Oh, I imagine *he* got an early start. No telling what he's doing to that boat of his. If he doesn't roll in by the time we've finished breakfast, I'll tell you where he parks that monstrosity."

After delivering the cereal and a napkin, Holly sat across from Maude. "So how are your feet this morning?"

"Oh, they're all right, I suppose."

She supposes? Holly leaned forward. "Are you in pain?"

"No, nothing you wouldn't expect after surgery. You know the old saying. Guess I'm just sick and tired of being sick and tired."

"Well, you know the other old saying: 'All in good time.'"

Maude laughed softly. "I was supposed to be back on my feet weeks ago. It's bad enough that I feel like a helpless old woman, having to rely so heavily on Parker."

"I don't know him very well, of course, but it doesn't seem to me that he minds a bit."

"Oh, he'd never complain, even if he did! It's just that he has so much to do, what with the charter business and all. And then there's helpless old me." She sprinkled sugar over her cornflakes. "And this writing project, of course." Maude shook her head. "I was stunned when he told me about his plan to write a book and donate all the money to the lighthouse and turtle projects."

Odd, Holly thought, *that despite her smile and jovial laughter, Maude seems so…sad.* "You're sure you aren't in any pain?"

"I'm sure."

Holly put their bowls in the dishwasher then refilled Maude's mug. "Will Opal be here with you today?"

"No, it's Henry's turn."

"Ah, your beau…"

Maude harrumphed. "So he'd like to think."

Holly didn't know how to respond. "Can I get you anything before I leave?"

"No, but thanks. Henry is nothing if not punctual." She glanced at the tail-wagging cat clock above the sink. "He said he'd be here at six forty-five, so I expect him in two shakes of a cat's tail." Laughing at her own joke, Maude slapped the table.

"I just need to run upstairs and grab my purse. Is it a long drive to Parker's boat?"

"To be honest, it'll take less time to walk, and you have the perfect weather for it."

Holly looked out the window, where white-gold sunbeams shimmered from every gentle wave that slapped the beach. In a few hours, seashell hunters, dog walkers, and joggers would pock the smooth sand with fingers, feet, and paws, but for now, the sand glowed pale blue, thanks to the cloudless sky overhead. "You know, that sounds like a lovely idea," she said. "I'll just grab a sweater, and then you can give me directions."

Upstairs, Holly slathered on some sunscreen then tucked sunglasses and a white hoodie into a small backpack. After threading her ponytail through the opening at the back of her favorite Orioles cap, she tucked a twenty-dollar bill into the side pocket of her jeans. Halfway out the door, she dashed back into her room and grabbed an umbrella, hoping as she darted down the stairs that Parker would still be with his boat by the time she got there.

Holly had barely stepped into the kitchen when a handsome,

gray-bearded man said, "Dr. Leonard, I presume." Grinning, he stuck out one hand. "Name's Henry. Henry Donovan, but my friends call me Hank. I hope that's what *you'll* call me, Holly. I've heard so much about you."

Holly figured she had the rest of the summer to find out why Maude called him *Henry* and, grasping his hand, said, "A pleasure to meet you."

"Headed down to the water, are you?"

Nodding, she smiled. "Hopefully, I won't get lost."

"You won't." Hank pointed. "You'll see a path at the end of Maudie's drive, and it'll lead you to a small pier near the lighthouse inlet. It's the only one out there, and so's his boat. He painted the name SEA MAVERICK on her hull in blue and gold."

Like the sunset? Holly wondered.

"Help yourself to some bottled water," Maude invited. "And take one for Parker too."

"Thanks," Holly said, sticking her head into the fridge. "Don't mind if I do." She tucked the bottles into her bag. "Anything we can bring you when we get back?"

"Nothing comes to mind, but if it does, I'll text Parker."

Hank chuckled. "You know he hates that, Maudie. Why not just call him?"

She chuckled too. "Because that old-fogy son of mine needs to fall into step with the times, that's why."

Waving, Holly wished them both a good day and headed outside. She'd barely reached the bottom porch step when she heard Hank say, "Maudie, if that boy of yours lets this one get away, he's out of his ever-lovin' mind."

If Maude replied, Holly didn't hear it, because Hank's comment increased her pace by twofold. Seashells, bleached white by the sun and shattered by time and nature, crunched beneath her tennis shoes. For an instant, a pelican soared overhead, casting a gray shadow as she hurried down the path, brushing aside reeds and ducking past sea oats. "Better look where you're going," she told herself, "or you'll end up with a nose full of sand." And wouldn't Parker enjoy *that*!

Just as suddenly as it had begun, the tilting wood fence that lined the path came to an end. Beyond it, the beach lay just ahead, untouched save a trail of big footprints leading from Parker's house to the weathered wharf that jutted out into the ocean, where, just as Hank had said it would be, the *Sea Maverick*'s blue-and-gold-painted hull gleamed in the sun.

The boat bobbed slightly in the Atlantic's froth, and above the soft *smack* of waves slapping at the boat, the quiet refrain of a familiar song and the husky baritone that tried—and failed—to stay on key. As much as she wanted to find out which onboard chore had put him in such an agreeable mood, Holly didn't want to startle him. "Ahoy, matey!" she called, laughing at the silliness of her greeting.

A moment of silence was followed by a ragged "Arggh, and who goes there?"

Parker peered over the rail, his grin the only part of his face visible in the shade of his cap. "Mornin'," he said, waving a fat sponge over his head. "What brings you out and about so early?"

She hopped onto the pier. "Well, you said something about getting an early start but never mentioned a time." Shrugging, she added, "I figured since I was up anyway, I might as well have myself a nice brisk walk and find out where, exactly, you do what you do."

Standing, he dropped the sponge into a bucket. Holly knew, because she heard the quiet splash and then saw him look down and frown. "Got your feet wet, did you?"

"Hey. It's a boat. Sooner or later, everything gets wet." Then he held up a hand. "Hold it," he said. "You just stay put, you hear? Don't take another step until I get down there."

"Why? Afraid I'll trip and fall headfirst into the drink?"

"Something like that," he said, grinning.

She watched him make his way to the side, marveling at how quickly and nimbly he descended the three steep wooden steps that led from the dock to the boat. *You couldn't do that on a bet, and there isn't a thing wrong with* your *leg,* she thought, frowning to herself.

"Give me the backpack," he said, wiggling the fingers of one hand.

"So I won't lose my balance and take a dive?"

"The dock doesn't move," he explained, "but the boat does. Add to that the gap between the boat and the dock and, well, it makes some people dizzy. Even people who aren't…"

Clumsy? she finished silently, grinning as she gave him her hand and the backpack.

Once Parker had helped her up the short flight of steps and she'd planted both feet firmly on the coarse boat floor, Holly nodded. "I see what you mean." She steadied herself on the shiny brass rail. "So," she said, looking around, "this is the famous *Sea Maverick.*"

"I'd hardly call her famous."

Parker had made it clear during their lunch that he didn't like talking about his background—the military stuff in particular. So she couldn't very well admit that, prompted by the appearance of the lady in the wheelchair and her handsome caretaker, she'd looked him up on the Internet before turning in last night. Her exploration took her to numerous websites, where in every photograph, he wore the same stiff-lipped smile, whether he and his teammates raised football trophies or superior officers pinned the Purple Heart and Silver Star to his chest. The only one in which he'd looked truly happy had him surrounded by grinning Boys' Club members who hoisted hammers and saws, fishing poles and reels...the tools he'd taught them to use as, together, they turned a forgotten old tub into a seaworthy charter boat. Someday she'd ask about the boys. For now, she pointed out to sea. "Is that the Morris Island lighthouse?"

He followed her gaze. "Sure is. She's a beauty, isn't she?"

Arms crossed over his broad chest, Parker leaned his backside against the rail and told her how it grew from an ordinary flame that warned 1670s sailors of the craggy shore, to the forty-two-foot "Charleston Light," commissioned in 1767 by King George. By 1862, the Confederates destroyed it to keep it from Union hands, but the North quickly took it over and used it to guide their troops. At the close of the Civil War, the lighthouse was rebuilt on Morris Island.

Holly had read all about it before coming to Folly Beach, but she didn't say that. "Then I guess your Save the Light project must be doing its job," she said instead, "because it doesn't look all that worse for the wear to me."

"Looks are deceiving," he said without turning around. "We're hundreds of yards from her, so you can't see the worst of it." He explained how, over the years, the rhythm of the Atlantic's waves had rotted the light's wooden base. Ocean microbes, various erosion-protection projects, and basic neglect had only increased its instability. "Save the Light is responsible for turning it into a historic landmark," he said, nodding. Funds from local governments and private contributors were working to keep it from crumbling into the sea. "But the work's far from done," he added, frowning. "If we want it there for future generations to enjoy..."

His voice trailed off, and for the first time in her life, Holly wished she was independently wealthy, so she could supply all the money required to protect the beautiful old relic forever.

＊＊＊＊＊

"I know I said we'd start on the turtle project today," Parker said, "but one of my regular customers called last night."

"Oh, I don't mind. Maybe I could help out—make sandwiches and act as your hostess. It'd be a great way to see how a charter business works."

"Well, they only booked a three-hour tour."

Holly launched into the *Gilligan's Island* theme. He didn't know which surprised him more—the fact that she had such a stunning voice, or that she remembered all the words. When she finished the last stanza, she donned a sober expression and said, "I hope the weather bureau isn't predicting any storms."

He went back to scrubbing the deck. "Me too."

Now her serious expression turned more real than feigned. "Why?"

"Because unless the wind blows us back toward land, we're doomed."

If her eyebrows rose any higher, they'd completely disappear under her bangs. "Doomed?"

He aimed the drippy sponge at the Atlantic. "No islands east of here."

"But what about...? Really? *No islands?*"

"Nary a one." Parker shrugged and put the sponge back into the bucket then extended sudsy hands, palms up. "Sorry."

"Sorry?" A nervous snicker punctuated her question.

"That's odd...."

"What's odd?"

"In all the years I've owned the *Sea Maverick*, this is the first time I've noticed an echo." He reached into the bucket again and wrung out the sponge.

"An echo?" She looked even more surprised than she sounded.

"Yeah, and it's a bad one."

"A bad ech—" And then she grinned as she got the joke. "Funny. Real funny. I have a friend whose uncle owns the comedy club on Water Street in Baltimore."

He didn't get it. "Comedy club?"

Holly nodded. "Yeah. If you're really nice, I'm sure I can arrange an audition."

"An audition?"

He was scrubbing the next section of deck when she said, "Well, sir, when you're right, you're right."

"Right? Right about wha—"

"There *is* an echo on this boat, and it's a bad one, I tell you. Bad!"

"Oh. I get it." He laughed. "Touché, professor. Touché."

She lifted her cap just enough to allow her to stuff her bangs under its brim. "So these regular customers of yours, are they Wall Street bankers? Hotshot attorneys? Real-estate moguls?"

"Bill and Sissy and their twins. They own Davis Management. At the height of the season, the properties they oversee keep them hopping and there isn't much time to goof off with the twins."

"Bill and Sissy and the twins? Is that another one of your jokes? 'Cause if it is, I have to say, it's not nearly as funny as—"

"Jokes?"

Slapping a hand to her forehead, Holly groaned. "Don't tell me we're starting up a whole new round of the echo game!" Laughing, she said, "Those names—you made them up." One brow rose as she met his gaze. "...Right?"

"'Fraid not."

Another giggle came, and then, "What are the kids' names?"

He winced. "I almost hate to tell you."

"Not—"

"Sorry..."

"Buffy and Jody?"

"'Fraid so."

"Oh my goodness! If you tell me they have a butler named Mr. French, I might just have to jump overboard."

Another shrug. "You want a hand up, or can you make it over the rail all on your own?"

She was laughing too hard to answer.

"All right," Parker said, "so the guy isn't a butler."

"Whew!"

"More like a supervisor. Or even a foreman."

She studied his face. "But his name is Mr. French?"

"Nah, but..."

"Thank heavens. I thought for a minute there I'd have to make good on my threat!"

"…but his real name is Vinnie DeMarco," Parker continued, "but because of all the other coincidences, he got stuck with the nickname of French."

By now, she was bent at the waist, with both hands resting on her knees. "Please," she squeaked, "stop. I can't breathe."

Difficult as it was, Parker tried to behave as though the whole thing wasn't the least bit funny. Frowning, he bit back a grin. "I never would have guessed that you're one of those people who makes offers willy-nilly, without following through."

"Willy-nilly?" The phrase started up a whole new gale of giggles.

"I don't see how you can perform hostess duties in your condition."

"I'll pull myself together before they get here." She wiped her eyes on a sleeve. "But just to be safe, when are they getting here?"

"They're not. We're going to them." Using his chin as a pointer, Parker said, "That's their place, just over the dunes. Soon as you're ready, we'll fire up the *Maverick* and motor over to their dock."

"They have a dock but no boat?"

"They have one, but it's a sailboat. Not nearly as conducive to fishing."

"I can hardly wait to meet this family," she said, rubbing her palms together. "I'm ready when you are…unless you want me to throw together some sandwiches first."

"No need," he said. "It's only a…"

"…Three-hour tour," they said in harmony.

And this time when she burst into merry laughter, he joined her.

Chapter Nine
....

A man waved to them from the shore, and Holly said, "Hey, Parker, isn't that Hank over there?"

He grabbed his binoculars and snapped off the protective lens caps. "Yep. Sure is."

"Why don't we pick him up? I'll bet he'd love to join us." She glanced around the boat. "There's room for one more, isn't there?"

"Yeah, there's room. But this isn't like driving a car, y'know," he said, grinning. "I can't just hit the blinkers to signal a lane change and then pull up alongside the beach and park this old tub."

Buffy pointed to a pier not fifty feet ahead. "But couldn't we stop there and pick him up?"

"First of all," her twin said, "we need to make sure there's a life vest for him." Jody lifted the padded seat and peered into the compartment where Parker stowed the jackets. "One, two," he counted then met his sister's eyes. "Well, that's one problem solved." He dropped the seat into place and faced Parker. "So how *will* we pull up to get him, Parker?"

Grabbing the loudspeaker, Parker said into the mike, "Yo, Donovan...you in the mood for a little fishing this morning?"

Even from this distance, Holly could see Hank's smile. The

older man waved and started jogging toward the dock. It took a few minutes to reel in the trolling lines, secure each rod, crank up the engine, and motor over to the pier. Soon enough, though, Hank climbed aboard and greeted each passenger with a bear hug. "Did you notice that there's something new painted on the old boat?"

"What old boat?" Holly asked.

"Just a johnboat," Hank explained. "The dumb thing washed ashore during Hurricane Hugo and nobody claimed it." He handed Holly the binoculars and showed her where to look. "So there it's been ever since, collecting one crazy saying after another. Why, I'll bet the thing weighs three times its original weight in enamel alone." He chuckled. "Every couple of weeks—sometimes more, sometimes less—somebody comes along and adds a saying to it."

"'CONGRATULATIONS, TIM AND MARLENE,'" she read. "And 'DUKE ROCKS!'" Smiling, Holly put the binoculars back on the hook beside the helm. "That's pretty neat," she admitted. "Has anyone ever seen who adds the messages?"

"Not that I know of," Parker said.

"Reminds me of Edgar Allan Poe's grave in Baltimore. For years and years now, on his birthday, somebody sneaks into the cemetery in the dark and leaves a single red rose and a bottle of cognac on his tombstone." She shrugged. "Without getting caught."

"What?" Bill Davis scoffed. "With all the gizmos and gadgets out there today? Sounds to me like one of those things people *choose* to overlook."

"Right," agreed his wife, "because not knowing the truth is a lot more romantic than finding out who's responsible."

"Well, in any case," Hank interrupted, "it's funny that you guys happened by today," he said, giving Parker's shoulder a fatherly squeeze. "I've been on the beach off and on hunting for shells. Must be some kinda storm brewing, because I didn't see a thing worth bending over for between here and your mom's place."

Sissy recapped her water bottle and asked, "What's the connection between a shell-free beach and an impending storm?"

"Y'know," Hank began, "I'm not a hundred percent sure." He threaded his arms through the sleeves of a life vest. "It's something my pa always said. Wasn't the most talkative fella," he added, fastening its buckles, "so I never pressed him for an explanation. Near as I can figure, the sea gets real quiet when a nor'easter is fixin' to roll ashore."

"The calm before the storm?" Jody asked.

Hank ruffled the boy's hair. "Probably, son."

Buffy looked across the glassy surface of the Atlantic. "Was your father a fisherman?"

As Parker motored toward deeper water, Hank helped Holly reset the hooks with bait. "Matter of fact, he was. Spent more time out there on the Atlantic than he did at home, so I reckon he'd know."

"Didn't you miss him?" Buffy asked. She glanced at her dad. "I hate it when Dad has to travel on business trips."

"Well, nobody liked it, least of all my mama. But the man kept a roof over our heads and food in our bellies, so we couldn't very well complain."

"Why were you lookin' for shells?" Jody wanted to know.

"I make stuff out of them. Glue 'em to candlesticks and picture frames, arrange 'em in jars of sand and the bases of glass lamps, and then I sell 'em to tourists."

"Wow," the wide-eyed little boy said. "People pay money for stuff made outta *seashells*?"

"Not enough to make me rich, but it pays for my fishing license every year." He looked at Parker. "What're we looking for today, son?"

"I heard on the radio earlier that they're pulling up a lot of redfish near Murrells Inlet. We'll float around over there for a while and see if it's true."

"Redfish are scaredy-cats," Hank said. "The least little thing will spook 'em."

"And if they aren't biting?" Bill asked.

"We'll try for sheepshead or sea bass."

Jody stepped up to the rod Hank had just baited with a live shrimp. "We gonna keep 'em, Dad, or we gotta throw 'em back?" he asked, watching as he secured the hook to an eyelet.

"If they're big enough, we'll keep 'em. Right, Parker?"

"Right."

"I heard in town yesterday," Hank said, "that a guy caught a forty-pound king, using blue crab as bait." He whistled.

"Now *that's* a fish story," Sissy teased.

"Nope. It's as true as true can be."

"Last time we went fishing," Buffy said, "you promised to tell us a *ghost* story, but there wasn't time. We have time now...."

"Oh, now, I dunno...your mama might think you're a tad young for such tales...."

Jody stood taller and crossed his arms over his chest. "We're almost ten years old! Tell him, Mom. We *are* old enough for ghost stories. Right?"

"I suppose," Sissy said. And wagging a forefinger at her children, she added, "But if you have nightmares, don't even think of waking me."

"Aw, Mom," Jody whined, "we aren't babies."

"Yeah, Mom," agreed his sister, "we know the difference between make-believe and something real."

Grinning, Bill shook his head. "You might want to take a nap when we get home, hon." He looked at his wide-eyed kids. "You know, just in case."

"Maybe *you* should take a nap," was his wife's quick retort.

Hank sat on the long starboard-side bench seat and draped an arm over each twin's shoulders. He spoke in soft, even tones, drawing—and holding—their attention as he described pirates and treasure chests and the legend of Civil War soldiers that prowled the shore in search of their severed heads.

Chuckling, Parker drew Holly's attention away from the family. "Better keep an eye on their lines," he said, smirking. "I'd bet my best rod that not one of them will notice if they get a bite."

"Yeah, it looks to me like maybe they'd *all* better take a nap."

"If I'd known what a first-rate first mate you'd be," he said, giving her a nod of approval, "I would have hired you for *that* job."

"Which reminds me…when are we going to get some writing done?" They'd compared research notes on the loggerheads, the lighthouse, and Folly Beach. Since they held similar opinions on all three topics, Parker saw no reason to rush into things. But she was right. In the few days that had passed by, they hadn't done a lick of work on his book. "We can start today…if you don't have other plans, that is."

Holly laughed. "The only people I know in Folly are right here on this boat." She glanced toward shore. "Well, except for your mom and Opal."

"Good point. So once I get Maude settled in for the evening, we'll head over to my place. Maybe work up an outline."

"I can't believe I hadn't thought to ask you this before, but if you don't even have an outline, what *do* you have?"

Without letting go of the wheel, Parker shrugged. "I have you. What more do I need?" Then he tapped the fish-finder screen, more as an excuse to look away from her steady gaze than to indicate that they'd located a school of redfish.

Switching off the motor, he gave Holly the signal to drop the lines. How like her not to hesitate even for a second. Parker watched as she expertly unfastened the first hook from its eyelet, glancing over her shoulder to make sure she had plenty of room to cast. The spinning reel whizzed as she released the line. It floated and reached thirty feet from the boat before plopping into the water, its sinker dragging the hook into the deep. She set the reel lock and didn't waste a minute, moving to the next rod and the next.

Then, her hands on her hips, she faced Hank and the Davises. "You guys gonna sit there all day listening to tall tales, or are you ready to catch some fish?"

It was all the excuse the kids needed to leave the scary stories behind. "Which rod is mine?" Jody asked, stepping up beside Holly.

"First come, first serve," she said. "Take your pick, mister!"

He chose the center rod, and his sister stood beside him.

"Keep a close eye on those rod tips," Parker advised. "We've got a whole school of fish right under us."

Bill's rod arched and bounced. "Got one!" he said, grabbing it.

"Hey, look!" Jody shouted. "Buffy's got one too!"

"Remember," Hank added, "these babies spook real easy, so—"

Squeals and shouts rose up as every rod tip bent. Holly and Hank helped the Davises reel in their fish, using the ruler on the ice box lid to determine which could go into the box and which they'd release.

Parker kept his eye on the horizon, where the low-hanging clouds had gone from burnt orange to blue gray. The wind had picked up too. Not a good sign, he knew. Not a good sign at all.

Holly didn't rebait the hooks, telling him that she'd seen the sky too. Instead, she handed out sodas and said, "Need to ask the captain if we're staying here or moving elsewhere." Then she jogged into the cockpit and leaned in close to whisper, "When are you going to tell them?"

"Didn't figure I needed to. They've got eyes, and they've been coming down here since before the twins were born. Soon as the shine of a cooler full of fish wears off, they'll want to head in even more than we do."

"I'll start packing up, then," she said, heading back onto the deck. One by one, she grabbed rods and prepped them for storage in the cabin's overhead racks. Without a word, she rummaged through the tiny cupboards until she found his supply of clear-plastic bags and twist ties. "Which is your sharpest knife?" she asked, opening the galley's only drawer.

"The one with the bone handle," he said, grinning. "Does that mean you know how to fillet fish too?"

She stood at attention and said, "Yessir, Captain."

Parker grabbed the wrist that held the knife, because, knowing her, she'd salute him next and end up gouging out an eye—or worse. "You know how to pilot a boat?"

"Yeah, I guess." Her brow crinkled into a tiny frown. "Why?"

"Because I think Hank has scared those kids enough for one day."

The frown intensified as she tried to figure out what he meant.

"They don't need to see your blood all over the deck...."

Her shoulders sagged slightly, and she gave a little nod.

He was still holding her wrist when he said, "I didn't mean to hurt your feelings. It's just that with the storm moving in and all, you might feel the need to rush, and—"

"No need to explain." She put the knife back into the drawer. "Or apologize. After all the crazy, clumsy things you've seen me do in the short while I've been in town, you wouldn't be much of a captain if you let me loose on deck with a sharp instrument."

She'd punctuated the statement with a short laugh, but Parker knew her heart wasn't in it. "You did okay with those fishhooks," he admitted. And nodding at the drawer, he added, "Just take your time. Okay?"

Her smile lit the dim cockpit, telling Parker he'd made the right decision in trusting her to the task. At least, he hoped it was the right choice. Because it was a good half hour from here to the dock and another fifteen minutes from there to the hospital.

* * * * *

"I don't believe I've ever seen a tidier job of packing up the day's catch," Hank said. He gave a final admiring nod as each Davis picked up their bagged redfish and climbed from the *Sea Maverick* to the dock. "You're just full of surprises, aren't you, Holly?"

She'd already said her good-byes to the family and was engrossed in hosing down the deck.

"I don't think she heard you," Parker said, laughing.

"That girl puts her whole self into things, doesn't she?"

He remembered the way she'd handled the rods and filleted the fish. How she'd noticed the storm at almost the same moment as he had. "Yeah. She sure does."

"Makes a man wonder what kind of wife she'd make, doesn't it?"

He looked at Hank, fully expecting to see the usual teasing glint in his eyes.

"Woman like that," Hank continued, "who doesn't do anything halfway?" He gave another nod of approval. "Man would be lucky to share his life—"

"I know, I know...with a woman like that."

Now the familiar grin lit the man's face. "So you've noticed too, have you?"

Hard not to notice, Parker thought as she rolled up the hose and stowed it in the under-seat compartment. He hadn't asked her to swab the deck, either, but she'd done it. Squeezed every drop of the water from the mop and hung it up to dry too. Then she rested both fists on her shapely hips and did a slow turn, no doubt to see if she'd missed anything. Parker read her lips: "Yep, all's well." And when a satisfied smile brightened her face, he thought his heart would thump clean out of his chest.

She looked up just then and blushed when she caught him staring. "Is everything shipshape?"

"Ah, yeah," he managed. "Thanks."

"Happy to be of service, Captain."

This time, instead of saluting, Holly winked…and started his heart pounding like a parade drum. Again.

"Well, kids," Hank said, giving Parker a playful elbow jab to the ribs, "I'd better head home before that monster reaches us."

Both Holly and Parker followed his gaze to the horizon, where nearly black clouds stretched as far as the eye could see and rose high into the heavens. "We'd better make tracks too," Parker said, locking the cabin.

From the dock, Hank said, "Yeah. Get that sweet girl some- place safe and dry. Sugar melts when it gets wet, y'know." And, laughing, he trotted back up to the spot on the beach where they'd first seen him hunting for shells.

"Think he'll make it home before the storm hits?" Holly asked.

"Yeah. His place is just on the other side of the dunes. He'll be hunkered down long before we will."

"Your place is closer," she said, "but I'm guessing we're going to your mom's first?"

Nodding, he fell into step beside her. "Yeah. Once I check her bandages and make sure she has everything she'll need to ride out the storm, we can head over to my place and see about hammering out that outline you were talking about."

"I'm the only guest at the cottage tonight."

He shot her a quick glance. "And your point is…?"

"We've put off working on the book for days. What's one more night?"

Chuckling, he shook his head. "You don't have to worry about

Maude. The woman was born and raised on the shore. Truth is, if Ma Nature knew what was good for her, she'd steer clear of Coastal Cottage."

"Maybe. Under normal circumstances. But she can barely get around on those feet of hers."

"All right. If it'll ease your mind, we'll hang around, at least until the threat of bad weather passes. I'm sure Maude will enjoy the company."

They'd just crested the biggest dune when she said, "Can I ask you a question?"

"Something personal?"

"Yeah, I guess you could say that."

"Ask away...long as you're okay knowing that I might not be able to answer it."

"Might not *want* to answer it, you mean."

"Is there a difference?"

"I suppose not."

They walked a few more feet in silence. Then Parker said, "So what's your question?"

"Why do you always call your mother *Maude*?" She let a tick in time pass before adding, "If I called my mom by her first name, she'd raise a terrible fuss!"

"I don't always call her *Maude*." He shoved his fingertips into his jacket pockets. "Do I?"

"Well, *I've* never heard you call her anything else." Holly waved a hand in front of her face. "Never mind. It was a dumb question. And what you call her isn't any of my business anyway."

Parker shook his head. "You must think I'm an insensitive clod, not noticing a thing like that."

"Mind if I make a casual observation? One friend to another?"

Is that what they were? *Friends?* Coworkers, he could deal with. Boss and employee, even. But friends? That's the last word he'd used to define the way he felt about Holly.

"I'll take your silence to mean you'd rather not hear my opinion on the subject."

He'd been woolgathering, and she'd caught him. *Doing a lot of that lately,* he told himself. "No. I mean, sure. Of course I want to hear what you think."

"This is just armchair-shrink stuff, and I'm probably way off base. But from the little I've seen and heard, there's a certain…"

She frowned and bit her lower lip, as if searching that amazing mind of hers for the right term.

"…There's a certain tension between you two. Nothing huge, mind you. But it's as though neither of you are really comfortable with the other. Like…like something happened in the past and one or both of you hasn't dealt with it yet."

They were, at most, two minutes from the cottage. No way he could explain the uneasiness between him and Maude in that amount of time. How could he help Holly understand something that he hadn't figured out himself?

It started to rain. Big, fat drops that landed inches apart, staining the sand. They fell harder, closer together, until looking through them was like trying to see through a thick fog. Within minutes, the beach was as wet as if the tide had come in, partly from the downpour and partly from the storm-stirred waves that slammed ashore.

Holly pulled up her sweatshirt's hood and, laughing, grabbed his hand and broke into a full-out run. It surprised him to see how fast those short little legs could go. Surprised him how tightly she squeezed his hand. There was more power in this tiny woman, he acknowledged, than met the eye. And he had a feeling that her strength wasn't purely physical.

Once they reached Maude's back porch, Holly ducked under its protective roof and shrugged out of her hoodie. She gave it a good shake then hung it on one of the pegs beside the door. "Hopefully," she said, whipping off her baseball cap, "the wind will dry it out a bit." She shook water from her long curly hair too, and then held out one hand, silently inviting him to give her his jacket, and he gave it to her without a second thought. When she hung it beside hers, something happened inside him. Something wild and weird and wonderful, because the only thought in his head was, if their soggy jackets looked that good side by side, how much better would his *life* look, with her next to him every step of the way?

"Once the storm passes, I'll run 'em both through the washer and dryer." She opened the door, hesitating on the threshold. "You have another one, right?"

"Well, yeah," he said, though he didn't have a clue where. "A couple of 'em, as a matter of fact."

"Good." She stepped into the foyer and held the door for him. "Then if it takes me a couple of days to get to it—and that is the more likely scenario," she said, laughing, "then you won't have to go digging in your attic."

"In the attic?"

"To haul out your winter coat."

"Ah. I see." Parker latched the screen door to keep it from

flapping in the wind, grinning as he closed and bolted the inside door. "I'm gonna check the windows and make sure nothing is open."

"Okay. While you do that, I'll put on a pot of tea." She rubbed her hands together. "That'll warm us right up."

Like he needed a cup of tea to warm him. *Oh, you're in trouble, Brant. Big trouble,* he thought, taking the stairs two at a time. He wondered how long it would take Holly to get back to the subject of his relationship with Maude. Never, he hoped, because he had no idea how to explain it. If anyone else had brought up the subject, he'd have wasted no time in telling them to butt out. But this wasn't anybody else. This was Holly, who'd soon become his writing partner. Who'd pitched in today as his first mate—and did a stellar job of it too—and who, as Hank so astutely pointed out, put her all into everything she did. He sensed that, if he had a mind to, she was a woman he could confide in and that she'd dish up some sane and sound advice. Why? Because, to put it simply, she was the woman who, despite his efforts to prevent it and without even trying, had stolen his heart.

Chapter Ten

....

The storm had raged for most of the night, and in the morning, Parker stumbled into the kitchen, sheet wrinkles lining his handsome face and his dark hair poking out in all directions.

"What time did you get up?" he asked, slumping across from Holly at the kitchen table.

"Oh, an hour or so, I guess." She stacked the daily newspaper and stood to grab a mug from the shelf above the stove. "Coffee's ready. Can I pour you a cup?"

Yawning, he scratched his bristly chin then grabbed the sports section. "I can get it myself."

My, but he looked cute, all tousled and sleepy-eyed. And it was nice to know he didn't wake up grumpy. That would certainly make early-morning meetings easier to bear. "I don't doubt that for a minute."

She placed a cup near his elbow as Parker said, "The O's have lost six straight games. Do I know how to pick a winner or what?" He tossed the paper back onto the stack and poked his long forefinger through the mug's handle. "What smells so good?"

"I took the liberty of rummaging around and found all the ingredients to make a sausage-egg casserole. It's in the oven, and it'll be ready in about fifteen minutes. How 'bout some juice while you're waiting? If memory serves, Maude has orange, cranberry, apple, and tomato in the fridge."

"She keeps the cranberry around for me," he said, a lopsided grin brightening his handsome features. "Even though I've never been particularly fond of the stuff."

There it was again...that peculiar edge that so often hardened his voice when speaking of his mom. Holly considered reopening the subject they'd started yesterday, before the rain had pounded down on them, but decided against it. He seemed the "elephant memory" type—which probably explained his attitude, now that she thought about it—and he no doubt remembered all too well that she asked way too many questions. If he wanted to answer them, so much the better. And if he didn't, well, maybe she'd find out what she needed to know as they worked together.

"If there's enough to go around, I wouldn't mind some OJ."

"There's plenty—for breakfast. Maybe later I'll hop in the car and make a run to the grocery store for your mom. I used the last of her eggs and all the sausage for the casserole."

"I can drive you." He sipped the juice she brought him. "Unless you'd rather go alone."

"I'd love the company! Besides, I have no idea where the grocery store *is*."

He blew a stream of air across the surface of his coffee. "Pretty tough to get lost in this town," he told her.

Is that how he'd look, Holly wondered, *if he puckered up to plant a kiss on my cheek?* She might have laughed out loud at the ludicrous thought if Maude hadn't rolled into the kitchen at that moment, smiling and sniffing the air.

"Have I died and gone to heaven? Coffee and a breakfast casserole, and I didn't have to lift a finger?" She parked her wheelchair alongside the table and patted Parker's forearm. "Thanks, sweetie."

"Don't thank me," he said, pointing at Holly. "She's the one who's been up since the crack of dawn, brewing and baking."

Maude's eyebrows rose. "But, Holly, you're our guest! You shouldn't be—"

"Now, now," Holly interrupted, "let's not forget 'the customer is always right' rule."

"Funny, but Parker used that same old cliché just a few days ago." Squinting, Maude added, "I forget why."

"Because Kate Sullivan has the power to stretch my patience to the breaking point," he ground out. To Holly, he said, "She's one of those people who makes me wish I was independently wealthy, so I could afford to tell her to take a hike when she calls to schedule a fishing trip."

"You give her that power, son."

"Mother knows best, I guess." Holly turned just in time to catch the merest glare emanating from his dark eyes. To his credit, Parker recovered quickly. If Maude noticed the sarcasm, she showed no sign of it. Then, thankfully, the oven timer dinged.

She'd barely opened the oven door before Parker said, "Well, I think that must have been the longest fifteen minutes in breakfast history." He drained his juice then got up and put his glass in the sink. He had to wait for her to move away from the stove in order to slide three plates from the cabinet. "Have a seat, Holly. Least I can do is serve up this great-smelling meal you made us."

"Oh, but really, I don't mind—"

"Humor me, then, okay?"

Was he smiling? Holly couldn't tell, because he'd turned around to gather flatware, napkins, and a pot holder that he then plopped in the center of the table.

"How do you serve up this stuff?" he asked, putting the dish on the pot holder. "Spatula? Spoon? Ladle?"

She jumped up to grab a wooden spoon. "This oughta do it."

She'd barely taken her seat when he said, "Do we just dig in? Slice it first?"

This time when she got up, it was to grab a steak knife from the cutlery drawer. "There y'go," she said, sitting again.

He bent over the table, but the blade never made contact with the food. "One slice at a time? Cut the whole thing at once?"

Gently, she eased the knife from his hand and proceeded to cut the casserole into twelve equal squares. "There!"

"Will the first piece fall apart, like pie or brownies? 'Cause if it does, I'll take that slice. It's only fair, after—"

Using the wooden spoon, Holly served each of them a slab. "Since you're closest to the fridge, you might want to grab the syrup. Some people like it sweet."

"Maude—I mean, *Mom*—doesn't keep the syrup in the fridge." He opened a cabinet door and withdrew the bottle. "I like mine plain, but there's different strokes, I suppose."

Conversation was light and happy all through the meal, and when Maude pushed away from the table, Parker started collecting the plates. "I'll do the dishes. Not the way I served up breakfast, either."

Laughing, Maude said, "I was wondering if you'd bring that up. You had the poor girl hopping like a toad on a hot rock, fetching this and that. Reminded me of an *I Love Lucy* episode. Remember the one where Lucy is pregnant and Ricky insists on serving her breakfast in bed?"

"Yes," Holly said, joining in her laughter. "The one where he can't find anything and Lucy has to keep getting up to go into the kitchen, and just when she's all settled back in bed, he needs something else, and—"

"All right, you two. The least you could do is wait until I've left to have a chuckle at my expense."

"Sorry, son."

"Yes, sorry, Parker."

"Fibbers," he said without missing a beat as he loaded the dishwasher. "Just remember that other old saying: 'What goes around, comes around.'" Then, "Hate to eat and wash and run, but I have an appointment in town." He folded the dish towel and hung it on the swing arm above the sink. "Catch up with you later, Holly? Maybe we can actually get that outline written before nightfall."

"Sure. What time should I meet you at your place?"

"I'll pick you up when I'm finished in town. Should be lunchtime by then. How about if I pick up a pizza?"

"The usual," Maude said.

"Pepperoni-mushroom, crispy crust, easy on the cheese, extra sauce." He bent to kiss her cheek then winked at Holly. "You two behave while I'm gone, hear?"

Maude snickered. "And what'll you do if we don't?"

"I'll bring home thick crust with extra cheese and light sauce, that's what."

He didn't wait for a reply, and when they heard the crunch of gravel beneath his shoes, Maude sighed. "Some days I think it's a miracle my heart doesn't just burst with love for that boy." She brightened and said, "Breakfast was delicious, Holly. Can I convince you to write down your recipe? It'll be a hit around here, I guarantee it."

"I'd be happy to." She refilled their coffee mugs then draped the casserole with aluminum foil. "It heats up great in the microwave, one slice at a time. And it's fantastic on toast with—"

"You don't need to sell me on it, girl. There's a tablet and pen in that drawer right behind you."

While Holly wrote down the ingredients and directions, Maude said, "When Henry was here earlier, he told me that you filled in as first mate yesterday. That's quite a job, especially for a little slip of a thing like you."

She looked up, but only long enough to say, "I was only too happy to help out." *I'd do more, so much more, if only he'd let me.* Holly wondered if, by summer's end, she'd understand what made Parker tick. Sighing, she turned her attention back to the recipe.

"I just have to say, you're nothing like his other girlfriends."

She almost laughed. "Girlfriends?" She handed the recipe to his mom. *Don't let Parker hear you say that!* she thought. *You'll jinx things!* But that would have been a silly thing to say, even if she believed in such things. And she didn't. Well, with the possible exception of Murphy's Law. And who could blame her for that?

Maude glanced at the paper before tucking it into her pocket, and for the next hour, she held Holly spellbound with stories of Parker's romantic past. Or, to be more accurate, his *un*romantic past. Her heart ached for him, for the way he'd been used and abused and even left standing at the altar once. No wonder he seemed so ill at ease around her.

"And what about you?" Maude wanted to know.

"What about me?"

"Well, I can't believe that a girl as pretty and sweet and smart as you are doesn't have some sort of romantic past. What are you, twenty-something?"

"Thirty," Holly said.

"Okay, thirty. You didn't get all the way to the ripe old age of thirty without making some poor man fall head over heels for you."

She debated whether to tell the woman about Jimmy. And Ethan. "There was only one 'head over heels' episode in my past," she said. "He was my best friend, my confidant, the answer to my prayers."

"Was?"

"We were in the Florida Keys when..." Holly didn't know if she had it in her to tell the story, especially to a near stranger. But then, maybe it would be easier, reciting cold, clinical facts to someone who had never met Jimmy, who didn't know her well enough to hear the agony in her voice. "I was working for the University of Maryland at the time, researching rays for an upcoming class on marine biology. And Jimmy was there doing an underwater photo shoot for *National Geographic*. A motorboat raced by overhead, stirred up the water, and agitated the rays. One speared him, and—"

Maude gasped. "You mean like that TV fellow from Australia who always did such dangerous and crazy things?"

"Exactly like that."

The woman reached across the table and blanketed Holly's hands with her own. "Oh, honey, I'm so sorry."

Holly only nodded.

"How long ago did it happen?"

"It was three years last month since..." She sipped her coffee, afraid that if she said another word, she'd burst into tears. And if Parker walked in while she was blubbering like a baby, well, how would she explain herself?

"Were you together long when...you know...?"

Holly nodded. "We were the stereotypical high school sweethearts. Attended the same college, got our doctorates at the same university, secured jobs in the Baltimore/DC area..." She exhaled a shaky sigh. "We were supposed to get married that year. In December. And take a Christmas cruise for our honeymoon."

Maude nodded too. "I know it's hard to believe, me being more than twice your age and all, but I know how you felt. How you still feel. Parker's father was the love of my life. When he left, I thought I'd just dry up and blow away like sand." She took a deep breath and sat up straighter. "But here we sit, survivors of the worst kind of heartache, none the worse for the wear."

Easy to say, Holly thought—but from where she sat, there wasn't an ounce of truth in Maude's words. If Ethan had come along at some other time in her life, they might have had a chance. How many times had he said that she seemed detached? How often had he accused her of still being in love with a dead man? Too many times to count. *Remember that, Holly,* she told herself, *next time you get all googly-eyed over Parker.* The poor guy had already suffered too many broken hearts. She couldn't in all fairness subject him to another, on the off chance she'd finally put Jimmy's memory to rest.

"He was a test pilot," Maude was saying. "Oh, what a dashing figure he cut in his uniform! I can't believe how young and foolish I was back then, telling myself that if he had to choose the Air Force over me, I'd win."

They heard the roar of Parker's old pickup, followed by the *creak-slam* of the driver's door. "He won't have any trouble believing we sat here this whole time, chattering like a couple of magpies," Maude said. "What he won't believe is that we barely scraped the surface!"

Her merry laughter echoed in the sunny kitchen and inspired a smile on Holly's face too. "I'll grab some napkins and paper plates," she said. "At least that way *one* of us will be in a different spot than we were when he left here."

"You're such a thoughtful, helpful girl," Maude said.

Thoughtfulness had nothing to do with it. And she wasn't doing it to be helpful, either, Holly admitted. The sole reason she'd put her back to the door was to give her time to erase any misery that her storytelling might have etched on her face, because the last thing she wanted to do was explain it all again to a concerned Parker.

More important than that, the last thing Parker needed, with his history, was to *hear* all about it.

* * * * *

"I can't believe my eyes," he said, grinning, as he slid the pizza box onto the table. "Have the two of you been here blabbing the whole time I was gone?"

"Not the *whole* time," Maude said. "Holly helped me to the powder room once. And talked to her mom for a minute on her cell phone."

"I hope you got all the gossiping out of your system this morning, because once we get started on this book, it's hard to tell when— or if—you'll get another chance at it."

"Gossip?" Maude groaned. "Of all the…well, I never!"

Holly handed out paper plates and napkins then lifted the lid on the pizza box. "What makes you think we were gossiping?"

He looked from Holly to Maude and back again. "You're women, that's what." If she knew exactly how *much* a woman he thought her to be, Holly might turn tail and run.

"What'll you have to drink?" she asked him. "I made iced tea and lemonade, and Maude has a few sodas in the fridge."

"Nice tall glass of ice water will satisfy me just fine."

"Make it two, sweetie," Maude said, "as long as you're up." And turning to her son, she added, "This girl is just one big ball of thoughtful, I tell you!"

From his point of view, there wasn't anything big about Holly. Except for her eyes. And her heart. And okay, the thoughtfulness that inspired her helpful nature.

"So what sent you into town?" Maude asked. "Another 'Save the Light' meeting?"

"No. That isn't until Monday." He glanced at Holly. "Might be nice if you sat in on it. You know, see what you can pick up that we might include in the book?"

Nodding, she took a bite of pizza—such a huge bite that he almost added "mouth" to his list of her big things. Chuckling, he continued explaining where he'd been all morning. "Stray cat showed up at my door night before last," he said. "Big friendly thing without a collar or an ID tag, so I took him to the vet to see if maybe his owners had implanted him with one of those microchips. Turns out they didn't. And the cat's a she, not a he." He helped himself to another slice of pizza. "I put some 3x5 cards in all the usual places, hung 'lost cat' signs on a few telephone poles.... And the vet said that if anybody comes into the clinic claiming to have lost a cat, he'll give them my number."

"What if no one calls?" Maude asked.

He shrugged. "Then I guess I've got me a cat."

"Have you named her?"

"No. I figure there's plenty of time for that if nobody claims her."

Maude sniffed. "I can't picture you with a cat, Parker."

"Why not?"

"Well, you're...you're—"

"More a dog kind of guy?" Holly put in.

"No, more like, he's not a *commitment* kind of guy."

That was hardly fair, considering his past, but he didn't intend to open that can of worms right here, right now.

"So where is it?"

"Took her back to my place."

"She isn't declawed, is she?"

"Matter of fact, she is. I couldn't have done it to her, but she gets a big kick out of trying to claw up the furniture, so I'm not about to judge whomever did."

"So she's over there with the free run of your house?"

"Yes, Maude," he said with as much patience as he could muster. Why the third degree, anyway? It was a stray cat, for the luvva Pete. "If it turns out she's staying, I'll make her one of those little swinging doors, so she can go in and out any time she—"

"Oh no, son. That would be irresponsible. She has no claws. How would she defend herself against dogs or bigger cats or whatever else might attack her?"

"She did all right before adopting me," he pointed out. "Vet says that by the looks of her, she's been on her own for months, that I'm lucky she didn't turn feral."

Suddenly, Parker had no appetite whatsoever. What was it with Maude, anyway, that inspired her to zero in on his sore spots and peck away like a starving hen? She'd nagged every man who'd come into her life, whether for a month or a year, making Parker wonder, even as a kid, why they'd put up with it for as long as they did.

He didn't like the resentful thoughts. Didn't like himself much for thinking them, either. Experience had taught him that if he didn't put a little time and distance between himself and Maude, so he could gather some perspective, he'd end up blurting out something he'd regret. Because for better or worse, Maude was his mom, and as such, she deserved his respect. The Good Book said "Honor thy father and thy mother." Period. God hadn't tacked on any qualifiers like "when respect has been earned."

On his feet now, he put his paper plate and napkin into the trash can and his water glass into the dishwasher. "I hate to rush you, Holly, but we've got a lot to do."

"Oh, don't give that another thought. I can be ready in two minutes."

Something in her sparkly blue eyes told him that she understood exactly why he'd decided to leave all of a sudden. He didn't know what it was, but he could have hugged her for it all the same. "You go ahead and do whatever you need to," he said, "and I'll get

Maude situated in the parlor." Almost as an afterthought, he said, "Any new guests checking in this evening?"

"Nope. I'm free as a bird for the next few days."

"Good. That way you won't be tempted to push yourself." He rolled the wheelchair into the parlor as Holly bounded up the stairs. "Couple more weeks off your feet and you'll be right back where you were before the surgery."

"Dear Lord," she said, laughing, "I certainly hope not! I limped around for years on these corn- and bunion-ridden feet before finally making the decision to have my old tootsies repaired!"

Thankfully he was behind her, so she couldn't see that he'd clenched his teeth to say, "Well, yeah, that's true. But you know what I meant, right?"

She reached back and patted his hand. "'Course I do. You're the best son any mother ever had. I know how blessed I am."

If that's true, he wanted to say, *then why do you jump at every chance to find fault with me?*

"Have I told you lately how proud of you I am?"

He put on the chair's breaks then gently lifted her from its seat and deposited her on the sofa. "I'll gather up a few snacks and something for you to drink," he said, handing her the TV's remote control. "You have a yen for anything special?"

She patted her belly. "I had one too many slices of that pizza, so no. I should be fine until Henry gets here. He's bringing my favorite movie. And popcorn!"

Parker chuckled. "What will this make, a hundred viewings? More?"

"A hundred. Listen to you." Laughing, she said, "If we watch it once tonight, it'll bring the total to seventy-nine."

And she could recite every line right along with the actors. *Well, whatever floats your boat,* he thought, heading into the kitchen. Holly was there when he entered, putting away the last of the pizza mess. "You weren't kidding when you said you'd be ready in two minutes, were you?"

"There are few things I hate more than to be kept waiting." She shrugged. "Golden Rule, y'know?"

He slid a tray from under the sink and filled it with chips, chocolates, and bottled water. Holly tossed a few napkins onto the pile and then dampened some paper towels and tucked them into a zipper bag. "In case her hands get sticky, eating the chocolates," she explained as she added it to the tray. "This might be a tad indelicate, but…"

"But what?" he asked, hoisting the tray.

"If she can't walk, how will she use the, ah, you know, the facilities? Do you think maybe we should work here? I brought my laptop. We could set it up right here, or in the dining room."

How like her to worry about something like that. "Nah. All my notebooks and research papers are at my place. Hank will be here soon and—"

"I'm sure he means well," she interrupted, "but Parker…he's a *man.* Don't you think your mom would be more comfortable taking care of, you know, *things* with another woman instead?"

"She's never complained."

"She doesn't seem the type."

He could tell that he was fighting a losing battle. If he had a white flag, he'd wave it. Grinning, Parker handed the tray to Holly. "It'll only take me ten, fifteen minutes to go home and gather up my stuff. After you deliver this to Maude, maybe you can set us up in the library. It's right beside the parlor, so if she needs, you know, *things,* you'll be able to hear her."

All his life, he'd been hearing the phrase "Her face lit up like a Christmas tree." But until that moment, Parker hadn't experienced it firsthand.

"We'll both be able to concentrate better," she said, backing out of the room.

She'd been gone a full minute before he unpocketed his keys and walked toward his truck. "Well, if that don't beat all." He couldn't help but chuckle a bit as he slid behind the wheel. "If that just don't beat all."

Chapter Eleven
....

"And here I thought I knew what an outline was," he said, leaning over the table. "I've never seen anything like this in my life."

"I sort of pulled it together from a bunch of how-to books I've read and seminars I've attended. So if you notice anything that might streamline it, say the word and we'll incorporate it into the plan."

"Hard to improve upon perfection," he said. And he wasn't just referring to her outline, either. "In just a couple of hours, we've nearly finished it." He sat back and, crossing both arms over his chest, nodded. "You're something else, Dr. Hollace Leonard."

"Cut it out," she said, laughing. "Blushing cuts off the blood supply to my brain." She met his eyes and, reading his smile, arched an eyebrow. "What? You don't believe me? Keep it up, Captain, and you'll see for yourself."

He couldn't say "uncle" before, but he could say it now. "Okay, you win. From now on, you'll get nothing but nagging and criticism from me."

"Oh, dear…"

Parker leaned forward again. "Oh, dear?"

"I don't work well under pressure, either." And then she launched into a merry rendition of "Good Time."

She had a really pretty voice—not that he was surprised— and a real knack for putting him in a good mood too. It amazed him that two people could laugh as hard as he and Holly had these past two hours and yet get so much done. Psychologists had been saying for years that positive outcomes could be expected when compatible people worked together, and now Parker had proof of it.

But she'd worked hard today and on the boat yesterday, and it was beginning to show. When Holly tried not to yawn and failed, Parker decided to call it a night. "I'm sure Maude won't mind if we leave this stuff here," he said, "since there aren't any guests scheduled for the next few days." He stretched and loosed an exaggerated yawn. "I don't know about you, but I'm beat. What-say we pick this up tomorrow, after breakfast?"

"After we make a grocery store run, you mean. I poked through the pantry, the fridge, and the cabinets and made a list. I'll show it to your mom in the morning and see if she has anything to add to it."

This time when he yawned, it wasn't fake. "I'll check on Mau— on Mom one last time when we're done in here, and then I'm going home to hit the hay."

Holly tidied their papers and saved their work on the laptop then sent him a tired smile. "I don't think it's going to take me a full minute to fall asleep tonight. I'll just stay good night to Maude, and then I'm hitting the hay too."

They walked side by side down the hall, stopping in the doorway to exchange an amused glance. There in the parlor, Maude dozed on the couch while Hank snored softly in the recliner. "I almost hate to wake him," Parker said.

"I know what you mean."

"But if I don't, he'll wake up with a monster crick in his neck."

"He really does look peaceful sitting there, doesn't he? Like he belongs right there beside her."

"Shh," Parker said. "If she hears that you approve, he'll be gone like that." He snapped his fingers, which roused Hank.

"Remind me to ask you about *that* in the morning," Holly said as the older man got to his feet and shuffled toward them.

"What's this I hear—you've got yourself a cat?" Hank whispered.

"She just showed up the other night, and it doesn't look like she has plans to leave anytime soon."

Hank nodded. "Yeah, Maudie told me you had it checked out at the vet's. That was good of you, Parker. Had me a dog once. I know what pets cost."

He waved the compliment away. "Anybody would have done the same thing."

"If that were true," Holly pointed out, "the cat wouldn't have been allowed to roam about and end up on your porch."

Well, he hadn't thought of it quite that way, but Parker supposed she had a point.

"How 'bout if I pop over first thing in the morning," Hank said, "so you can introduce me to her?"

"Sounds good to me."

Holly stood in the foyer, one hand on the door jamb, as both men descended the porch steps. Looking more like the hostess than a guest at the cottage, she said, "I'll lock up good and tight and check on Maude before I go upstairs."

"Thanks," Parker and Hank said together.

She started to close the interior door then stopped. "You know what she needs?"

"What?" they harmonized.

"A baby monitor."

The men exchanged a puzzled glance as she explained. "Leave the base near Maude; take the receiver with us. That way, it'd be like someone is always right there beside her."

"That's a great idea," Hank said.

Parker nodded his agreement. "We'll pick one up when we're out tomorrow." He grinned up at her. "Now shut the door, turn off the porch light—and that brain of yours—and go to bed, will ya?"

It wasn't easy, putting his back to her, but Parker managed it. Mostly because he knew that in less than twelve hours, he'd see her again.

And until then, he'd see her in his dreams, because at least there, he had half a chance at a future with her.

* * * * *

It was barely past six a.m. when Hank arrived with a sack of donuts in one hand and a cardboard carrier with two Styrofoam cups of coffee in the other. He put them both on the redwood picnic table and tilted a terra cotta planter to retrieve the extra key Parker had hidden. "One of these days," he muttered, grabbing it, "somebody with bad intentions is gonna find this, and then—"

A quiet *meow* interrupted him, and he looked down at the orange-and-white-striped tabby that wove a figure eight around his ankles. "Ah, you must be the little orphan I've heard so much about." The cat looked up and, blinking big golden-brown eyes, chirruped happily.

He stuck the key into the bolt and said, "I distinctly remember Parker's mother telling him it was a bad idea to let you roam around outside, with no claws to defend yourself." The door opened with a quiet *click* as the cat sauntered inside with a flick of her tail.

"So where's the captain?" he asked, turning on the light above the stove. "Isn't like him to sleep in."

"Didn't sleep in," Parker said from the next room. "Got up at five and ran one mile up the beach and another mile back."

"And now I suppose you're climbing the rock wall in your living room. You know, to give your arms the same workout your legs just got."

Laughing, Parker strode nonchalantly into the kitchen, his bare feet slapping across the hard wood. "When you said you wanted to stop by first thing, I didn't figure you intended to get here before sunup."

"If you weren't such a lazy slob," Hank shot back, "you'd know that the sun *is* up." He snickered and pointed at the coffee and donuts. "Brought some sustenance." Bending, he picked up the feline. "Now, how about an introduction to Miss Kitty, here?"

Parker opened the donut bag and grabbed a chocolate-glazed cruller. Hoisting one of the coffee cups, he said, "Hank, meet Cat. Cat, this is Hank."

She reached up and rubbed Hank's cheek with the side of her face, purring all the while. "Oh, she's a charmer, Parker. If you don't keep her, I will."

"You know, that's not a bad solution to this problem."

"What problem?"

"Of who'll take care of her when I go to Afghanistan."

Hank sat at the kitchen table, and Cat settled on his lap. "You found the boy?"

"Not yet. But it could happen any day. And I'd be gone for a couple of weeks. Cats are resourceful, so my friends who own them tell me, but they can't take care of themselves for that long."

Hank scratched between her ears. "She's litter-trained?"

"Yep," Parker said around a mouthful of donut.

"Then if nobody claims her, let me know."

"Why wait? She seems to be in love." Parker chuckled. "And if you want my honest opinion, so are you."

"Might be nice having someone to talk to besides myself at night."

"I said the same thing the night she showed up. You're welcome to all the stuff I bought her: bowls, food, collar, toys...."

"I hope I won't live to regret this, but you've got yourself a deal. I only see one problem."

"Which is?"

"You scribbled your number all over town. How will her owners get in touch with me? If they show up, that is."

"Don't worry, Hank. I'll get word to you." Parker chuckled. "You FBI agents think everything to death. No wonder you retire early."

"Hey. Don't knock the Agency. It was my connections that hooked you up with the bigwigs who are working on getting you and Ben together."

"And I'll never be able to thank you enough for that."

"Even if it doesn't happen?"

* * * * *

Hank's question hit Parker like a sucker punch to the jaw. He didn't want to believe in anything less than a successful outcome. But reality wasn't always pretty, and he had the scars and the limp to prove it. "Even if it doesn't happen."

"So what time are you meeting with Holly?"

Clever, Parker thought. And then he smiled, because it felt good, knowing that someone understood him well enough to recognize the signs of uneasiness when he saw them. "I didn't give her a time, just said I'd stop by this morning. I promised to take her to the grocery store so she can restock Maude's kitchen and pantry."

Hank grinned. "I must be getting old and senile, because I would have sworn that Holly is a Coastal Cottage guest."

"You *are* old and senile," Parker teased, "but that doesn't make you wrong. It's just something she wants to do, and if I didn't drive her, she'd drive herself. And with that breath-mint-sized car of hers, it'd take a dozen trips. I'd never be able to live with myself, knowing how much gasoline she was wasting."

Hank whistled. "You said a mouthful there!" He popped the lid off his cup. Suddenly the jovial smile was gone, and in its place was a fatherly frown. "Maude told me an interesting tale last night about Holly's past. Things I think you ought to know, since you'll be working so closely with her all summer."

"What kind of things?"

"You can't let on that you know. Maude'll skin me alive."

Unless the man said she was married, Parker could handle

it. He held up the Boy Scout salute. "I'm all ears, and my lips are zipped."

"If you're ever invited to a costume party, that might make quite a mask. I'd wager you'll be the only one there with—"

"Hank, neither one of us is getting any younger."

"Sorry, son," he said, chuckling. "When you're right, you're right." He started with the sudden and violent death of Holly's fiancé. "Seems her family rode her pretty hard to stop living in the past. She feels guilty about what happened between her and the last fella she dated."

"Guilty? But what would Holly have to feel guilty about?"

Hank only shrugged. "I don't know what they expected. I only know what she told Maudie and what Maudie told me. The guy cheated on Holly, and Maudie is convinced that the poor girl only started seeing other people so her family would quit worrying that she'd mourn her fiancé forever." Hank's eyes narrowed. "You want my opinion?"

The man had never been anything but straight with him, even when it wasn't comfortable, and his advice had been some of the best Parker had ever heard. "Yeah," he said, "I do."

Hank leaned forward, which didn't set well with the cat. She leaped down from his lap and looked up, sleepy eyes seemingly accusing him of disturbing her peaceful nap. She strutted off, tail flicking, and found a nonmoving place to sleep on Parker's favorite chair. "Sorry, Cat," Hank said. Chuckling, he added, "Haven't even taken her home yet and already she's got me jumping through hoops."

He met Parker's gaze. "Now, don't get me wrong, I think the world of your mother, son, but she can be..." Hank frowned, searching for the right term. "She's unlike anyone I know. She'd give you her last meal and the shirt off her back. Why, I'd wager the woman would share just about anything she has with anyone who needs it—except her heart."

Parker nodded. He'd often wondered why Hank stuck by her, knowing she'd never love him as much as he loved her.

"I know what you think," Hank continued, "that I shouldn't put up with her arm's-distance treatment, that I should demand that she give as good as she gets. But your dad was the love of her life. If I don't measure up, well, that's more my fault than hers, now isn't it?" He shrugged. "I figure, if I hang in there long enough, she'll decide that second-best is good enough."

Sadly, Hank was right, and Parker knew it. Everything from the man's posture to the pained expression on his face made it clear that he was hurting. "And if she never does?"

"Then I'll go to my grave a better man for having known her."

Parker could only shake his head. He remembered what Hank had said about Holly—how lucky any man would be to have a woman in his life who didn't do things halfway. He hadn't made the connection then, but he made it now. It was Hank's secret wish for himself and Maude. "I wish I knew what made her tick, Hank, believe me, I do." His elbows resting on the table, he leaned forward and quoted Hank. "You want my opinion?"

"Sure. Let me have it."

"If she ever loved my father—and nothing she's said or done backs that up—it turned to hate over the years. My best guess is that time took the hard edge off the hate and turned it to…I don't know…disgust?" He sighed, tipped his coffee cup, and saw his rippled reflection on the surface of the dark liquid. "No point in beating yourself up, Hank. She is what she is. Nobody would blame you if you...y'know..."

"I appreciate that, son, but I'm not going anywhere." He winked. And smiled. "Who knows? God might decide to answer my prayers and wake that woman up once and for all." He chuckled. "Wouldn't I feel like the fool of the century if He did it after I'd stomped off to make some stupid point!"

Parker wanted to admit that his mother didn't deserve loyalty and affection like that. Instead, he said, "She's lucky to have you."

Bobbing his head, Hank glanced at the clock. "Holy moly. Where has the time gone? I have a doctor's appointment in fifteen minutes." He got up and tossed their empty coffee cups into the trash. "As the cowboys say, we're burnin' daylight. And if I don't get out of here, you'll be burnin' the midnight oil, making up for lost time."

The cat sat up then arched her back and meowed, as if to say, "Aren't you forgetting something?"

"Routine physical?"

"Yeah, something like that." Then he said, "How about if I come back for the cat and her stuff afterward?"

Parker walked him to the door. "You know where everything is."

"Speaking of that key," Hank said. "You have to find a new hiding place. That one's just—"

"A very wise man once told me that if you can think of a place to put a key, a burglar has already thought of it."

"Touché. I guess. But it wouldn't hurt to move it around once in a while. You know, confuse the would-be robbers. Why make it easy for 'em?"

"You're the only one who has ever used that key. Where do you suggest I hide it?"

Hank frowned. "Let me think on it and get back to you." He gave the cat a quick pat on the head then huffed down the back porch steps. "Have fun shopping," he said, laughing.

Fun, Parker thought, closing the door. *Yeah, right.* Knowing what he did about Holly's past, how was he supposed to make *that* happen?

* * * * *

He'd never been to the grocery store with anyone but Maude, and that had been so long ago, Parker could barely remember it. He pushed the cart as Holly dropped things into the basket, chattering the entire way.

At first, thinking she'd been talking to him, he'd said, "Sorry, didn't hear you" and "Really?" But he knocked that off pretty quick when she met every question with a confused and wide-eyed, "What?"

Strangely, he enjoyed trailing behind her, watching her frown as she inspected the fruit and squint as she did the mental math to determine which products were the better deals, listening as she grumbled to herself about things like price gouging and captive audiences. Near as he could figure, she'd aimed that particular barb at the store's manager, who knew that the tourists didn't have much choice but to fork over whatever amount was stamped on every can of peas and box of noodles. Parker didn't have to ask who "he" was when, in the dairy aisle, she'd muttered, "How can the man sleep at night?" And the same was true in the frozen-foods department, where she'd thrown up her hands and said, "Doesn't he have a *conscience*?"

She'd worn a sleeveless white blouse into the store, and Parker found himself thanking that conscience-less store manager for setting the AC so high that Holly had to untie the University of Maryland sweatshirt she'd wrapped around her waist. There was a lot to like about Holly Leonard, not the least of which was the way she filled out a pair of khaki shorts. Her little white sneakers squeaked now and then as she made quick starts and stops on the polished linoleum, and once, she'd stooped to retie the laces. "I'll never understand why they stopped making them out of cotton," she said, tugging at the tidy bow. "These acrylic things are just downright annoying."

Acrylic. The word annoyed him for an entirely different reason, because it reminded him that he hadn't had time to uncap a single tube of paint in weeks. Maybe this fall, when the fishing excursions ended, he'd attempt to capture Holly's glittering eyes and happy smile. He hoped so, anyway, because then, at least, he'd have the painting to remember her by when she went back to her busy life in Baltimore.

"What's your favorite ice cream?"

The question caught him by surprise, mostly because she was looking right at him when she asked it. "Who, me?"

Holly laughed. "Yes, you. Who else?"

He shrugged. "Oh, I dunno…maybe the invisible shopper you've been talking a blue streak to since we walked into the store?"

"You're cute when you grin like that," she said. "And who knew you had dimples?"

She put a fingertip into one, and it took all his concentration to keep from grabbing her wrist and pulling her into a hug.

"You really ought to smile more. Lots more." She went back to shopping. "Very flattering. Erases ten years from your face too."

Parker harrumphed quietly, but he didn't fail to notice that he was smiling when he did so. "Fudge ripple," he said.

Holly turned around so fast that she nearly spun clean off her feet. "Huh?"

He caught her before she careened into the shelf behind her. "Got a thing for Paul Newman?"

Did she have any idea how much it made him want to kiss her when she wrinkled her nose that way? Parker inhaled a calming breath. "You were about to get real cozy with him just now." He nodded at the neat row of salad-dressing bottles.

She glanced over her shoulder then bobbed her head as understanding dawned. "Remember when I said my friend's dad could get you an audition at his comedy club?"

"Yeah…"

"Well, I take it back." Her merry laughter drew the attention of several other shoppers—one who smiled, one who frowned, one who rolled her eyes. "Oops," she said, slapping a hand over her mouth.

Why did he still have one hand on her shoulder and the other on her hip, when she'd regained her balance a full minute ago? He let go of her and reached into the cart, rearranging the loaf of bread and package of biscuits she'd tucked into the kid compartment. Admittedly, his hands weren't anywhere near as warm now as when they'd been in contact with Holly. The thought, for some odd reason, reminded him that she'd kicked off this whole scene by asking him about his favorite ice cream. "Fudge ripple," he said again, hoping to distract himself from the weird emotions roiling in his heart. "The more fudge, the better."

"Wow."

"Wow?"

"Yeah, wow."

"What on earth does that—"

"It's my favorite too." She met his eyes.

Coincidence? He didn't think so. Considering the hundreds of flavors out there, he had to agree. "Wow."

Grinning, she tossed a half gallon of the stuff into the cart. "We have everything on the list," she announced, "so I guess we're finished."

What a shame, he thought, because he would have been content to follow her around the store for another hour—or two—without complaint. That surprised him, because Parker had always hated shopping. Hated stores and standing in line and parking lots too. He shrugged. Yeah, there was a whole lot to like about Holly Leonard, all right.

Chapter Twelve

·····················

The volunteers had ripped an enormous pile of plant material from the sand, and it continued to grow as the morning progressed. Vitex, Holly knew, was sometimes used by beachfront communities to aid in erosion control. It had earned its nickname as "the kudzu of the coast" because it grew fast, covering the dunes and choking out more desirable plants like sea oats and grass. Worse, it hampered the loggerheads' ability to nest.

Strike one.

Folly Beach was prone to erosion, and the dunes weren't particularly stable either.

Strike two.

The weather this May had also hindered the loggerheads' activities. Unusually cool and stormy, the air and water temperatures delayed the turtles' approach.

Strike three.

Thankfully, the volunteers' determined efforts kept the negatives under control, and there was evidence, finally, that the turtles had begun their annual trek ashore. Ruts carved into the sand by front flippers and heavy-shelled bodies led straight to the nests, where mothers used their back flippers to dig nests then deposited a hundred eggs or more before covering them up and heading back out to sea. The eggs on the bottom had the best chance of hatching… provided that heat, bacteria, ghost crabs, and other invaders didn't interrupt the growth cycle.

Even with the hard work of volunteers, only a small percentage of the eggs would hatch to make the long crawl to the Atlantic. Of those, even fewer would survive sharks, fishing nets, boat propellers, and pollutants. Without them, the endangered loggerheads would sink into extinction. Holly said a silent prayer of thanks to the dedicated people who'd joined the Folly Beach Turtle Watch program, because despite what the name hinted at, their duties were rooted in determined, vigilant beach preparation rather than turtle watching.

She used her cell phone to take pictures and scribbled copious notes into her spiral tablet. Thirty-one nests at last count—not bad, so early in the season. In another forty-five days, sixty at most, the babies would start the great migration that, thanks to inborn tracking talents, would lead surviving females back again when it was their time to nest.

Holly hoped she'd be one of the lucky volunteers who, while reminding tourists and residents to turn off their porch lights and shooing dogs, raccoons, and birds from nests, would witness one of the miracles of God's creation. If she was fortunate enough to see one of the enormous females lumbering in from the Atlantic, so much the better.

Parker limped up the beach, dragging a wad of Vitex. He tossed it onto the already-huge mound collected by other volunteers then trotted up to Holly. "You ready to head out?"

"Sure. But we'll come back, right—tonight?"

"Won't be anything to see tonight."

"We could get lucky and spot a loggerhead on her way to build a nest."

He nodded. "We could, I suppose." He waited until she stuffed her supplies into her backpack before sliding an arm around her waist and leading her toward the dock and the planking that led to where he'd tied up the *Sea Maverick*. "I figured we could motor out to Morris Island so you can get an up-close-and-personal look at the damage. And photographs. We'll need those for the book too."

Their outline included a whole section about the lighthouse and another about the turtles. There would be twelve chapters in all, starting with the name change from Coffin Island to Folly Island. The famous Edwin S. Taylor Fishing Pier and pavilion, the board-walk and amusement park, the story of how Gershwin rented a cabin in Folly and wrote *Porgy and Bess*, even the hurricane-battered boat that had become a Folly landmark would be featured. Parker's goal, he'd told her by e-mail even before she'd come to town, was to prove to tourists that Charleston wasn't the only beautiful and historic city on South Carolina's coast. And now having spent more than a month here, Holly was inclined to agree and only too happy to do her part to make travelers aware of this quaint and picturesque town.

"How long do you think we'll be on the water?"

"An hour, two at most." He slowed his pace to ask, "Why?"

"No reason, really, except that I was going to offer to pack us a lunch...if it was going to take longer, that is."

Parker glanced at the cloudless blue sky. "Last time I checked with my appointment secretary, there were no meetings scheduled.

If you want to float around out there a while after we've finished working, that's okay by me."

"Might be nice to get a few shots of the Atlantic…and the sunset."

He looked at his watch. "It's barely noon."

Holly shrugged. "I like it out there. Can you blame me?"

"No. But the way you're dressed," he said, giving her shorts and sleeveless shirt a quick once-over, "you're just begging for a bad sunburn."

"So I'll put on some sunscreen before we go out. After I slap together some sandwiches. And throw a few bottles of water into a cooler."

Parker stepped into her path. "Tell you what," he said, placing his hands on her shoulders, "you go on back to the cottage and slather on some lotion and let me take care of the food and drinks."

She looked up into his handsome face, hoping he couldn't hear her heart pounding away like a parade drum. What was it about this guy that could change her behavior from a feet-on-the-ground scientist to that of a giddy teenager just by looking at her with those dark-lashed chocolate eyes of his?

"Don't look so shocked," he said. "I can slap together sandwiches too, y'know."

So he'd read her silly expression as surprise, had he? Well, good. Because that sure beat having him know how empty-headed and weak-kneed she felt in his presence. Especially lately. In the weeks she'd been in Folly Beach, her feelings for him had gone from detached and professional to friendly to something dangerously close to warmly romantic. "Pardon me," she joked, "for forgetting your complex warrior training."

Chuckling, he drew her into a light hug and then pressed a brotherly kiss to her cheek. "Go on," he said, giving her a gentle shove, "before I change my mind."

Holly nodded and half ran across the sand, wishing that when he'd kissed her, Parker had aimed a little *left*.

＊ ＊ ＊ ＊ ＊

Holly paged through the pictures she'd taken with her digital camera, smiling as the lighthouse, the sparkling Atlantic and its shore, and the sunset flicked by. "Leave it to your son to get a shot of the green flash," she said, handing the camera to Maude. "Most people live a lifetime without ever seeing it, and he manages to capture it on film."

"A multitude of hidden talents, that boy of mine."

"The whole time we were out there on the water, while he talked about the lighthouse and the turtles and the moods of the Atlantic, I kept asking myself if there's anything he *doesn't* know."

"He doesn't seem to know when he's sitting on a gold mine...."

Holly met Maude's dark eyes. "A gold mine?"

"You, silly girl. You're the best thing that's happened to him in recent memory, but he's too immersed in all his 'projects,'" she said, drawing quote marks in the air, "to have noticed."

Holly didn't know what to say, so she went back to shuffling through the photos she'd taken from the bow of the *Sea Maverick*. "Funny, but I never thought to ask him why he chose that name for his boat." Hopefully that would change the subject, and quickly.

Maude pointed at the bureau across the room. "There's a picture in that old dresser I'd like you to see."

Holly took the hint and walked toward it. "This one?"

Nodding, Maude said, "It's in the second drawer, under a bunch of old magazines and newspapers. Silver-framed black-and-white snapshot. One of my favorites."

Holly dug around in the drawer, trying not to make too big of a mess of the tidy stack. Why would Parker's mom hide a much-loved photo under all this junk? Finally, the corner of a silver frame peeked out from beneath an ancient issue of *Life* magazine. Holly rubbed her thumb over the glass. Surely she was mistaken— this couldn't be the man she'd seen in the Charleston restaurant, could it? The man whose wheelchair-bound mother thought Parker looked like him. That would be too much coincidence, even for somebody like her who believed in fate and chance meetings. Holly hadn't said so at the time, but she'd agreed with the woman…her son and Parker *did* look a lot alike. She held up the photo and said to Maude, "Is this it?"

"Yes, yes it is." One hand extended, Maude said, "Bring it here to me, will you, sweetie?"

Holly left the drawer open, thinking that Maude would probably want to bury the photo again, once she'd told its story.

Patting the cushion beside her, Maude said, "Sit."

And Holly did.

"This is Daniel Brant."

Holly's heart started beating double time.

"That's right, Parker's father."

She couldn't take her eyes from the photograph. "But…but I thought he was killed years ago, testing a fighter jet."

"That's what I allowed Parker to believe."

Turning slightly on the cushion, Holly faced his mom. "What you *allowed* him to believe?"

Tears pooled in Maude's eyes as she nodded. "Oh, sweetie, I'm afraid it's a long, sad story. And in all these years, I've only shared it with one other person."

Did that mean she planned to share it with *her*, here and now? Holly didn't know if she wanted to hear the story. Surely Maude would expect her to keep it to herself. But what if his mom said something that Holly thought Parker ought to know?

"Parker doesn't know, then? That Daniel is his father, I mean?"

"Oh, he knows *that*. I just never got around to telling him everything else."

Holly groaned inwardly. How would she get out of this gracefully?

"Isn't he just the most handsome man you've ever seen?"

"Second only to your son," she admitted.

Maude tugged at the sleeve of her sweater and used it to blot her tears. "Will you put it back for me, sweetie? I'm feeling a little sleepy. Think I'll just lie down here and take a nap."

She placed the photo on the coffee table long enough to plump Maude's pillow and cover her with the lightweight blanket. As she was tucking the photo back into its original hiding place, she spied another picture. This one wasn't framed, and she took care in sliding it from the stack. Instantly, she recognized a much-younger, much-happier Maude, sitting on Daniel's lap, her eyes sparkling. Daniel, on the other hand, looked anything but cheerful. Something between "afraid" and "trapped" described his expression far better. But why?

The mantel clock chimed six times. Holly had promised to meet Parker here at six to put the finishing touches on the book's foreword and dedication. It would be just her luck to be standing here, poking through his mother's antique bureau. She slid the pictures back where she'd found them and covered them with back issues of *The Saturday Evening Post, Look,* and *Ladies' Home Journal.* Maybe someday she'd page through a few of the issues and try to figure out why Maude had saved them all these years. *Surely not simply to hide her sad past,* she thought, sliding the drawer closed.

"You all ready to get to work?"

Holly stifled a squeal and faced the doorway. "Parker," she whispered, "you scared ten years off the end of my life."

Winking, he grinned. "I guess you owe me a thank-you, then."

She joined him in the hall. "A thank-you? For scaring me half to death?"

"I know it's small consolation, but I hear those are the ten worst years anyway."

Groaning, she headed into the library, where their materials still sat exactly as they'd left them yesterday.

He sat down across from her and picked up the last pages she'd printed out. "I know exactly what you're thinking."

"How lucky we are that none of Maude's guests are nosy?"

"Really? That's what you were thinking?"

No, Holly thought as Daniel Brant's image flashed through her mind. "What did you *think* I was thinking?"

"That you'd changed your mind. About that friend of yours getting me an audition at his comedy club."

A silly giggle popped out of her mouth, making her sound even goofier than she felt. "Oh. That." Another giggle, and then, "No. Comedy was the farthest thing from my mind."

"Ouch," he said, wincing. "You sure know how to hurt a guy."

If only you knew, Holly thought. "Pass me the dictionary, please?"

He did, and then said, "What're you looking up?"

She found "comedy" and, pointing at the passage, handed the book back to Parker.

"'Something amusing or funny,'" he read, before returning it to their book stack. "Guess you've told *me*," he said, grinning.

No, Holly thought, *I haven't told you. Yet.*

Chapter Thirteen
....

She hadn't expected to run into Hank, especially not at the gas station. But there he was, smiling and waving as the wind blew his white hair into his suntanned face. "What brings you out here so early of a Saturday morning?"

"Just topping off the tank," she said.

"Same here. Heard on the news this morning that they expect the price to rise. Again."

"Well, at least we aren't paying twelve dollars a gallon the way they are in Europe."

"Yet. But don't get me started." He laughed. "Say, I'm headed to the diner for some breakfast. Nothing sadder than an old man eating alone. What-say you join me? My treat."

Holly wondered if Hank was "the only other person" Maude had told about Daniel. She couldn't have orchestrated a better opportunity to find out. "I'd love to," she said, "but I have no idea where the diner is."

"Just follow me. In case we get separated, just ask anybody how to get to the Lost Dog."

Ten minutes later, they sat at a table near the windows in Folly's most notable breakfast spot. Every waitress acknowledged Hank with flirty grins, fluttering lashes, and terms of endearment. A white-aproned woman whose name tag said AGNES handed them menus and napkin-wrapped silverware. "Hey, dollface. How are you today?"

"I'm good. And you?"

"Better...now that you're here." She gave Holly a once-over. "Who's this little chickie, your daughter?"

Laughing, Hank said, "No, no. This is Dr. Hollace Leonard, in town to help Parker Brant with some book project he's working on."

"He's okay with you moving in on his territory, is he?" she teased.

"I'd never do that," Hank said. "Parker's half my age and twice my size."

Agnes laughed. "Coffee?" she asked, looking at Holly.

"Yes, please," she said. "Black for me."

"And you know how I like mine."

"You bet I do, Handsome." She winked. "Back in a jiff," she said, snapping her gum, "to take your orders."

"So," Holly said, grinning, "I understand you're about to adopt a pet."

"Looks that way. Shocked me, how fast that cat took to me."

"I'd be more shocked if she *didn't* take to you."

"Well, thanks for the compliment." He grinned. "I figure we'll make a good pair, that stray cat and me. Ain't like anybody else wants us."

"Please. The way every woman in here has been flirting with you?"

He shrugged off her compliment, and Holly knew it was because the only woman he wanted didn't seem to want him. *How sad,* she thought, *because they'd make a lovely couple.* "Maude showed me a photograph yesterday."

"Oh?"

"Big secret, buried deep in an old dresser." She cringed inwardly, because she hadn't planned to launch into the discussion that way. *A little finesse might be nice, Hol.*

"I'm not surprised, kiddo. You're easy to talk to."

Did that mean he knew about the picture?

The waitress arrived with their coffee. "Juice?" she asked, palming her tablet.

"Tomato for me," Holly said.

And Hank responded, "The usual."

"Y'all ready to order?"

"You first," Hank said.

"One egg over easy, bacon, white toast, and home fries."

"I'll have the same, only—"

"—two eggs over easy," Agnes finished for him. "You got it, cutie-pie." And winking, she sashayed away.

"That Agnes," he said, blushing.

"I wonder..."

"What?"

"If Maude would play so hard to get if she knew how many other women found you appealing?"

"I'd just as soon not win her over with jealousy." He chuckled. "I'm a little long in the tooth for black eyes and split lips."

Maude didn't seem the type who'd resort to such behavior, but she didn't point it out. Holly had a feeling Hank knew that even better than she did.

"So how much did she tell you? About Daniel, I mean?"

Was it her imagination, or did Hank's voice take on a bit of an edge just saying the man's name? "Nothing, really, except that he's Parker's father. It was weird," Holly told him, remembering how Maude's eyes had filled with tears and how she'd suddenly grown weary enough to require a nap just by looking at the black-and-white reminder of her past.

"He's more than that. A whole lot more, I'm afraid."

If there'd been any question about how Hank felt about Daniel, it was gone. Hank definitely had issues with the man who still seemed to hold control of Maude's heart.

Agnes brought their food and invited them to call her if they needed anything. When she was gone, Hank told the story as he knew it: it was love at first sight for Maude, who was young and naive when she'd met the good-looking soldier. Before she knew what was happening between them, she was pregnant. "She tried to tell him about the baby but chickened out when he said he'd been promoted, that he'd been reassigned to a base out West, where he'd get the chance of his lifetime, test piloting fighter jets."

Holly felt horrible, making him relive it all by telling her what he knew. "I don't know anything that tastes worse than cold eggs," she said.

"Your breakfast is getting cold too," he said, and then he picked up where he'd left off.

"She was about to break the news to him when a pretty Air Force nurse asked if he was ready for takeoff."

"And she jumped to the conclusion that Daniel and the woman were an item."

"Something like that." He shook his head then pierced the yolk of his egg with a fork tine. She'd been raised by her grandparents,

Hank said, who'd scrimped and saved to keep the wolf from the door. "Daniel, on the other hand, was born with the proverbial silver spoon in his mouth."

Nodding, Holly said, "And she figured they'd think she got pregnant on purpose, hoping to get a matching spoon out of the deal."

"Which is why they never married."

How sad, Holly thought, sighing as she shoved her plate away. "Do you ever wish you weren't so easy to talk to, Hank?"

"All the time, kiddo. All the time."

"Well, if it's any consolation, I feel the same way."

"Wishing Maudie hadn't hung her dirty laundry out for you to see, are you?"

"Not for the reasons you might think."

"Oh, I think I know why."

She met his eyes and waited for him to explain.

"Now that you've got this overloaded basket in your lap, you can't decide what to do with it: tell Parker what you know, or keep your mouth shut."

"Exactly."

"Want a piece of advice?"

She grabbed his hand and gave it a gentle squeeze. "Please."

"Pray for patience and the wisdom to know when to tell him…if you should." He returned her squeeze. "You're exactly what that boy needs, Holly. When the truth comes out—and it's just a matter of time before it does—he's gonna need somebody like you to lean on."

"Hard to believe a man like Parker would ever need to lean on someone, but if you're right, I hope I'll be strong enough. He's already been through so much, with heartaches and war wounds and growing up without a father."

"See there?"

"See what?"

"What you said just now—it's all the proof I need to tell me you're a godsend." He chuckled.

Grinning, she said, "What's so funny?"

"I don't know if Parker ever prayed for help in choosing the right woman, but it looks to me like the good Lord read his heart and sent her to him, anyway."

"I feel so silly saying this, because I've known him such a short time, but—"

His cell phone rang, interrupting her. "Speak of the devil," he said, grinning as he answered. "Hey, Parker. What's up, son?"

She watched Hank's face go ashen as he nodded, listening intently to whatever Parker had said. "We'll be there in ten minutes," he said, snapping the phone shut.

"It's Maudie," he said, answering Holly's unasked question. "She's had a heart attack."

Chapter Fourteen

....

Seeing how shaken the news had left Hank, Holly slipped Agnes a twenty-dollar bill and she led him to her car. She didn't want to come right out and say that he was in no condition to drive, so she told him he'd be doing her a favor, acting as her navigator.

"Clumsy as I am, there's no telling when I might need to make a quick trip to the ER," she said, hoping to ease his worry at least a little bit. There would be plenty of time for worry once they arrived at the hospital and got all the details about Maude's condition from Parker.

"Your problem isn't clumsiness, kiddo; it's intelligence." He pointed. "Make a right at the next traffic light."

Despite the serious situation, she couldn't help but laugh at that. "You're joking, right?"

"I've had plenty of time to read about all the great inventors and scholars—being Maudie's boyfriend allows a man lots of time alone—and without exception, they were awkward. You know why?"

"No, but I'd love to hear!"

"Take the next left," he said. Then, "Because their brains never stopped. Always thinking of the next experiment or test, they were easily distracted. Didn't see what the rest of us dummies see, so they tripped and dropped things and walked into walls." He gave her arm a gentle nudge. "Get it? If you weren't brilliant, you'd be as graceful as a gazelle."

"Hank Donovan," she said, "if your heart didn't already belong to Maude, I'd pray for the means to make you mine."

"I'm flattered, but you're all wet, you know that?" Chuckling, he said, "The hospital is just around the next curve. On your right." And then he said, "But you can't kid a kidder, kiddo. *Your* heart belongs to Parker, and nothing this old FBI agent can do will ever change that fact."

"Goodness," she said, steering into the parking lot, "does it really show that much?"

"Only to people who take the time to look." He got out of the car, and when Holly joined him, he linked his arm with hers. "You remember when Agnes asked if you were my daughter?"

As they walked into the lobby, she nodded.

"Well, if God had seen fit to bless me with a daughter, I hope she'd have been exactly like you."

"You're sweet." She stood on tiptoe and kissed his cheek.

"Sweet's got nothing to do with it. Just tellin' it like it is, that's all." Then he asked the woman behind the desk to look up Maude's name in the patient directory, and she told them where they could find her.

Parker saw them the instant the elevator doors opened. "Thank God you're here," he said, stepping between them. Flinging an arm over their shoulders, he led them to the waiting area where he'd been sitting. "They've done a preliminary exam and think it's a blockage. They've got her in the Cath Lab now, looking to see how bad it is."

"But she just had a full physical," Hank said, "and the EKG didn't show a thing wrong with her."

"That's because that test doesn't show blockages," Holly said. "My dad went through something similar a couple of years ago. It took a sonogram to determine where the blockages were." She squeezed Hank's forearm. "They're doing the right tests," she assured him. "And they're pretty quick about getting back with the results."

She *didn't* say that her father's episode had sent him to Johns Hopkins, one of the nation's best-equipped, best-staffed institutions. "Why don't we relax over there?" she said instead, pointing to the row of chairs across the way.

Parker and Hank sat side by side as she added, "How about if I see if the nurses will share some stale coffee with us?"

"None for me," Parker said.

"Me either," said Hank.

"Then, bottled water or a soda or—"

The double doors at the end of the hall whooshed open, admitting a white-coated doctor. He slid off his surgical cap and stuffed his stethoscope into a deep lab coat pocket. "Mr. Brant?"

Parker stood, and so did Hank. Holly, who hadn't had a chance to sit yet, stood between them.

The doctor extended a hand. "Bill Williams," he said when Parker shook it. He looked at Hank. "You must be the boyfriend."

Hank's white eyebrows lifted in surprise.

"She told me you'd be here, and that I was to tell you not to worry."

When Holly heard Hank swallow, she grabbed his hand.

The doctor explained what they'd found so far, adding that the only solution was open-heart surgery. He told them how they'd remove veins from her leg and use them to replace the arteries damaged by the blockage. A six- to eight-hour operation, he added, provided that there were no complications. He asked if they knew their blood types and then nodded when all three claimed Type O. "Good," he said to Parker. "That's the universal donor, and your mother's blood type as well. We'll run some quick tests—which I'm sure you'll all pass—then get a pint or two from each of you just as a precaution. Give me a few minutes to arrange it."

And with that, he disappeared through the double doors again.

"Well, that was fast," Parker said, slumping onto the nearest chair.

Hank sat beside him. "I suppose there's one good thing to come of this."

Frowning, Parker looked over at him, as if to say, "Are you nuts?"

"At least now we know she'll get the flat-on-her-back rest she needs," Hank said, "for those feet of hers to continue healing."

Several minutes later, a nurse carrying a clipboard stepped into the quiet hall. "You three," she said, pointing, "come with me."

Exchanging puzzled glances, they followed her. "Reminds me of my days in boot camp," Parker whispered from the corner of his mouth. "'Just do what you're told and don't ask questions.'"

"Now that's what I like," the nurse said, winking, "obedient patients."

"Patients?" Holly cleared her throat. "There must be some mistake. We're here for Maude Brant."

"You're all Type O, right?"

"Yes, but—"

"Then you're my patients." She handed Hank the clipboard. "You fill out that form, honey, while I get these two hooked up."

Parker and Holly leaned back in pink vinyl chairs and sipped the OJ the nurse had thrust at them. "Ladies first," the nurse said, wrapping a tourniquet around Holly's bicep. She hung an empty IV bag on the pole between the lounges before saying, "Make a fist, honey." Uncapping a needle, she reassured Holly. "This won't hurt a bit." After piercing the tender flesh in the bend of Holly's arm, the nurse checked the clear tubing that led from the needle to the bag. Satisfied that things were working as they should, she stepped up beside Parker.

"Ready, good-lookin'?" she asked. Before he had a chance to reply, she ran him through the same paces Holly had just completed then took the clipboard from Hank and handed it to Parker. "Fill that out while I take care of Handsome over there, and when you've finished filling out your form, hand it to your girlfriend." She gave them all a hard stare. "If everybody does his or her job just right, we can be finished here just in time for my coffee break."

Another nurse poked her head into the room. "Mrs. Brant is asking for Dr. Leonard. So when you're finished here—"

Their nurse blanched. "Doctor?" she echoed. "Why didn't you say something? If I'd known you were a doctor, I'd have—"

"Relax, lady," Hank butt in, "she ain't *that* kinda doctor." He shook his head. "But it's nice to know that your bedside manner changes depending on who your patients are."

"As I was going to say," the nurse began, "before I was so rudely interrupted, if I'd known she was a doctor, I would've saved her for last." She wigged her eyebrows and snickered. "You know, enhancing the whole 'misery loves company' sensation."

She wasted no time in getting Hank hooked up to an IV. "So tell me, if you're not a medical doctor, what type of doctor *are* you?" she asked Holly.

"PhD," Holly answered.

"She's too modest," Hank said. "The lady's a marine biologist."

"Is that a fact?" She didn't sound impressed. Didn't look impressed, either, as she rechecked the tubes and bags. "Drink that orange juice, gang. I wouldn't want anybody passing out on me."

"I could use a refill...," Hank said, holding up his empty juice bottle, "...*Florence*."

"Oh. A funny man, eh?" But she chuckled, and this time it almost seemed sincere. "Happy to oblige, Handsome." With that, she shoved through the door and called over her shoulder, "I've got orders to get a full bag from each of you, so behave, or I might just make that *two*."

"She isn't fooling me," Holly said.

Parker looked up from the clipboard to say, "What're you talking about?"

"She saw how tense we were and distracted us by behaving like Dorothy's wicked witch." She sipped her juice. "And it worked, didn't it?"

Hank and Parker exchanged a bored glance. "Yeah. I guess so," Parker admitted.

"Maybe we oughta send her a thank-you card."

"Good one, Hank."

"And flowers."

"Let's not get carried away."

Doctor Williams burst into the room. "Good, good," he said, inspecting the tubing. Stepping up beside Parker, he added, "Your mom is doing great. We've given her some light sedation to keep her calm while we finish the tests and wait for the results, so don't be surprised if, when you're finished here, she's a little drowsy." He looked at Holly. "Did the nurse tell you that Mrs. Brant wants to see you?"

"She did."

"Alone?"

"No." Holly licked her lips. Why would Maude want to spend these last minutes with her instead of her son—or Hank, who loved her so much that he would have happily traded places with her?

"Ever given blood before?"

"Yes."

"Good. Then you know that sometimes dizziness can sneak up on you." He patted her hand. "So make sure you give yourself plenty of time before you see her. We don't need two patients from the same family tonight."

Nodding, Holly smiled. "Thanks. I'll remember that."

"Don't stay too long, now. I'm sure she'll want to see these two before she goes off to surgery as well, and we don't want to unnecessarily tire her."

It was all happening so fast. *Maybe that explains the dizziness,* Holly thought. "I won't."

"When will you start the operation?" Parker wanted to know.

Williams pulled back his sleeve and looked at his watch. "I'm guessing it'll be another hour or two before we have all the test results. As soon as I've had a chance to review everything, I'll book an OR and come find you."

"Thanks, Doc."

Nodding, he disconnected Holly from the tubes.

"I'm not finished already, am I?"

"Yeah, you are." After pressing a bandage to the needle prick, he added, "It's my professional opinion that when a patient's face is as white as the pillowcase under her head, she's given enough blood."

Holly groaned. "Of all the times to behave like a weakling."

"Happens to the best of us. Last time I donated, I passed out cold. Took two orderlies and a burly nurse to get me back up onto the chair." He made a last check of the men's tubes. "I'll have the nurse bring you a soda. The sugar and caffeine works better for some reason than OJ." On his way out the door, he laughed. "Nobody go anywhere now, hear?"

"Hmpf. And Nurse Ratchet called *me* a comedian," Hank muttered as the door opened again.

"Goodness," said their nurse. "I've starred in two movies in less than a half hour." After handing them each a can of cola, she fluffed her hair. "Maybe I've missed my calling." She disappeared for a moment and returned pushing a wheelchair. "Hop on, my pretty," she told Holly. "You and I are going for a little ride."

"Speed limit in the hospital is *five*," Hank called after her.

"That's only if you're a patient. Or a visitor." And the last thing they heard before the door whooshed closed was her enthusiastic, "Woo-hoo!"

* * * * *

Maude's eyes fluttered open when she heard the *tick-tick-tick* of the wheelchair rolling into the draped cubicle. "Holly? Is that you?"

"Yeah, it's me," she said, squeezing Maude's hand as the nurse pushed a chair closer to the bed. Holly thanked her and sat down. "The doctor said you wanted to talk to me?"

Maude nodded. "I have a favor to ask."

"You know I'd do anything for you."

"It's a big 'un," she said, smiling weakly, "so if you feel differently after you hear what I have to say, I won't hold it against you."

Under different circumstances, Holly might have admitted that the woman was scaring her. At times like these, she wished her mom was nearby, so she could get some solid, straightforward advice, the kind only a loving mother could give.

After pushing several buttons on the bed, Maude sat up a little straighter and began with an apology. "I'm sorry to foist this on you, sweetie, but there isn't anyone else I'd trust to carry out my wishes, you know, in case…"

"Maude, really," Holly scolded gently. "The doctor says you're going to be just fine. He told us he has performed this operation a hundred times, and—"

"That's good to know, and I'm planning to come through this with flying colors. But things happen, you know? And I like to be prepared."

"But what about Hank? I'm sure he'd be honored to—"

Maude laughed softly. "Parker thinks a lot of Henry, I'll grant you that, but he's in love with *you*." She paused as if to give her words time to register in Holly's confused brain. Then she started out by blaming herself for Parker's poor choice in women, for the way he held everyone—even herself and Hank—at arm's-distance. "He isn't like that with you, Holly. I've seen the way he looks at you, the way he hangs onto your every word. He trusts you, and that's why I know I can trust you too."

"But, Maude, trust me with *what*?"

"With watching out for him, that's what. He's spent so many years playing the part of the big, tough fighting man that he isn't even aware of his own vulnerabilities. He'll need you, sweetie, when he finds out that..." Maude licked her lips and swallowed.

"Can I get you something to drink?"

"No, they've cut me off, I'm afraid. Too close to surgery time." She patted Holly's hand. "I can handle a little thirst, knowing you're going to take care of Parker."

And then she launched into the story Hank had told her in the diner, adding that her boy had a right to know that he wasn't fatherless—and that Daniel had a right to know he had a son. "If I make it through this, I'll tell him myself." She held up a forefinger to forestall Holly's attempt to assure her that she *would* make it through this. "But on the off chance that I don't, I want Parker to hear it from someone who loves him as much as I do."

For the second time that day, Holly said, "Does it really show that much?"

"It's written all over your face...and in your voice, and in the gentle way you do things for him. He needs you, Holly, and I have to believe that he'll admit it before too much longer."

"Nothing is going to happen to you—well, except that Dr. Williams is going to unclog your blocked arteries—but you have my word that if something does, I'll do everything you've asked." She scooted the chair closer and added, "If God ever blesses me with children, I hope I'm half the mother you've been."

"No, no...I'm a terrible mother. I've kept this awful secret for so long, and I'm the most impatient woman you'll ever meet."

"That's nonsense. You didn't keep that secret because you're self-ish. You kept it because you were afraid. Afraid that Parker might suffer the pain of rejection you felt when you thought Daniel chose the Air Force over you."

"When I *thought* he chose jet planes over me?" Maude laughed. "That's exactly what he did, dear girl, and you know what? After this is over, I'm going to throw away every copy of *The Ghost and Mrs. Muir* and change every plaque on every door at the cottage. The ghost of Daniel is finally gone!"

From the other side of the striped curtain, a woman's voice said, "Mrs. Brant?"

"There's another lie I have to make right," Maude whispered. "Poor Parker," she cried softly, "what'll he think when he finds out he was born out of wedlock?"

The curtains parted and two masked, gowned nurses entered.

"It's time," the tallest one said, unlocking the bed's wheels.

The second nurse whipped back the curtain. "It'll all be over before you know it."

They took up their places, one on either side of the bed, and pushed Maude into the hall. "Mr. Brant?" the tall one called. "You and your friend can walk with us as far as the surgical suite if you like."

Holly watched Parker and Hank hurry down the hall, each taking one of Maude's hands and murmuring words of assurance as they reached her. The nurses stopped outside the OR doors and gave them a minute to kiss her cheeks and forehead.

The men stood side by side as she was rolled into the OR, their shoulders sagging as the doors hissed shut.

Tears filled Holly's eyes as she bowed her head and prayed.

Prayed that Maude would come out of there fine. That Parker and Hank would stay strong in the meantime. That she'd have the courage to keep her promise to Maude in case things didn't go as planned.

Most of all, she prayed as she never had before that Parker's love for Maude would overshadow any hurt and anger that the truth about his conception and birth might awaken.

Chapter Fifteen

They'd been waiting for more than three hours with no word from the OR. Holly took it upon herself to approach the woman manning the desk, to see if the surgeon had called up a progress report.

"Sorry," the lady said, "nothing yet." She glanced over at Hank and Parker, pacing in opposite directions in the middle of the room. "Tell you what," she whispered. "I'll call down there and see what I can find out." She picked up a pen. "Sometimes they get so busy that they forget the patient has family up here worrying."

"Thank you," Holly said.

She clicked the pen. "What's the patient's name?"

"Maude. Maude Brant. And Dr. Williams is her surgeon."

After scribbling the information on the tablet beside her many-buttoned phone, the woman picked up the receiver. "I'll call you even if there's no news yet."

"Thanks," Holly said again. She walked back to Parker and Hank. "You two are going to wear out the rug if you keep that up."

Parker slapped a hand to the back of his neck. "They said there would be reports."

"Every hour or so," Hank added.

"That nice lady," Holly said, pointing, "is trying to get us some information right now." She shook her head and sighed. "I know you're scared. And concerned. But it could be another four or five hours yet. You'll wear *yourselves* out if you don't sit down."

Nodding, Parker sat on the chair closest to him, and Hank chose the one across the way. The television blared with a story about tornado damage in the Midwest and fires in Texas. If the constant noise and bad news was driving her to distraction, Holly wondered what it was doing to Parker and Hank.

"While we're waiting, I'm going to drive back to the cottage and see if Maude has any guests checking in. If there are, I'll call the people who've registered and explain things. Under the circumstances, I'm sure they won't mind moving to the Shoreside Inn. It's nearby."

She returned to the help desk, where the nice lady had just hung up the phone.

"She's doing fine," the woman said, "and I asked the nurse if she'd call back in an hour or so."

"That's wonderful news," Holly said. "I'm going to run an errand for the family. But I wonder if I could bother you with another request—would you turn down the volume on the TV?"

"Oh, thank the good Lord," she said, grabbing the remote. "I'm not allowed to choose channels and things like that, but if a patient's family asks me to, I can click this thing till the cows come home." She pressed the Down arrow on the volume control and let it go after a second or two. "There. Is that better?"

Holly nodded. "Much."

"What about the show? You're the only ones in here, so if you'd rather not watch the news...."

Holly glanced over at Parker and Hank, who weren't fooling

anyone by pretending to read—Parker, a sports magazine, and Hank, the morning paper. "I doubt they're paying attention anyway, so feel free to turn it to whatever you'd like to watch." Smiling, she thanked the woman, gave a little wave, and left.

It took nearly two hours to make sure that everything was taken care of at the B&B, and when she returned, Holly went directly to the help counter and then joined Parker and Hank.

"That nice lady says Maude's doing fine," Holly told the men, "and that the nurse told her it'd be another hour or so before the doctors wrap things up."

Both men nodded.

"Everything okay back at the cottage?" Parker asked.

"Yes. She only had one couple checking in tomorrow, so I called and made a tentative reservation at the Shoreside in their name. They were really nice about it and told me to let you know they'd be praying for Maude."

"That's nice of them."

Parker didn't sound very convincing, but Holly chalked it up to nerves.

"Thanks, Holly," he said. "I don't know what we'd do without you."

"That's for sure," Hank agreed. He folded the paper, placed it atop the stack of tattered reading material on the table nearest his chair, then slowly rose to his feet. "Think I'll head down to the vending machine. Either of you care for coffee or a soda?"

"Nothing for me," Parker and Holly said together.

After he'd rounded the corner, Holly whispered, "I'm a little worried about him."

"So am I."

I'm a little worried about you too, she thought, sitting beside him.

He closed his magazine and let it dangle from the fingertips of one hand.

He stared at some unknown spot across the room and shook his head. "Maybe this will be her wake-up call."

Holly wasn't sure what, exactly, he meant, but she didn't press him for an explanation. Instead, she scooted as close to him as their armed chairs would allow and sandwiched his free hand between hers. "Now I'm *really* sorry I pulled that all-nighter," he said softly.

She'd thought he looked a little rougher around the edges than usual but had blamed it on worry. "What were you doing when the hospital called?"

"Wasn't the hospital that called. I'd been up all night, painting. Hadn't touched those canvases in weeks, and I lost track of time." Pinching the bridge of his nose, he groaned. "Feel like a first-class heel for the way I handled things."

"Handled what?"

"When the phone rang, I was really into it, and, well, I..." He shook his head. "Then she said she was having chest pains." He tossed the magazine onto the table and ran a hand through his hair. "Don't remember hearing her sound like that before."

"Sound like what?"

"Scared. Quiet. *Weak.* And that scared *me.* So like an idiot, I barked at her. 'For the love of all that's holy,' I said, 'go lay down. I'll call 911 on the way over.' And I hung up. Didn't even say good-bye."

Several seconds passed before he continued. "I got there four, maybe five minutes before the ambulance did." He gave her hand a squeeze. "She looked bad, Hol, real bad. I feel like such a heel. What if that was the last time—?"

"Don't talk like that," she interrupted. "Maude knows you better than you know yourself, and she understands why you were... abrupt. And anyway, she's in good hands now. *God's* hands."

He exhaled a shuddering sigh then leaned his head into hers.

It was such a small thing, and yet Holly's heart swirled with tenderness. *Help me know what to say, Lord.* When his nervous grip on her hand relaxed a little, she said a prayer of gratitude. She took it to mean that all Parker really needed right now was the quiet understanding of a friend.

By the time Hank returned carrying a cup of coffee and a candy bar, Parker's breathing had slowed. So it was no surprise to see Hank's eyes widen and his brows rise. "*Sleeping*?" Hank whispered.

She would have told him how Parker had been up all night, painting, when the terrifying call came. And how afraid he'd been. Or that the stress of seeing his mom in a life-threatening situation was taking its toll. But, afraid of waking him, she smiled and sent an "Oh, well" expression Hank's way.

"I'm not asleep," Parker mumbled. "And I can smell that coffee from over here. When was it brewed...last week?"

Until he sat up, Holly hadn't acknowledged how good it was, knowing he'd felt comfortable enough to lean on her.

"Trust me," Hank said, "it smells way better than it tastes."

"Then why don't we all go down to the cafeteria? I'm sure they have a whole row of fresh-brewed pots lined up." Realizing that the men might not want to leave the waiting area, she got up and headed for the counter, adding, "I'll just leave my cell phone number with this nice lady."

"Oh yes," the woman said. "I'm happy to call if there's any news."

After she'd written down her number, she rejoined Parker, who was watching Hank pour the contents of the waxed paper cup into the drinking fountain. "I hope the hospital's pipes are copper, 'cause that stuff's liable to eat clean through anything made of PVC."

Chuckling, they made their way down the long hallway toward the bank of elevators. As they waited to get their car, Holly thought of her family. She'd been putting off talking to them, mostly to avoid hearing them complain about how much time she'd been spending away from home lately. They'd lecture her about doing a better job of staying in touch. Tell her that avoiding them wouldn't help her "put the whole Jimmy thing" behind her. But the first chance she got, she intended to call. Enduring their scoldings would be a small price to pay for the assurance that all was well in Baltimore.

"Why so quiet?" Parker asked when the elevator doors hissed shut.

"Just thinking it's been a while since I talked to my mom," she admitted.

Hank's thumb lit up the Number One button as Parker nodded. "Yeah, you really ought to call her."

"I will, just as soon as Maude is in the recovery room."

No one spoke again until they were standing in line at the coffee counter. "I think I'll skip the coffee," Hank said, grinning a little as he rubbed his stomach. "What would you say if I drove to your place to check on Cat?"

Parker paid the tab and dropped the change into the "Help the Children" jar on the counter. "I'd say that's a great idea. I blew out of the house so fast this morning, I didn't even think to check if she had food or water."

When Holly handed Hank her key ring, Parker's brows rose slightly.

"We were having breakfast at the diner when you called," Hank answered his unasked question. "Little Miss Thinks of Everything, here, figured I was in no shape to drive."

Parker cut her a quick glance, and in that instant, she saw something—approval? affection?—glittering in his dark eyes. "You want to pack up Cat's stuff and take her to your place today?"

He walked with Holly and Parker to a nearby table. "Think I'll wait until things settle down a bit, if it's all the same to you. No point in uprooting her in the middle of all this chaos." He jangled the keys and winked at Holly. "Thanks, kiddo. I'll top off the tank for you on my way back here."

Holly would have told him that there was no need to do that, but he was gone before she could find her voice.

Parker watched Hank hurry toward the exit. "I see what you mean."

"About what?"

"His behavior does raise some concern, doesn't it?"

"He'll be his old self again once the surgeon tells us Maude's going to be fine. And in the meantime, we'll keep a close eye on him and make sure he takes care of himself."

"Yeah, I guess that's—"

Holly's cell phone rang, startling them both. "Really? That's wonderful," she said into the phone before snapping it shut. "Maude is in the recovery room already. The lady said you can see her if you want to." She relayed the directions from the cafeteria to the cardiac-care unit and reminded him what Dr. Williams had said about the condition Maude would be in—completely out of it, thanks to anesthesia, and attached to tubes and monitors—after surgery.

He gulped his coffee then got to his feet. "Don't worry," he said, chucking her chin, "I won't keel over."

"I think while you're in there, I'll call Hank. I'm sure he'll be relieved."

"Good idea."

She walked with him to the elevators. "And then I think I'll go to the chapel."

Parker stared at the red-lighted numbers above the door and shrugged. "Can't hurt, I suppose."

Oh, Lord, she prayed, *bless him with some peace of mind and ease his fears?* She grabbed his hand as the white U p arrow dinged. "She's strong and stubborn, Parker, with a whole lot to live for. She's in good hands with Dr. Williams, so don't worry." The doors opened, and she gave his hand a squeeze. "She's going to be fine."

He stood in the shaft's opening and, for what seemed like a full minute, studied her face. Then Parker kissed her knuckles, let go of her hand, and stepped into the elevator. "See you in the chapel," he was saying as the doors swooshed shut.

As she waited for Hank to answer his cell phone, Holly couldn't decide if Parker had looked more sad than scared, or the other way around. Maude's influence had imprinted deeply on the men in her life, that much was certain. And something told her that somewhere out there was yet another man who'd been forever changed by knowing her.

* * * * *

Parker stepped into the hushed chapel and slid into the pew beside Holly. And although they were alone, he whispered, "Dr. Williams wasn't kidding when he said she'd look scary."

Holly pretended she didn't notice the way he sat, linking and unlinking his fingers in his lap. "I remember how my dad looked after open-heart surgery. Well, not *right* after, because they wouldn't allow anyone but my mom in there at first."

Nodding, he stared straight ahead. "So you called Hank?"

"Yeah. Left a message on his cell phone." She snickered quietly. "Guess he's giving the cat some TLC."

"Did he tell you he might take her home and keep her?"

"No." That surprised her a little, because when Parker had talked about the stray, he'd seemed attached to it right from the start. "What made you change your mind about adopting her yourself?"

"Didn't." He shrugged. "Just figured Hank needs the companionship more than I do."

But Hank had Maude, and Parker had…

Holly stared straight ahead too, at the big wooden cross hanging from the ceiling. *Help me understand him, Lord,* she prayed.

"Did they give you any idea when Maude might come to?"

"Two, maybe three hours." He gave another shrug. "Even then, she won't be able to communicate with that lousy ventilator tube down her throat."

She remembered the woman in the ICU cubicle beside her dad. The poor thing had panicked when she woke, groggy yet alert enough to realize that something had blocked her airway. Thrashing and trying to cry out for help, she'd repeatedly frustrated the nurses' attempts to take her off the machines, and they'd been forced to threaten to put her back under. Holly had prayed that the whole "people hear things while unconscious" theory was true and that her dad's brain would pick up enough of the confusion taking place on the other side of the curtain to spare himself the same ordeal.

He had not.

Thankfully, her mom had stepped out to use the ladies' room when he started to come around, sparing her the feelings of helplessness that surrounded Holly as she watched her formerly strong and capable father whimpering like a frightened child. She stepped out too, to spare him the humiliation of having his daughter see him that way. To this day, Holly had never shared the upsetting memory with anyone.

And she wouldn't share it now, either.

"Getting hungry?"

"Not really." But his stomach chose that moment to betray him, and the hollow growl echoed in the nearly empty chapel.

What started as a grin built gradually, from a quiet snicker to a merry giggle, and the more effort she put into *stopping,* the harder and more loudly she laughed. It must have been contagious, because soon Parker joined in.

"Nervous laughter?" he managed, knuckling tears of mirth from his eyes.

"Something like that. I'm just thankful there's no preacher in here to scold us," she admitted once she'd caught her breath.

"Really. Why's that?"

"Because when I was a girl something like this happened, and I was the laughingstock—pun intended—of the church for weeks."

She told him how, at the ripe old age of eleven, she and her friends had convinced their parents that they were mature enough to sit in the front pew—unsupervised. Halfway through the service, a little voice rang out. "Mommy," it said, "I just belched." And as if to prove it, the child burped again, the sound of it reverberating from every hard surface and inspiring whispers that floated around the building like a soft wind. "I didn't *start* the giggle fit," Holly admitted, "but I was every bit as guilty as the other girls for what happened once it got rolling." The stern looks and clucking tongues of adults seated around them did little to squelch their merriment.

"So what did it take to finally quiet y'all down?"

Holly feigned a shiver. "If I close my eyes, I can still see Pastor Cummings's angry glare."

Parker chuckled. "I'll bet you were something as a kid."

"That might be something you'll want to take up with my parents."

He turned toward her slightly. "You planning any visits home during the months you're working here?"

She wrinkled her nose. "Not really."

"Not really? What sort of answer is that?"

"Because like E.T., I don't get very good reception when I phone home."

He sat blinking for a second or two. Then, grinning, he slid an arm around her shoulders. "I don't know anyone else who could make me laugh at a time like this." He pressed a kiss to her temple.

Oh, how she wished they weren't in the chapel...and that his lips had aimed a little south and a little right.

"I wasn't kidding about what I said earlier," Parker continued. "I don't know how I'd get through this without you."

"Please," she said lightly, waving the compliment away. "You fought a couple of wars and survived. I'm sure you'd muddle through on your own."

"Maybe." He was staring at the cross when he said, "And maybe not." Then he looked at Holly. "But it sure is nice not having to muddle through all on my own."

His stomach growled again, even louder than before.

"We'd better get some decent food into you before someone calls Animal Control."

"Animal Contr—" He chuckled. "Ha. I get it, funny girl."

"Before we go back to the cafeteria, will you pray with me?"

His eyes narrowed slightly, and so did his lips. "I'll listen," he said, giving her hand another squeeze. "You pray."

She supposed it was only natural that a man who'd been through as much as Parker had wouldn't wholly believe in the power of prayer. *Well, no matter,* Holly thought. Eventually, everything that was upside down in his world would right itself, and then he'd see that the Lord loved him simply because he lived and breathed.

At least she hoped that was the case, for his sake as well as her own.

Holly bowed her head and closed her eyes. "O Father in heaven," she began, "we ask that You guide the decisions of Maude's doctors as they see her through this uncertain portion of her recovery. Watch over Your servant Maude, and heal her quickly and completely so that she can return to her happy, active life. Watch over Hank too, and give him the strength and patience to wait for Maude to admit her feelings for him."

Pausing, she took a breath, and when she did, Parker squeezed her hand yet again.

"Bless Parker, Lord, who has dedicated so much of his life and time to his mom. Provide him with the answers to the questions that plague him and give him much-deserved ease from the pain of his injuries.

"We thank You, Lord God, for showing us Your steady presence in our lives...and for reminding us daily that You are with us, loving us, always. Amen."

For a long time, Parker didn't move. Didn't speak. Holly leaned forward and looked into his troubled face. Smiling, she said, "I thought maybe I'd gotten a bit long-winded for your taste and you'd fallen asleep on me."

"No way," he said, shaking his head. "That was really, ah, really thoughtful. And sweet. Just like you." He stood in the aisle and held out his hand, and when she took it, Parker said, "Thanks, Holly, for...for everything."

"No thanks necess—"

One corner of his mouth lifted with the hint of a smile. "You're just lucky we're in a church."

"Chapel."

"Whatever," he said, grabbing her hand and leading her toward the exit. Outside the big double doors, he stopped just long enough to ask, "Well?"

"Well, what?"

"Aren't you curious to know why I said you were lucky you were in a church?"

"Chapel," she teased.

Parker rolled his eyes. "Chapel," he echoed, drawing her into a loose hug.

"Why was I lucky that we were in a church?"

"Because," he said, "I might have been tempted to do this."

And then he pressed his lips to hers. It wasn't the romantic kiss she'd wished for earlier, or even a chaste new-love type of kiss. No, this was more of a peck, like the ones her dad and cousins might deliver while wishing her happy birthday or to say hello or good-bye. Then Parker stepped back and punched the elevator's Down button, while Holly did everything in her power not to let him see her disappointment.

Chapter Sixteen

....

Once Holly saw Maude, her worries for the woman's recovery ended. Pink-cheeked and bright-eyed, Maude didn't even seem to mind the expected after-surgery discomforts.

The first question Parker's mom asked when he left the room was, "You didn't tell him yet, did you?"

"No." *Thank the good Lord I didn't have to,* she thought, remembering that she'd promised to deliver the bad news—but only if the unthinkable happened to Maude. "And you aren't going to tell him anytime soon, I hope."

"Ah, you'll make a wonderful mother someday."

That was a strange way to reply to her comment, but Holly didn't say so.

As it turned out, she didn't have to.

"Because you're pretty good at making a question sound like an instruction. You know, like 'Have you made your bed' or 'You haven't done your homework, have you….'"

Holly leaned on the bed's side rail and smiled. "At my age, I'm beginning to wonder if I'll get the chance!"

"Oh, don't you worry, sweetie. Your day is coming. And if I know that boy of mine, it's right around the corner."

Holly recalled the brotherly kiss he'd pressed to her lips, thinking, *Not at that rate, it isn't!*

"And just so you won't worry, I won't tell him until I'm home and get the all-clear from the doctor."

"Good." *For more reasons than one,* Holly thought. Maybe between then and now she could find a way to get Parker back into the habit of praying, because he'd never need it more than he would when his mom told him the truth about his background.

"Have you seen Hank lately?"

"Just this morning, as a matter of fact. He spent a lot of time in here watching you sleep. It took Parker, two nurses, your surgeon, and me to convince him that he needed to go home, have a meal, and get a good night's sleep."

"What sort of story did y'all have to tell? To get him in here, that is."

"Parker sort of gave them the impression that you and Hank are engaged."

"Sort of?" Maude groaned. "Never mind. I don't think I want to hear the details."

"That isn't really so far from the truth...is it?"

"Oh, I don't know...." Then, "How'd *you* get in here?" Maude had no sooner asked the question than she added, "Don't tell me... same insinuation?"

Holly felt herself blush. "Basically."

"Well, nothing wrong with that. The way I see it, it's only a matter of time before *that* story, at least, is true. Besides, Parker needs you here every bit as much as Hank thinks he needs to be with me."

He doesn't think *it,* Holly wanted to say. *Hank really* does *need to be here.*

Suddenly Maude didn't look so pink-cheeked anymore. Her eyes glazed over and the monitor started beeping up a storm. Holly didn't ask questions. Instead, she hurried into the hall to make sure the nurse had heard the same thing she had. Sure enough, the blue-garbed woman was jogging down the hall, her stethoscope bouncing as she spoke into a walkie-talkie.

"Don't worry," the woman said, "this happens fairly often following open-heart surgery. I'm sure it's nothing."

"But I assume it's a good idea to tell her son and her fiancé what's going on?"

She rolled a blood-pressure machine into the cubicle. "Yeah. No reason to alarm them, but they might want to be here just in case."

The instant she hit the hospital lobby, Holly dialed Parker's cell phone number. He'd left an hour or so ago to shower and grab a nap. He picked up on the first ring.

"What's wrong?"

"The nurse says it's probably nothing, but you might want to come back as soon as you can."

"Why? What happened?"

Holly admitted that she didn't know and explained what had happened while she and Maude were chatting.

"I'll be there in ten minutes," he said before hanging up.

"Let him drive safely, Lord," she prayed while she dialed Hank's number. "Pick up," she whispered. "Please, please, *please* pick up...."

His voice was sleep-groggy when he answered with, "Donovan."

"Hi, Hank. It's Holly. No need to be in a terrible rush or anything, but you should probably get here soon." She repeated what she'd told Parker.

"Thanks, kiddo. Be right there."

She hurried back to the cubicle, thinking that someone familiar ought to be there until Parker and Hank showed up. When the nurse saw Holly, she slid the glass doors closed and led her down the hall, out of Maude's line of sight. "They're rushing her back into surgery," she explained. "Dr. Williams thinks maybe one of the sutures didn't hold and she's bleeding into her chest cavity. She's asking to see her son. No, let me rephrase that. She's insisting on it. Says she won't go into the OR until she talks to him."

"Good grief," Holly growled. She knew exactly why Maude was stalling: she aimed to tell Parker the whole sordid story...in case something awful happened during surgery. "Well, fortunately, he's on his way." She'd no sooner said it than Parker stepped off the elevator.

"Your mother is asking for you," the nurse said. "Make it snappy, will you? We've got the OR booked."

"But...I—I don't...what's—"

"I'll just let your pretty little girlfriend here explain the pre-liminaries. Dr. Williams will give you the details just as soon as he can." A monitor beeped from somewhere down the hall, signaling another patient in distress. "If you'll excuse me, I have to run. Good luck to your mom," she called, running backward.

Parker frowned and entered Maude's cubicle. "What," he teased, kissing her forehead, "you didn't get enough attention after that last emergency go-round?"

She laughed weakly and waved Holly closer. "Pull up a chair, son. I have something to tell you. Don't interrupt now, you hear, because I don't have much time."

Holly hesitated. "I should probably see if Hank's on his—"

"He'll get here when he gets here," Maude interrupted.

The no-nonsense expression served as a reminder of how Maude had stressed that, once the truth was out, Parker would need Holly as he'd never needed anyone. As if orchestrated by a Broadway choreographer, Hank showed up as Holly nodded her consent, and they gathered close as Maude began the sad tale.

The color drained from Parker's face as he stood stiff and straight, gripping the side rail so tightly that his knuckles turned white. Holly couldn't decide if it was anger that made him clench and unclench his jaw, or raw, unbridled pain. His dark eyes darkened still more behind the sheen of unshed tears.

Hank, for his part, hung his head, and Holly got the feeling that he would have given anything to trade places with Parker. So would she, for that matter.

All of five minutes had passed before Maude rasped, "That's it. Now you know." Tears leaked from the corners of her eyes, and then she looked at Hank and Holly. "Will you two give us just a minute alone, please?"

Hank stepped up close and pressed a kiss to her cheek. "Anything you say, Maudie. Love you." Then he straightened, led Holly into the hall, and closed the sliding door.

"Sometimes I think I'll never understand that woman."

Clearly, Hank was angry, but Holly couldn't find the words to comfort him. Much as she liked the man, it was *Parker* that her heart ached for. In all her life, she'd never seen a man look more lost and alone. Why, after letting him live his entire life in the shadow of her lie, had Maude found it necessary to tell him the truth *now*?

It seemed beyond unmaternal and unloving, unburdening herself at her only son's expense.

Hank looked up and fixed his gaze on mother and son, there on the other side of the glass partition. "I've always known she's got a selfish streak, but until now..."

It seemed he didn't have the heart to complete the sentence.

"Just look at him," Hank said, using his thumb as a pointer. "Looks like he's carrying the weight of the world on his shoulders. What was she *thinking*, waiting until a time like this to dump all that on the boy? And what could she possibly add to it all *now*?"

He drove a hand through his thick white hair and, holding it there, met Holly's eyes. "Thank God he's got you in his corner, kiddo, that's all I can say."

She opened her mouth to tell Hank what she'd told Parker earlier... that he'd survived war and battle injuries all on his own. But this was different, very different, and she knew it would take the strength of Hercules to endure it. "I'm not going anywhere," she said, meaning it. "I only hope he isn't too proud—or too hurt—to *let* me be there for him."

Hank laid his hands on her shoulders and gave Holly a gentle shake. "You've gotta be strong, kiddo, stronger than you've ever been. No matter what he says or does, you have to make sure he knows you're there to lean on."

Nodding, she glanced at Parker, who had his head down and his shoulders slumped, looking like a man who'd just lost everything. And in a way, he had. "I will."

"Won't be easy, you know. Men are odd ducks. Think they're better off alone at times like this, which is the *last* thing he needs.

He'll probably say some hurtful, angry things, hoping to drive you away." He gave her another little shake. "But you be tough. Be stubborn, you hear? No matter what, you hang in there, because he won't mean a word of it."

She was about to tell Hank that she understood when he said, "He's a good and decent man, that Parker Brant. None better, in my opinion. If I had a son…" Eyes shining with unshed tears, he added, "He's hurting, but it's gonna come out looking as if he's mad."

"He has every right to be both," she nearly snarled. "I can't imagine what must be going on in his head, in his heart."

"See there?" Hank drew her into a fatherly hug. "I knew you were a godsend." Holding her at arm's length, he looked deep into her eyes. "This isn't gonna be easy, what you're about to face, but I promise, Parker is worth it."

Two beefy orderlies half ran past them and into Maude's room. As they wheeled her into the hall, she reached for Holly's hand. "Don't let him be alone," she said, gripping it with a strength that belied her condition. To Hank, she added, "Same goes for you, okay?"

"Couldn't love him more if he were my own," Hank said, kissing her knuckles, "but you already know that, don't you?"

She closed her eyes. "Yes, yes I do." Then, "Parker?"

He stepped up beside the bed, looking as haggard and ragged as if he'd just completed a 15K run. "I'm right here, Mom. You just concentrate on getting through this," he said, his voice foggy with tears. "And after that, you'll concentrate on getting better. The rest…" His voice cracked with emotion. "The rest will sort itself out."

Maybe Hank had been wrong and this sad yet calm demeanor meant that Parker would be all right, after all. That he wouldn't need to resort to fury and self-imposed seclusion to cope with the awful news. *Maude doesn't deserve a son like him,* Holly thought. And more than ever, she wanted to talk to her own mother, who didn't have a selfish bone in her body, who'd never done anything but love her child with all her heart. If a little nagging and scolding were part of her mothering tactics, well, Holly would gladly, gratefully, accept it from now on.

"Love you, Mom," Parker said and kissed her cheek.

"You too," she said as the orderlies rolled her toward the OR suite.

"Doc Williams will send somebody out to update you," said the biggest orderly as the doors closed.

"Did either of you get a chance to eat while you were gone?" Holly asked.

"Had a couple cookies," Hank said.

"And I grabbed an apple."

"Well, that's no good. No good at all." She linked arms with each and led them to the elevator. "We're going to the diner," she said, "and I won't take no for an answer. I saw chicken soup on the menu, and my mouth has been watering for a bowl ever since."

"Soup," Parker said. "But it's 80 degrees outside."

"If memory serves, the diner is air conditioned."

She pretended not to see when they exchanged an "Oh, brother" look over her head. Her goal right now was getting their minds off Maude. Off the horrible story. If she had to swing from the diner's hanging lamps and chatter like a chimp, she'd do it.

And, God willing, she wouldn't do something clumsy and further complicate poor Parker's life.

* * * * *

Parker wasn't sure how Holly managed to talk him into going to the beach, but now that he was here, it felt good, felt right. The volunteers who'd combed the sand during daylight hours, clearing weeds and any debris that washed ashore, had handed their batons over to others who walked softly and carefully, making sure nothing got in the turtles' way as they lumbered from the water to make their nests.

Like the volunteers, Holly stood still and silent beside him. All around them, a light June breeze blew in from the east. It felt good, felt right too, even though everything in him told him it should feel anything *but*. She'd witnessed the most humiliating moment of his life. If he had a lick of pride left, he'd send her packing, book or no book. *What was it she said?* he asked himself. *That if I could survive combat and war wounds, I could survive anything?* That might be laughable…if it wasn't so doggoned *sad*.

Holly grabbed hold of his arm and used her free hand to point toward the clear black sky. "Look," she whispered, "isn't that Delphinus?"

He stared into the inky heavens and shook his head. "Sorry, I'm not up on constellations."

She moved closer still, saying, "It represents the dolphin. California's Chumash tribe said it means 'to go in peace and protect.' The way their legend goes, when they were getting ready to migrate to the mainland, their grandmother built them a rainbow bridge. Hutash warned them not to look down while crossing or they'd fall into the sea and drown. Some couldn't help themselves, and because she loved them so, Hutash turned them into dolphins before they hit the water."

"Really."

She nodded. "Early Christians called it 'Job's Coffin,' and the Arabs named it 'Riding Camel.' In Australia, the Aborigine see the dolphin as a wise older brother, swimming the world's oceans to guide and protect their siblings who've chosen to go through life in human form. To this day, killing one is considered sacrilege."

"Isn't *all* this mythological stuff sacrilege?"

"Well, sure it is, if you *believe* it. I just think it's fascinating, all the tall tales God's stars inspire. This one especially, since it's not particularly big or bright." Using his fingertip, she drew the dolphin's outline. "Now that you've seen her, you'll never forget where to find her."

"Her?"

Holly harrumphed. "Well, if you can call your boat and your pickup a *her*, I think it's all right for me to refer to a star formation that way."

Despite all that had happened that day, Parker chuckled quietly. "Good point." Then, movement up ahead caught his attention— a giant sea turtle, plodding across the sand. "Look," he whispered, "isn't that a loggerhead?"

He didn't just hear her gasp, he felt it as Holly pressed closer. "Isn't it just magnificent? I've seen it before, six or eight times, and it never fails to mystify me."

As though he'd been doing it for years, Parker's arm slid around her waist. "That's an odd word to describe it."

She gave a little shrug. "I suppose. But the whole life cycle, from egg to hatchling to turtle that makes this demanding trip a dozen times in her lifetime, using the exact same route…maybe *miraculous* is a better word."

"What kind of scientist are you," he asked, laughing softly, "talking God and miracles? I thought y'all were into *dis*proving everything religious and spiritual."

"That's true for some," she admitted. "Their loss."

"How so?"

"I'd think that believing only in things that can be validated and verified would be a very cold and lonely way to live. It's comforting to know that God's love is all around us. Like up there," she said, pointing at the constellation again. She aimed that dainty finger at the Atlantic and then at the turtle making slow but steady progress toward a sand mound. "And there and there." She put herself in front of him and pressed her palms over his heart. "And there."

No, he wanted to say, *God isn't in* me. Especially now, with all the angry, hateful thoughts hammering at his brain. But she was looking up at him, big eyes aglow with hope and faith. She really believed every word she'd said, and Parker didn't have the heart to take that from her. If he uttered so much as a syllable that diminished her beliefs, he was no better a human being than Maude.

He hoped she was resting comfortably, getting better, breath by breath, because—

"I wonder how your mom is doing?"

Man, it was unsettling, the way she seemed to be able to read his mind! "She's fine, I'm sure." After the reparative surgery, and after she came around in the recovery room, Dr. Williams had assured them all was well, especially considering that the leakage hadn't been a harbinger of a bigger problem, but the result of Maude's getting out of bed to pour herself a cup of water. Now that the staff knew that she was the type who'd sneak around, dismissing doctor's orders, they had tied her to the bed. "Provided that she hasn't undone her bindings," he finished.

Holly frowned and shook her head. "I'm sure she didn't mean to cause any trouble, getting out of bed. She probably just wanted to spare everyone the bother of waiting on her. Before her foot surgery, she was pretty independent."

Independent? Not if he counted the hundreds of things she was always asking him to do around the cottage and the errands she was forever getting Hank to run. A random thought slammed into his brain: why had it been so easy to believe that his father had died while testing a fighter jet? If he'd questioned the story at some point, maybe—

"Are you thinking we should get back there, to make sure she's all right?"

"No." He didn't have the stomach or the patience to fake something amiable with Maude just now. She'd deprived him of a relationship with his father. She'd lied to Daniel too. The man didn't even know he *had* a son. If he'd known, what sort of father would he have been?

Frustrated and furious, Parker exhaled a shaky breath. "No, let's give her the night to rest up." Hopefully, by morning, he'd have summoned the backbone to put on a good front. Because despite the lies—or maybe because of them—she was the only family he had in the world. He'd never been angrier, not even on the battlefield, when the enemy, believing they had Right on their side, literally tried to kill him and his fellow soldiers. But he wanted to see Maude healthy again. If for no other reason than to find out if his legal last name was Brant or if she'd lied about that too.

The turtle had found a sweet spot in the sand by now, and those back flippers were all business, flicking sand in a high, wide arc to create her nest. Before long she'd have a hole deep enough, and she'd deposit her eggs, one atop the other, and cover them over. Pure instinct drove her, and it would drive her back into the Atlantic too. It wouldn't inspire a backward glance, and she wouldn't give the eggs another thought. In her mind, she'd fulfilled her maternal duties and was now free to go back to looking out for her own best interests as she encountered sharks, boat propellers, fishermen's nets, and other dangers lurking in the ocean.

It wasn't a particularly flattering comparison, but the loggerhead reminded Parker of Maude, whose single-minded struggle for survival overshadowed her son's needs. She'd provided the necessities: a roof over his head, food, clothes. How much of that had come from love for him…and how much was to protect her own reputation from the gossipmongers who waited for the single mother to make a mistake?

"You're awfully quiet," Holly said, interrupting his thoughts.

"Don't mean to be. Sorry."

"I didn't bring it up to elicit an apology. I know you have a lot on your mind. I just want you to know that when you're ready to talk about it…"

He nodded and turned slightly then drove both hands deep into his jeans pockets. "I know. Thanks."

She linked her arm with his and started walking. He fell into step beside her, and for the second time that night, it felt good, felt right. But what hope of a future did he have with someone like Holly, who grew up in a house filled with family members who genuinely cared about one another? Whose faith in a Supreme Being gave her comfort even during those dark hours after she'd lost the love of her life? She'd expect things like that from him, but he didn't have them. Didn't know if he could find it in himself to get them. Didn't have a clue where to look for them if he did.

"Maude… She…" She huffed and started again. "I know it doesn't seem like it right now, considering—"

Considering she'd lived a lie for thirty-two years *and dragged me into it?*

"—but Maude loves you, Parker."

Bitter laughter burned in his throat, but he bit it back. He recited his turtle analogy for her. Maybe that would help her understand how he saw Maude's capacity for *love*. By the time he finished, they were standing at the end of the flagstone walk leading to her cottage. She must have seen him looking a few hundred yards farther down the beach, where the dim lights of his own house glowed.

"Are there any eggs in your fridge?"

"I'm pretty sure."

"Bread and butter?"

"Yeah."

"Sausage? Bacon or ham?"

"Both, I think." It seemed weird, talking about food right now. A spin-off on the old adage that the way to a man's heart was through his stomach? Maybe she believed a big country breakfast would distract him from his troubles. "Look, Holly, I appreciate what you're trying to do, but—"

"Whoa," she said, cutting him off. "If you think for one minute I'm asking on *your* behalf, you've got another think coming. Night air gives me an appetite, I guess, because I'm famished."

He didn't believe that any more than he believed that the loggerhead would come back in a day or two to make sure nothing had disturbed her babies. "Well, after all you've done today, I guess the least I can do is feed you."

She looked up at him and, seeing his grin, smiled. Relief coursed through him, and Parker decided to hold onto it for as long as it lasted, knowing it was temporary at best.

Chapter Seventeen

....

Holly stuck her head in the fridge and began stacking breakfast fixings in her arms. "Why don't you take a long, hot shower while I fix us something to eat?"

"Holy mackerel," he said as the coffeemaker sputtered, "aren't *you* good for a guy's ego."

She turned so quickly to see his face that she nearly dropped everything. "That wasn't a subtle hint that you *need* a shower. I just thought—"

"I know." He grinned. "But just for clarity's sake, that wasn't a subtle hint."

Relieved that she hadn't insulted him, or worse, hurt his feelings, Holly plopped her load onto the counter. "I don't suppose it was, was it?"

"It's a good idea, though, and I think I'll take you up on it." With a wave of his hand, Parker said, *"Mi casa, su casa.* Anything you need, just help yourself."

What she needed, Holly decided when he rounded the corner, were ideas. Solid, foolproof plans that she could put into play in the days and weeks to come to help him cope with the awful mess Maude had made of their lives.

Opening and closing lower cabinet doors, she found two frying pans and began layering bacon in the largest. While it warmed up, she dropped a pat of butter into the smaller one. She turned down the heat as she remembered how Parker had compared his mom to the loggerheads. It made her cringe, hearing him say that, mostly because he wasn't totally off base. Holly couldn't think of a scenario that would prompt her own mother to so much as *consider* doing anything that might hurt her child.

He kept his plates right where she'd stored hers in the Ocean City condo, and in her Ellicott City townhouse too…in the cupboard above the silverware drawer. Gathering what she'd need to set the table, Holly glanced at the ship's clock above the sink. It was too late to call home now, but first thing tomorrow, she'd *make* time. And between now and then, she'd pray that God would give her the words to make sure her folks knew how much she loved and appreciated them. Maybe they'd agree to drive to South Carolina for a long weekend. She knew firsthand that none of Maude's guest rooms would be rented over the July Fourth holiday.…

Four slices of bread stood at the ready in the toaster, and beside the stove were serving plates for the bacon and eggs. He didn't have enough juice for two full servings, so she swirled a drop into one glass and stood it beside her plate. That way, when he sat down, he'd think she'd already downed hers and she wouldn't need to explain why she didn't want to divvy it up equally. He'd been deprived of enough in his lifetime. If she could provide him with a full ration of *something*, Holly intended to do it!

The only thing left to do was fry the eggs and pour the coffee. Well, that and to come up with something bland yet un-boring to talk about so that he could eat the meal without getting heartburn. No way he'd get a decent night's sleep with heartburn to cope with on top of Maude's bulletin.

While looking for napkins, she'd noticed a tiny white container of Maude's pain-reliever-sleep-aid pills. Maybe, she thought, smirking, she should crush one up and enforce a good night's sleep. Then she shook her head. What was she thinking? That wouldn't just be unfair to Parker, but wholly wrong, as well. If she resented the little bit of control her mom occasionally tried to exert, how much more would he resent it if she did something like that?

She'd just have to trust God to get him through the rough times ahead. And possibly, in the process, he'd learn to trust Him too.

Sighing, Holly poured herself a mug of coffee. Thankfully, he'd had just enough decaf to brew one pot. She'd seen a jar of instant decaffeinated tucked in behind the mugs. With any luck, they wouldn't have to resort to using that, because if Parker felt the same way about the stuff as she did, well, she'd just as soon skip it.

He padded into the kitchen just then, all six-two and towel-dried dark hair of him. My, but he looked handsome in his plain white T-shirt and baggy black jog pants. "Have a seat," she said, pulling out the chair at the head of his table. "I just need to fry up the eggs and butter the toast."

He eased the spatula from her hand. "Why not let me do that while you make the toast?"

The barest hint of a grin lifted the corners of his mouth. If only she could coax a full-blown smile onto that gorgeous face. Stories about her childhood had amused him in the past....

"I remember the very first time I ever cooked eggs. I was on a camping trip with all my cousins and—"

"How many cousins?"

"Off the top of my head, I'd say, twelve? Fifteen? Ranging in age from, oh, forty to thirty-two."

"Ah, so you're the baby of the family. No wonder they hover."

Holly snorted. "That's a lousy excuse for hovering if ever I heard one."

"All I know is, if I had a kid sister or little-girl cousin or whatever, and she was forever getting into trouble the way you are, *I'd* hover."

Like dominos toppling, Holly thought of all the ways she'd gotten into trouble just since arriving in Folly Beach. She dropped bread into the toaster and watched him crack an egg into the pan. "So let me tell you about the very first time I made eggs."

"I hate to be repetitive, but I think we're gonna have to work on your subtlety."

We? Well, a girl could dream....

"Over easy, right?"

Nodding, she grabbed the toasted slices as they popped up and began buttering each slice while he cracked the second egg.

"How is it you know me so well already?"

Already? They'd shared meals and coffee and hours, hunched over tall stacks of research notes, pounding out the book, one computer keystroke at a time. "I might not be big on subtlety," she said with a smirk, "but I've honed my observation skills to a keen edge."

After carrying the toast to the table, Parker grabbed the coffee carafe, filled his empty mug, and topped off hers. Then, with one tine of a fork, he removed the bacon from the big skillet and laid the slices side by side on a paper towel–covered plate.

"Who taught you how to do that?" she asked, flipping the eggs.

His voice cracked slightly when he said "Maude." She tried to read his expression, to see if his expression matched the dry grate of his tone, but he'd already settled onto the seat of his chair.

"You were telling me about your first egg-frying experience."

Somehow she'd have to find her way back to a chatty, upbeat mood, not only to blot out the dour reminder of what his mother had done, but to keep it at bay throughout the meal. He'd just uncapped the grape jam when Holly slid two perfect eggs onto his plate.

"What, no eggs for you?" he said when she joined him at the table. Pushing his plate closer to hers, he added, "Here, take one of these. I don't need—"

"I tell a better tale when I'm not distracted by food." And with that, Holly launched into her camping story, which started with a stormy night in the Allegheny Mountains of Maryland that all but flattened their tent and ended with undercooked eggs fried in a pie tin over a sputtering fire pit. "Half of what I fried up stuck to the pan, and the other half…?" She laughed. "It's a minor miracle that we didn't all end up in the hospital with botulism or salmonella poisoning."

Bite by bite his midnight breakfast disappeared, and by the time the coffee urn was empty, she'd told him about the time she sewed the hem of her dress to the sofa slipcover and the upturned dresser fiasco, as well.

"What's a minor miracle," he said, "is that you weren't crushed when the thing fell on you. What were you thinking, using the drawers as stairs?"

"I was four. I *wasn't* thinking."

He studied her face for a long, silent moment, as if imprinting every bit of it onto his brain. But why? Holly wondered. Was he planning to end things before they had a chance to begin? *Not that, Lord, please not that.* Hank had warned her that Parker might try to put distance between them, and that he might employ harsh words to accomplish it. *He's in for a rude awakening if he tries that,* she thought, because having grown up surrounded by rowdy cousins, she'd taken the taunting "Sticks and stones might break my bones, but words will never hurt me" phrase to heart.

"What," she said, smirking, "do I have bacon stuck between my teeth?"

His voice was anything but gruff when he said, "No, nothing like that." He tucked a lock of hair behind her ear. "I was just thinking."

"Uh-oh. That isn't good news."

Pressing his palm to her cheek, he added, "I'm glad we didn't meet back then."

"Because I was such a ditzy little klutz?"

That inspired a rich, full-bodied laugh, and Holly drank in every note of it.

"No, because I would've been right there in line with your family, trying to protect you from yourself." His thumb was drawing slow circles on her jaw when he added, "I never could have let myself feel this way about a girl who was like a sister to me."

Surprised and elated at his tender admission, she leaned into his hand. "How do you feel about me, Parker?"

The drowsy, relaxed expression vanished like the smoke of a spent match, and in its place appeared a serious, standoffish look that made her heart ache. As he sat back and started stacking plates, she thought, *Will you* ever *learn when to keep your big mouth shut?*

He gathered silverware into one hand and carried them to the sink. "I'll say this…you're still a klutzy little ditz, so it's tough *not* to feel like a big brother toward you."

A discordant, too-loud laugh bubbled from her, and she did nothing to stifle it. She hadn't known Parker long, but in the weeks they'd spent together, his gentle nature and thoughtful heart had become more and more apparent. Though this big bear of a man had donned a uniform and hefted powerful weapons to defend his troops against unseen, unknown enemies, he would never consciously hurt her. For proof, she needed only to think back to the loving way he'd treated Maude as the orderlies wheeled her toward the operating room after her revelation. Who would have blamed him if, instead of kind reassurances, he'd stormed off, leaving hateful, accusing words in his wake!

If Parker ever aimed tactless words Holly's way, it would prove something else: that he cared enough about her to push her away while he tried to get a handle on his churning emotions. He deserved better from her than to cower and waver because of a few stinging barbs. So she'd pray, pray as she'd never prayed before, for the strength to get him through this.

Because it scared Holly to death, thinking what might become of him—and of her—if she failed.

Chapter Eighteen

....

"I hope you won't mind," Hank said, folding and unfolding a small square of paper, "but I've made a few calls."

Parker looked up from the keyboard. "What kind of calls?"

Hank straddled the chair beside Parker's desk and leaned his forearms on its back. "I still have some friends in high places at the FBI," he began, "who owe me big favors."

It wasn't like Hank to beat around the bush this way, and as much as he hated to admit it, the stall tactic made the hairs stand up on the back of Parker's neck.

"After what Maude told you, I figured…" Running his fingers one last time across the paper's longest crease, he held it out.

It didn't escape Parker's notice that, since his mother's confession, Hank hadn't called her "Maudie," not even once. He felt bad for the guy, because like Hank, he too had clung to hope that the women from his own past might change, and, like Hank, he'd felt the sour sting of regret when they didn't. Heart thumping against his ribs and hand shaking, he reached out to accept the notepaper.

The name, address, and phone number, penned in Hank's architect-style printing, would take him straight to the door of Daniel Brant. Below that, Hank had written two more phone numbers and the Charleston marina slip where the man had docked a boat called the *Sea Stallion*.

"Weird, isn't it, how you chose such similar names for your boats?"

Parker only nodded as Hank said, "He retired from the Air Force after thirty years when his wife was diagnosed with cancer."

"What kind of cancer?"

"Breast. She's in remission."

Well, good for her. And for Daniel too, because Maude shouldn't have had the power to squander *his* chance at a normal, happy life.

"Any kids?"

"Three. Two sons and a daughter."

Parker ground his molars together. So he had brothers. And a sister. And Maude's deception had kept them all apart all these years.

"When did they divorce?"

"Never married," Hank said.

"*What?*"

Hank told the part of the story that Maude had left out that day in the hospital, about how just as she started to tell Daniel that she was pregnant, some woman walked up. "She told herself the both of you were better off without a man like that, a man who'd use women and cast them aside. And then there was the matter of Daniel's background."

Parker was having trouble wrapping his mind around the fact that his saintly mother had led him to believe, all these many years, that she and Daniel had been married when he died. So he hadn't just grown up without a dad, he was illegitimate, to boot. "What about his background?" he steamed.

"Daniel's father owned a manufacturing company that made

parts for the big car corporations. Branched out into parts for the airlines. And the trucking industry. The family rubbed elbows with the rich and famous, and Maude was afraid they'd think she got pregnant on purpose, to trap Daniel into marrying her so she could get a piece of the pie."

He was about to say, "It's good to know she had *some* scruples," when it dawned on him that Hank knew an awful lot about…about everything. "How'd you come by all this information?"

"Like I said, I have friends in high places. Called in a few favors. Asked the questions I'd have wanted answers to, in your shoes." He shrugged. "But you're under no obligation to do anything with it."

Isn't it ironic, Parker thought—that Hank knew him better than his own mother did. He thumped the note. "Must have taken hours, digging up that much stuff."

Hank chuckled. "How else was I gonna occupy my idle hours?"

True enough, Parker conceded. With Maude in the hospital, Hank hadn't been anybody's errand boy for weeks and had no obligations or responsibilities to anyone but himself. And the stray. "How's Cat?" The question inspired the first genuine smile Parker had seen since Hank walked through the door.

"She's good, and getting better every day." He leaned forward and looked right and left. "You won't believe this," he said conspiratorially, "but she comes when she's called. And she plays fetch. And sits upright on the couch, like a person."

"You don't say."

Parker wasn't looking forward to the day when he'd look as pleased, talking about a feline or canine companion. His e-mail program dinged, alerting him to a new message. Swiveling his chair to face the monitor, he clicked the tiny envelope. "It's about Ben!" he said.

Hank moved his chair closer and read over Parker's shoulder. "He's a little skinny, but no worse for the wear." Sitting back, he slapped his thigh. "Well, that's just about the best news I've heard in months. Does your friend say whether you can bring him here anytime soon?"

"I'm still tangled up in miles of red tape."

"I might know a way to cut through it."

Parker faced him. "How?"

"Old buddy of mine, a former agent, ran for office after he was wounded in the line of duty. He's a big-shot congressman now. Bet he could pull a few strings."

The picture of Ben, smiling down at him from the shelf above his computer, made him say, "Call him. What's the worst that could happen?"

"He could say yes."

"What's that supposed to mean?"

"You given any thought to what it'll be like, raising an Arab orphan in today's world? You could be opening him up to a world of hurt. Yourself too."

Parker had every confidence that he could shield Ben from most of life's blows. But bigotry and prejudice…could he protect the boy from that? Maybe. Maybe not. But he owed it to Ben to try.

"What about Holly?"

"What about her?"

"Ever wonder how she'd feel about helping you raise a war-scarred young boy?"

In all honesty, it had never entered his mind, because to this point, he hadn't let himself believe he *could* raise Ben. As for Holly's part in it, well, he'd been all over that ground a hundred times, as he tossed and turned during the nights. "She deserves better than the likes of a has-been gimpy soldier. Make that a has-been *illegitimate* soldier," he ground out.

"I don't think you're giving her near enough credit. She's no bigger than a minute, I'll give you that, but the girl is stronger than most men I know."

True, but that didn't mean he'd consider foisting his sorry self on her.

"Maybe you ought to let her decide what's best for her."

"And maybe you ought to butt out. No offense intended."

"None taken." Hank got up to leave but stopped long enough to say, "You'll regret it the rest of your life if you let her get away."

The lock clicked into place with a hollow *thunk,* reminding Parker of the sound he'd heard a time or two in the past when he'd whacked his head crawling through a tunnel or ducking under a door frame. Maybe that's what it would take these days to get things through his thick skull…a good hard thump on the noggin.

He couldn't say if the man was right or dead wrong. But before he could even consider the possibility of taking Hank's advice, he had a lot of work to do to get his head straight and his life in order. He owed that much to Holly, didn't he?

* * * * *

"And I miss you too," Holly gushed, meaning every word.

"Will you have time for a visit soon, I hope?"

Under other circumstances, she probably would have made the drive north two or three times between arriving in South Carolina and the end of the book project. But with Maude just home from the hospital and Parker in his brittle emotional state, Holly didn't want to leave. "No, I'm afraid not, but I have a great idea. How about if you and Dad drove down for the Fourth of July weekend? There are a lot of terrific things to do, and you could stay right here at the cottage."

She'd already explained that Maude's double medical emergency made it necessary to arrange other accommodations for the B&B guests, and she told how she'd been helping out since Maude's release from the hospital. "She says she'd love to meet you and that you're more than welcome to stay as long as you like."

"That's a lovely idea," her mom said. "I can't think of any reason we couldn't come, but let me talk it over with Dad and get back to you."

Holly didn't tell her that she'd already booked them the Lucy Suite, directly across the hall from her own room, and paid for a full week's stay. "Is Dad home?"

"Yes, but you know your father. Hard to tell whether he's tinkering in his garage or puttering in the shed. Hold on a minute."

Holly heard the *rustle-rattle* of her mother's hand covering the mouthpiece. "Bob," she called out. "Bob, it's Holly on the phone. She has something to ask you."

A moment later, she heard a *click* as he picked up the extension. "How's my girl?"

She could hear the smile in his voice. "I'm terrific. Listen, Dad, I was just telling Mom that you two should drive down here for the

Fourth. I'd love to show you around Folly Beach. It's the most amazing town."

"What do you think, Laura?"

"I'd love it."

"Wonderful!" Holly said. "Maybe, if you can stay awhile, we can take in some of the sights in Charleston. You've both been saying for years that it's one of those places you'd love to see."

"Can we get back to you on that, honey?"

"Sure, Dad. No rush. You can even come a few days ahead of the holiday, you know, to miss the worst of the traffic."

"With gas prices what they are today?" Her dad laughed. "We'll probably be the only car on the road."

"Well, I'd better run. I'm supposed to meet Parker to—"

"Aha," her mother interrupted. "This sounds promising."

"What, calling her boss by his first name?" her dad chimed in.

"Your secretary calls you *Bob*," Holly pointed out. "And Mom, you've called your editor *Marv* for as long as I can remember."

The sound of her parents' laughter was music to her ears. Oh, how she loved them! "All right, then," her mom said, "get to your meeting."

"We'll call you in a day or so to let you know when we'll be there."

"Sounds good. I can hardly wait to see you. And guys? I love you like crazy!"

When she hung up, Holly felt the need to share her good news. Parker didn't pick up, so she dialed Hank, who agreed to meet her for breakfast on the condition that she let him pick up the tab this time.

Once Agnes finished her usual flirtatious routine, she told him about her parents' visit…and the reason she was particularly excited to see them. "I'm ashamed to admit that I took them for granted. All the little things they've done over the years that I saw as meddling and bossiness, well, even if that's exactly what it was—what it is— they meant well."

"Let me tell you, kiddo, if you were my daughter, I'd be *all* up in your business."

"It's a shame you never had kids. You would have made a terrific dad."

"God knows what He's doing. The little woman didn't have the strength to carry a baby to term, but even if she had, she couldn't have been a proper mother. Not for want of trying, mind you, but because of her health."

He'd already told her that his wife had been diagnosed with a rare form of leukemia shortly after they were married, and that after years of struggle, she joined her Maker in heaven. Holly understood his point of view, but if they'd had even one child before her death, Hank would have a family of his own now instead of filling that empty spot in his life with Parker and, to a lesser extent, herself.

"Have you talked with Parker in the past few days?"

"Well, sure. We've added a good thirty hours' worth of work to the book."

Hank snickered. "But have you *talked* with him lately?"

She knew exactly what he meant. Parker had a penchant for zeroing in on a project to the degree that he barely saw or heard anything not related to it. And since Maude's bombshell, his tendency for focus had only sharpened. "Why?" She forced a grin. "What do you know that I don't?"

"That little kid he met on his last tour in Afghanistan?"

"Ben?"

"One and the same. Well, it seems he's safe and sound after all, and Parker's working the bugs out of the paperwork so he can get him and bring him home."

"That's just wonderful! He must be thrilled. Does Ben know?"

"Not sure, but it's doubtful. I wouldn't tell him if I had any decision-making power in the situation." Hank shrugged. "No point in getting his hopes up in case things fall flat."

"Well, we'll just have to pray like crazy that things *don't* fall flat, won't we?"

"Yep. So I hear you're getting involved over at our little church."

Holly laughed. "Not really. I volunteered to bake some brownies and said I'd man a table during the white-elephant sale."

"I heard they, ah, *persuaded* you into singing a solo this Sunday too."

"Yeah, but only if Emily Parsons's laryngitis isn't better by then." She leaned forward and looked from side to side. "Just between you and me, I'm praying that she's in full voice by then."

"Well, you can bet I'll be there, just in case."

"Do you think there's a chance that Parker might come?"

"A month ago, I might have said maybe. Now?" He loosed a raspy sigh. "I wouldn't count on it."

She nodded. "That's what I figured."

"Aw, now, don't look so glum. You never can tell. Miracles happen every day." He finished the last of his coffee and waved Agnes over. "So what's on your slate for this afternoon, kiddo?"

"I'm going to do some grocery shopping. Maude's cupboards are as bare as Old Mother Hubbard's, and Parker's aren't much better." She saw no point in telling him that Parker had been avoiding the cottage—or that she didn't much blame him—so except for sleeping, she'd been spending most of her time at his house. "Can't expect Maude's nurse to run errands, with everything else she has to do, and I figure with the holiday just around the corner and my folks coming to town, I'd better stock up. If I wait until the last minute, it'll probably be the same as when the weatherman predicts snow in Baltimore."

"The old 'we might run out of milk and toilet paper' run, eh?"

"Yeah, you don't want to be in the stores at the eleventh hour."

Until she heard his dour tone, Holly had almost forgotten that until the big confession, it had been Hank who'd run most of Maude's errands. She started to apologize when Agnes stepped up and slapped the bill on the table. "No need to leave me a tip, Handsome," she said with a wink, "if you sit with me at the church social on Sunday."

Grinning, Hank shook his head.

"That Maude," Agnes said, "is one lucky duck. I hope she realizes what a prize you are."

He waved the compliment away. "Agnes, you're incorrigible."

"Why? Because I call 'em as I see 'em?" She snickered. "You tell that woman I'm just waiting for her to get her strength back." She rolled up nonexistent sleeves. "Once she's got her game face on again, it's every woman for herself." She faced Holly and added, "If he doesn't tell her, *you* do it. It's only fair the woman get some warning, after all." And with that, she sashayed away, snapping her gum.

"Well, as I live and breathe," Hank said, watching her go.

"She's right, you know."

His brow furrowed with confusion. "Right? About what?"

"You are a prize, and Maude's lucky to have you, especially..."
Holly couldn't bear to admit her true feelings, especially after what
Maude had done to Parker.

"She had her reasons, I expect." His frown deepened.

Holly thought it best to change the subject and relieve Hank
of the self-imposed duty of defending Maude's indefensible actions.
"So what're *you* doing for the rest of the day?"

"Going to the pet store for some toys and treats for Cat."

"Cat? Is that the name you decided on?"

"She seems to like it."

"I think what she likes," Holly said, "is *you*. With good reason."

"C'mon now, you'll start me blushing like a schoolgirl again."
She picked up the tab and faced the cashier's counter. "You know
how hard that is to hide under this snow-white hair?"

Laughing, Holly joined him in the aisle and gave him a big hug.
"Have a great day, Hank."

The last thing she heard before the big glass door swung shut
was, "You, too, kiddo. See you in church!"

The words made her cringe, because she had a sinking suspicion
that Emily wouldn't be ready to sing that solo by Sunday, and knowing that Parker wouldn't be there to cheer her on, Holly's heart just
wasn't in it.

Chapter Nineteen

....

Parker didn't think he'd ever seen Holly happier or more animated and doubted that he could generate that much enthusiasm over *anything* family-related, not even if he lived to be one hundred. If he *had* a family, that is. His recurring daydream, where a couple of rambunctious kids and a loving wife raced down the walk to greet him, well, it would remain a dream. Even if he could find a woman willing to overlook his questionable parentage, he'd begun to worry about history repeating itself. What if he'd inherited his father's oblivious tendencies, or worse, Maude's self-centered streak? No way he'd inflict that on an innocent kid.

"So when will your folks get into town?"

"On July first."

He could see that she was trying to curb her excitement, and he believed he knew why: Holly, whose energy was rivaled only by her empathy, saw the stark contrasts between her background and his and had convinced herself that by downplaying her strong family ties, he wouldn't feel so left out or left behind. If he'd met her a year ago, before Maude's confession blew his world apart, well, because Holly didn't do anything halfway, she would have followed the "for better or worse" part of her wedding vows to the letter.

"Wow. July first is just around the corner."

Cupping her elbows, she trembled with pleasure. "I'm not supposed to know this, but a couple of my cousins are coming too, to take turns driving for Dad. I'm putting them in the Miles Fairley suite. It's not as big as the Captain Dan or as elegant as the Lucy, but I'm sure they'll be very comfortable."

"There are three other rooms. Why make them share a suite?"

"Because it'll give them a chance to reconnect. Adam has been going through some rough times since his separation, and I think being with Frank will help him deal with all that."

Then she smiled, sending Parker's heart into overdrive. Again.

"Adam served in Iraq, you know. Two tours. So you guys can bond over big guns and bombs and war and all that other *man* stuff."

"Maybe he's one of those guys who doesn't like talking about combat."

Now she laughed, adding to the heat in his cheeks. Oh, but he wished she'd quit looking at him that way!

"Well, if that's your way of saying *you're* one of those guys, then I feel it's only fair to warn you not to say the word 'soldier' around Adam."

Great, he thought. *Just great. Holly's cousin and me at our own private pity party.*

"Oh, now, don't look that way. Adam kept it all bottled up at first, which is precisely the reason he and Jessie separated. He wants things to work out between them, he really does. So much so that he agreed to see a counselor—he's still seeing the guy, I think—who advised him to open up. And believe me, he took the advice to heart!"

Different strokes for different folks, Parker thought. *Physical* therapy was one thing. But seeing a shrink? He'd stomached the rigors of rehab, but what kind of a man would he be if he couldn't muddle through this Maude mess on his own?

One eye squinted, Holly leaned against his deck rail and counted on her fingers. "Let's see, I need to put clean linens on the beds and fresh towels in the bathrooms, and then I have to go to the grocery store to restock Maude's kitchen."

Parker had the feeling she was thinking out loud rather than talking to him. But then she locked that big-eyed gaze on him and said, "Say, I have an idea. Why don't you come with me?"

"Why? My pantry isn't bare."

"Please," she countered, frowning. "You can't call a can of tomato soup and a half dozen eggs a stocked kitchen. Besides, I have a favor to ask you, and if you say yes—and I'm really, *really* hoping you will—you'll need more than a bottle of root beer and a tub of margarine."

"Favor?"

"Well, see," she began, pointing, "you have that big fancy gas grill and this enormous deck overlooking the Atlantic. So I was thinking… how nice would it be to have a cookout up here? Just my mom and dad, Adam and Frank, your mom and Hank, you and me and—"

"On the Fourth."

"Well, yeah."

When her eyebrows drew together, Parker knew she'd picked up on his "I'm not into family gatherings" clue.

She took a step closer. "Look. Parker. All you'll have to do is *be* here. I'll do all the cooking, the setting up and taking down, the—"

"Setting up and taking down? Sheesh, Hol, what kind of shindig are you planning?"

"Just your typical, average, everyday fami—" She cleared her throat. "An ordinary cookout, that's all. No biggie. A few hot dogs, burgers, potato salad, baked beans, apple pie," she singsonged, "some Old Glory-type decorations…"

"Decorations."

"You know, red-white-and-blue stuff. Tablecloths, paper plates, and napkins, a couple of streamers, a few flags…" Grinning, she grabbed his hands and brought them together with a *clap*. "It'll be fun, you'll see. Especially once it's dark, when they start shooting off fireworks. And how lucky will we be, that we'll just have to face your deck chairs toward the fishing pier!"

Parker had never been the type to wish his life away, but right now, he wished he could be a little more like Holly and just enjoy the little things life had to offer. Was it fair to rain on her parade just because he couldn't? He shook his head. "So what time will everybody get here?"

"Is that a yes?"

Though the chances that he'd ever have a daughter were slim to none, something told Parker that a kid of his own would inspire similar do-anything-for-her sensations in him. Besides, how bad could it be, putting it up with inane party banter for a couple of hours? If he could hold his own despite frigid temperatures in cramped quarters, never knowing when the enemy might strike or what he'd look like when he did, he could—

"Well, is it? A yes, I mean?"

Maybe Holly's cousin wasn't the only one who needed a shrink, because how far gone was a guy who compared the hardships of *war* to a backyard barbecue? Chuckling, he said, "Aw, why not?"

Holly threw herself into his arms. "Oh, wow, Parker. Thanks. You're the best."

Eyes closed, he buried his face in her mass of golden curls, inhaling the light, flowery scent of her shampoo, memorizing the way her pretty little face nestled into the crook of his neck as if made to fit there, committing to memory the way she sighed and snuggled close, so close that not even the warm wind blowing in from the Atlantic could have come between them. *What a shame,* he thought, *what a stinking, rotten shame that Maude had suddenly decided to come clean.*

His mother's confession squealed through his brain like an old-fashioned tape recorder on fast-forward. If it hadn't meant letting go of Holly, he would have clamped both hands over his ears to blot out the awful noise. Why was it that being hit with shrapnel, rifle fire, and the remnants of IEDs hadn't left him feeling anywhere near as weak as being *informed*?

"I promise," Holly said, her sweet voice muffled by his T-shirt, "you won't have to lift a finger."

Here he stood, holding in his arms the best and most beautiful thing life had ever given him. *So close,* he thought, holding her at arm's length, *yet so far. So very, very far.* He studied her face: the gentle arch of her eyebrows, thick lashes that dusted freckled cheeks, that slightly elfin nose, a smile that lit every dark corner of his heart, and bright blue eyes that he was certain had read every story written on his battered soul...

...and yet she loved him.

Even if he'd been blinded when that shell exploded, he'd feel that love beaming out at him. "I'm yours for the taking" was the silent message that traveled the invisible thread linking her gaze to his.

"You really are the best, you know," she said, smiling.

The best, indeed. What was that old saying? "You can't take your happiness at the expense of others." Well, if he took Holly up on her loving offer, that's exactly what he'd be doing. Which would make him exactly like *Maude*.

"I'm thinking baked beans..."

Was there a chance that what he saw glowing in her eyes was wishful thinking? That it wasn't love shining out at him, but the simple and genuine *goodness* that lived in her soul?

"...and that flag cake recipe I saw on the cover of a magazine at the grocery store."

Nope, not a chance that he was wrong. Parker would have bet the boat and the house and Ben's future on it. So he had two weeks, as he saw it, to do the right thing. He didn't know *how* he'd accomplish it, only that he owed it to her to help her realize that she'd have a better chance at happiness even with that clown she'd dated after losing her fiancé than with the likes of *him*. For now, to make sure she enjoyed every minute of her family's visit, he'd be on his best behavior. She deserved that. But once they were gone, he'd—

"What's *your* favorite, Parker?"

Favorite?

"Grilled chicken? Pork chops? T-bones? Baby back ribs?"

"I thought we were gonna keep it simple, just burgers and dogs."

"Well, those too, of course. I just thought"—she traced the logo on his T-shirt then bored into his eyes—"that it might be nice to add your favorite to the menu."

Parker could count on one hand the number of times he'd cried since entering adulthood, but if she kept this up, he'd have another time to add to the list, because it was killing him that he couldn't make her his own.

"Y'know, since you're so generously offering up your house for the—"

"Holly?"

"Hmm?" She tilted her head and batted her eyes. Was he seeing things? Or was she flirting with him?

"Holly," he repeated.

"Parker?"

"You'd better knock it off."

She grinned, proving him right: she *was* flirting with him. Blatantly. And if that wasn't bad enough, she'd pressed a palm to each of his cheeks. "Knock what off?"

Blanketing her hands with his, he ground out, "You know very well *what*."

"I do?"

"Holly…"

"That's my name; don't wear it out," she singsonged, reminding him of every bratty girl he'd ever gone to school with.

He had two choices: tell her to take a hike and spare himself having to do it after her family went back to Baltimore, or kiss the daylights out of her, right here, right now.

Thankfully his cell phone rang, because Parker had a feeling it would have been the latter, which would only have made his "take a hike" speech doubly hard to deliver. "News about Ben," he whispered as she stepped back.

Smiling, she leaped into the air with a jubilant fist pump then folded her hands and closed her eyes, mouthing a prayer.

"He's safe and sound and in Germany with my buddy," Parker said, snapping the phone shut. Mostly to himself, he added, "Don't that just beat all."

"How wonderful," Holly said, taking hold of his hands. "Thank the good Lord!"

If it turned out that *God* had anything to do with it, Parker decided, he'd be the first to thank the Big Guy. For now, he'd give credit where credit was due: Hank Donovan and the links in his amazing owe-you-a-favor chain.

"How soon can you bring him home?"

"Couple of weeks at best. Red tape has us all tied up, but Hank is working on that too."

"Hank?" she echoed. "*Too?*"

Holly looked stunned when he explained Hank's part in bringing about this happy result. "The way he was talking earlier, I just naturally assumed you were working on this all by yourself."

Parker nodded. "That's Hank. Humble to a fault."

"As soon as the July Fourth festivities are over, I'll have to start planning a *real* party."

"A… What? *Why?*"

She looked at him as if he'd grown a third eye. "To celebrate Ben's arrival, of course, and to show our gratitude to Hank for all he did to make everything possible."

"Wouldn't a simple welcome and thank-you suffice? Do we really need to—"

"Yes. We do."

He didn't know when or how she'd ended up in his arms again, but if Hank was right and he'd regret letting her go for the rest of his life, Parker aimed to enjoy this for as long as he could.

* * * * *

After a restless night of tossing and turning and pacing the house, Parker ate a light breakfast of cornflakes and coffee. He told himself, as he slid in behind the wheel of his pickup, that if he ever hoped to have peace of mind again, he needed to stop fixating on Maude's confession and start remembering all the good things she'd done over the years. But bitterness and resentment, he realized, was a hard habit to break.

He'd hoped that spending some time alone with her would get him on the right track—bring those good things to the front of his brain and, with any luck, blot out the bad. So he'd stopped off at the florist's on his way to her rehab center and bought a big, bright GET WELL balloon, a bouquet of summer blooms, and a box of chocolates. He drew the line at the blank-inside card—the only kind available on the spinning rack beside the counter—because the last thing he'd needed was to add yet another lie to those already separating him from his mom.

She'd looked good, all things considered, limping around on her almost-healed feet, and he did his best to smile and laugh while bringing her up-to-date on the book project and Holly's comings and goings and what the turtles had been up to lately. They might have been total strangers, sitting there discussing the weather and politics and how the sagging economy had all but dried up donations to the lighthouse project. Thirty minutes of that had been exactly twenty-nine minutes too many, and once he arranged her gifts on the windowsill, Parker gave her a quiet kiss and a light hug and all but bolted for the door.

He deliberately hadn't mentioned the whole Daniel debacle, and he couldn't help but wonder, as he sat in the Charleston marina parking lot, why *she* hadn't brought it up. *Just more classic Maude,* he told himself. Unfortunately, the admission did little to make her cavalier attitude easier to bear.

Parker got out of the truck, telling himself it would only be for a minute and only to stretch his legs. The next thing he knew, he'd made his way down the wooden walkway between two boats, one a sloop called *The Water Wench,* the other a schooner with *Sea Stallion* emblazoned on her stern. That clanking on board hadn't been caused by the rigging, and he scanned the deck and spied movement in the cockpit, where a shadowy figure was bent over the pedestal. *Adjusting the compass,* Parker thought, *or adjusting the throttle.* He didn't know what made the man look up just then, but when he did, Parker immediately recognized him as the man from the restaurant. He remembered how the woman in the wheelchair had insisted they looked alike. He'd agreed then, and he agreed even more so now. But was this Daniel Brant? Daniel Brant, *his father*?

Straightening, the fellow slid his eyeglasses from where they rested atop his head down to the bridge of his nose. "Say, aren't you that young fella from the restaurant?"

Nodding, Parker shaded his eyes from the sun. "Permission to come aboard?"

The man gave a wave. "Careful, there," he said as Parker climbed onto the deck. Pointing to Parker's leg, he added, "Sprained ankle?"

"IED," he answered. "Afghanistan."

He showed Parker a long, gnarled scar that wrapped from his wrist to his bicep. "'Nam," he said. "I'm retired Air Force. You?"

"Army."

"Name's Dan Brant."

Parker accepted the offered hand. "Parker."

"So, Parker, what brings you to my humble float?"

Where to start? he wondered. "Maybe this wasn't such a good idea."

"Nonsense. Take a load off, son. Let me grab you a cold water. Sorry I can't offer anything stronger." He jabbed a thumb into his chest. "Recovering alcoholic. What can I say? Pilots. We all had this *reputation* to uphold."

Yeah, Parker had run in to a few of those reputations during his stint with the army. Not all of them had been pleasant, and booze had usually been the cause of conflict.

Dan shrugged. "Day by day, right?" He nodded at Parker's leg. "But you know something about that, I reckon."

He should have thought this through. Come up with a plan of some sort. Figured out what he'd say if he ever met his father face-to-face.

His father.

His father.

It would be a long time, getting used to saying *that*.

Handing Parker a bottle of water, Dan uncapped one for himself then perched on the bench across the way. "So what, exactly, wasn't such a good idea?"

"I—I don't know where to start."

"Well, you know what they say."

Parker chuckled. "'At the beginning.'"

Dan chugged a gulp of water. "Spit it out, soldier. I've got brass to polish and cleats to tighten."

Parker took a deep breath and said, "I'm told you knew a woman named Maude."

Dan's brows rose high on his forehead. "She was hardly a woman, but yeah, there was a Maude in my past."

"She's my mother."

Nodding, Dan said, "Yeah, now that you mention it, I see a resemblance. Mostly around the eyes."

But what's that got to do with me? was Dan's unasked question.

"She, ah, well, I don't know how to say this, but—"

"Whoa. You tryin' to tell me you're my son?"

"Tryin'. Not doin' a very good job of it, though."

Dan recapped his water bottle and ran a hand through graying-brown hair. "Whoa," he said again. "I mean, whoa." He met Parker's eyes. "I'd ask for proof, but looking at you...it's like looking at a photograph of myself taken thirty-some years ago." He shook his head. "Man." He whistled. "Whoa."

"Sorry to spring it on you this way."

"Is there any other way?"

"No, I don't reckon there is."

Several moments ticked silently by before Dan said, "Mind if I ask you a question?"

Parker only shook his head.

"Why now? I mean, if memory serves, you'd be, what? Thirty, thirty-one?"

"Thirty-two."

"Why *now*?" Dan repeated. "You in some kind of trouble, money-wise?"

"No, no. Nothing like that. I own a boat too. The *Sea Maverick*.

Fishing charters, mostly. I've sold a few paintings over the years. Nothing to brag about. And I make furniture. These scars also bring me a decent pension check every month, so no, I'm not here because I want a loan."

"What *do* you want, then?"

It was a good question. "I wish I knew. I only just found out about you a couple weeks back." He told Dan about Maude's foot surgery, the back-to-back heart operations that inspired her confession, and the part about how she'd led him to believe that his father had died testing a fighter jet. "If I had the sense God gave a goose, I would've waited until I had a better handle on this to… Maybe if I'd given it a month, six, a year, even, I wouldn't have had to come here at all."

"I don't know which is craziest, that Maudie would let you grow up thinking your daddy was dead, or that nonsense you just spouted."

Parker looked up, stunned.

"I didn't know her all that well, or even all that long, for that matter, but it surprises me that she'd ease her own conscience by burdening you with—I don't rightly know what to call it—in the middle of your worries that she might not survive surgery." He whistled. "I'm trying to put myself in your shoes here, and all I can say is, whoa, that's rough."

"I didn't come here for money; didn't come lookin' for pity, either."

"'Course not. You were a soldier!" He took another slug of water. "Seems normal enough, though, you wanting to meet me. I have two boys of my own." He held up a hand. "Make that two *other* boys, and I can't imagine either of them growing up without a father." He looked long and hard at Parker. "Seems like you turned out pretty good, though. Who gets the credit for that?"

Another good question. "Guess I'd have to say it's 50-50."

"Half to Maudie, half to...?"

"An equal split between me and the army."

"Fair enough."

"So what do we do now?"

"You got me by the feet." Chuckling, Dan stood and tossed his empty water bottle into the trash can near the wheel. "But for starters, I'd say a hug is in order."

And with the strength of a man half his age, Dan pulled Parker to his feet and wrapped him in a bear hug. Then he called his wife and told her he had some great news to share with her when he got home, but not to hold dinner. Next, he pulled out his wallet and showed Parker photos of his stepmother, who was a school librarian; his sister, who taught kindergarten; and his twin brothers, one of whom ran the marina, while the other was serving a tour of duty in Afghanistan.

They exchanged home and cell phone numbers and addresses, and it was fully dark by the time he walked Parker back to the pier. "Can't wait to introduce them all to you, and you to them."

Dan sent Parker on his way after making him promise to call every day, until they could get together. As he drove home, Parker's eyes alternately stung and misted with tears. *A strange way to react to good news,* he thought, but as Dan had said, day by day...

Before long, Ben would be with him again. He'd found his dad. *Found his dad!* Piece by piece, the jumbled puzzle that had been his life was beginning to form a doggoned good-looking picture. He couldn't change the fact that he'd been conceived by hot-blooded, non-Christian youngsters, but Parker no longer felt illegitimate. In fact, he'd never felt more acceptable in his life.

The twenty-minute drive between Charleston and Folly Beach seemed ten times that, because Parker was chomping at the bit to tell Holly...everything. Maybe, just maybe, God would see fit to let her stay.

Chapter Twenty

It had only taken a few hours to get the guest rooms ready for her family's visit, and when she finished dusting and vacuuming the parlor, Holly started in on the dining room. Wouldn't Maude be surprised when she saw that Parker and Hank had helped her turn the library into a first-floor guest suite for the lady of the manor!

"I don't know why I never thought of it," Parker said, admiring her handiwork. "Especially after she insisted on having both feet operated on at the same time."

And Hank agreed. "You'd never know this was ever anything *but* a guest room."

It had taken hours and dozens of trips back and forth to move Maude's extensive collection of books and movies to the parlor shelves, and hours more to rearrange the settees and tables to make room for the rolltop desk and lounge chairs that had lined the library walls. Now both rooms looked bigger and brighter, and when the doctor gave Maude the green light to leave her rehab facility, she'd only need to climb the stairs when a new guest checked in.

"Hard to believe," Parker said, "that after all you've done, you still insist on paying the weekly fee to stay here."

"I don't mind, really. Our work on the book is nearly done, and I'll bet we don't spend an hour on the turtle project. It gives me something to do besides…"

She clamped her teeth together, hopefully before either of them asked what she'd *almost* said. Because the last thing Holly needed with her family coming to town was more strain between her and Parker. Especially after all that talk about the impropriety or acceptability of calling her boss by his first name.

On his way out, Hank suggested they trade rides for the day. "It's a gorgeous day, and I can't remember the last time I drove around town in a convertible, letting my mane flow free in the wind." Chuckling, he handed Holly the keys to his mini pickup truck. "Besides, if you use your car to stock two kitchens, you'll need to make six trips to the grocery store."

"I'd let you use mine," Parker said, "but I have to meet someone in Charleston."

Hank's brows rose. "Do tell," he said, smirking.

Parker only chuckled, and Holly didn't know what to make of his guilty expression and flushed cheeks. Surely he wasn't meeting a woman….

Well, what business was it of hers? She'd come here to work for the guy, not marry him. Those cozy, borderline-romantic moments had probably been more a figment of her imagination than anything else. If he felt anything beyond friendship for her, wouldn't he have reacted differently the other day?

"You're such a ditz!" she said, thumping the steering wheel as she remembered. Well, no more of that. She'd continue behaving in a courteous and polite manner. Friendly, even. But that little episode on his deck, when she'd barely stopped short of grabbing his face and planting a big fat kiss on his lips? Not a chance!

Between his mother's myriad health issues and the news she'd so recently blasted him with, the prospect of adopting a war orphan, his volunteer work with the lighthouse and turtle projects, and running his charter business, all while trying to write a book, it was a wonder the poor man had the presence of mind to put one foot in front of the other. The last thing he needed was some silly blond bimbo throwing herself at him.

The hours flew by, and before she knew it, her parents' arrival date was here. She'd planned the menus for every meal, from supper on their first night in Folly Beach to breakfast on the morning they'd head back to Baltimore. Hank and Parker had agreed to join them for supper, but she and the visiting Leonards would share the rest of their meals without them.

If they didn't run into construction or, God forbid, an accident along the way, they'd roll into Folly Beach by eight, and at that hour, they'd be too tired to eat anything heavy. A quick snack of fruit and veggies with a slice of spinach quiche would do nicely, and by four o'clock, the only thing left to do was reheat the egg dish.

On her last check of their suites, she decided something was missing: fresh-cut flowers on the nightstands. And wasn't it her good fortune that the roses surrounding the cottage's terrace were in full bloom? She found a wide, low-sided basket on a laundry-room shelf and clippers in the utility drawer, and set out to gather the bouquets.

As she snipped those first few buds, Holly smiled. "Thanks, Mom," she whispered, tucking the silky blooms into the basket, because if her mother hadn't added this chore to the list of things that helped Holly earn her summer allowances, she might have made a mess of the lovely shrubs.

Humming as she worked, Holly tried to ignore the fat bumblebee that buzzed around her head. "There are enough flowers for the both of us," she scolded, "so stop being such a hog."

"Talking to yourself again?"

The suddenness of Parker's voice startled her, and when she jerked back her hand, she scraped her arm on a thorn and drew a bloody pinstripe on her arm. The sudden movement startled the bee too, and it stung her square on the pad of the heel of her hand. She dropped the shears first, then the basket, and tripped over its handle while backpedaling away from the bush. If Parker hadn't been there to catch her, Holly would have landed flat on her back in the damp grass. But if Parker hadn't been there, none of it would have happened in the first place...and she wouldn't be sitting in his lap, like a little girl waiting for her daddy to read her a bedtime story.

"Sorry," he said, finger-combing bangs from her forehead, "I didn't mean to scare you. You okay?"

Before she could summon the presence of mind to answer, he began inspecting the thorn damage and then, as quick as an eyeblink, plucked the stinger from her hand. "Well, there's one bee that won't be pestering anyone again," he said before tossing it to the ground. "Now let's get you inside, so I can—"

"I'm fine, really, and I'll have this mess cleaned up in no time."

"Humor me, will ya? This mess never would've happened if I hadn't sneaked up on you. It'll take the edge off my guilty conscience if you let me bandage you up."

Heaving a sigh of frustration, Holly scrambled from his lap. After picking up the shears and the basket, she began collecting the roses she'd clipped. "Good," she said, putting them back into the basket, "none of the stems are bent or broken." He held the back door open as she said, "What are you doing here, anyway?"

"What's this," he said, chuckling as the door banged shut behind them, "the reverse of 'Here's your hat, what's your hurry?'"

"Oh. I. Well." She groaned as a blush warmed her cheeks. "I didn't mean it to come out that way. Sorry. I just didn't expect to see you today, that's all. Or to give you another entry for your Holly Folly list."

Parker harrumphed. "List. Ha. I have a whole file on you, sweetheart."

The comeback stung more than she cared to admit, and to hide it, Holly decided to tend the roses.

"Can't that wait until we get your arm cleaned up and put some ice on that bee sting?"

"This won't take but a minute. I want to get them into water so they don't wilt." She twisted the drain stopper and turned on the faucet then stood tiptoe to grab a vase from the cabinet above the sink. "I'm going to put vases on the guest-room nightstands," she said, her voice straining as she extended her reach. "Oh, to be a half-inch taller," she complained, opening the lower cabinet for use as a footstool. One foot on its shelf, she tried again…

…and when he grabbed her waist to steady her, he scared her a second time. Arms windmilling, she accidentally punched him on the jaw—hit him square on the right eyebrow too, before regaining her balance. Turning, she gasped at the bright-red splotches already forming on his face. "Oh, good gravy, you look like you've been in some sort of street brawl...and lost."

"At least I'm not bleeding. And swollen." He pulled out a chair and led her to it. "Please. Sit. And do me a favor?"

"Don't move until you get back," she droned, "with the first-aid kit."

"That's my good girl."

Oh, great, she thought. *You've just blown any chance you might have had to...*

To what? Hypnotize him? That was about the only way he'd remember all the gritty scientific work she'd already completed this summer, or the painstaking attention to detail she'd given his book, which—if she hadn't replaced hard-to-digest phraseology with fun and clever twists—would still read like a sixth-grade essay.

"Oh, that's just plain mean," she said under her breath, "and unfair." Flustered, Holly whacked herself in the forehead, setting off a series of throbs and aches in her bee-stung hand. "That's what you get," she muttered, "for trying to convince him that you're—"

"I could be wrong," he said, plopping the box onto the table, "but wasn't talking to yourself what got this whole disaster ball rolling in the first place?"

She'd completely forgotten having turned on the water...until he stepped up to the sink to wash his hands. Something unintelligible passed his lips as he plunged his hand into the water to pull the plug. He spoke all too clearly when he added, "Good thing this wasn't hot water."

In place of a reply, Holly decided to make herself useful and take that first important step toward proving she was more than a silly, awkward girl...by taking the top off the shoe box. But he stopped her by wrapping the fingers of his big, still-damp hand around her uninjured wrist, and for the next ten minutes, she sat in dazed silence as he made quick work of cleaning and wrapping the gouge carved into her arm by the thorn. "Not much you can do for the bee sting," he told her. "Ice, maybe, and if it starts itching, some calamine lotion."

"Right. Thanks." She started tossing unused cotton balls, antibiotic ointment, and gauze back into the box, and as he rearranged them, she said, "You never did tell me why you're here."

"Seemed like a pretty good story when I walked in here." He shrugged and put the lid back on the box. "But now it'll be anticlimactic, at best."

"How about you let me be the judge of that?" Holly got up and poured them each a glass of iced tea and then rejoined him at the table, where he held her spellbound for the next half hour, telling her about Daniel Brant and the family that had welcomed him like the prodigal son.

* * * * *

Holly was upstairs, doing one last check to make sure that everything would be perfect when her family arrived, when she heard the sound of slamming car doors and ran to the window of her cousins' suite. Her mom had barely closed the passenger door when she said, "Oh, Bob, isn't it just the *loveliest* place!"

Both forearms resting on the car's roof, he nodded his agreement. "No wonder Holly didn't want to leave it, even for a weekend back home."

By the time Holly raced down the stairs and burst through the front door, her cousins had opened the SUV's hatch and were depositing suitcases on the flagstone driveway.

"Hold on, Laura," her dad teased. "Here comes Holly Folly...."

But it was her oldest cousin whom Holly reached first. "I thought you guys would *never* get here!" she said, throwing her arms around Adam's neck. She hugged Frank, then her dad, and. after embracing her mom, grabbed the handle of the nearest suitcase and led the way up the walk. "Let's get your things into your rooms and show you around, and then we can relax." She held open the screen door. "I'll bet you're all just exhausted. How was the drive? Not too much traffic, I hope. I read on the Internet that there was some construction on I-95 just outside of Richmond. It didn't clog things up too badly, did it?"

"Down, girl," her dad said, grinning as he wheeled a bag over the threshold. "We're here, and we're fine. Thanks for those last-minute directions, by the way. Got us around those bridge repairs easy as pie."

"I can't take credit for that," she admitted. "Parker's the one who—"

Her mom kissed her cheek on her way by. "I'll be sure to thank him, then, first chance I get. Will he be here tonight?"

"Probably not." He hadn't said so outright, but Holly got the feeling that after checking on the progress Hank's contacts had made in bringing Ben home, he'd spend the evening in Charleston, getting better acquainted with his new family. "But I'm sure he'll stop by tomorrow. He's eager to meet you guys." She gave her mom a sideways hug. "You're going to love him, I just know it. And I'm positive he'll love you!"

"We'll just see about that," Frank said, winking.

"Right," Adam agreed. "Do you have a 100-watt lightbulb?"

Holly laughed. "I was just upstairs, checking your rooms when you arrived, and all the lights were just—"

"Not for the lamps in our rooms, silly girl," he said, tweaking her nose. "For the interrogation. If this *Parker* dude hopes to partner up with my little cousin, he's gotta pass muster first."

Laughing, Holly said, "You're the silly one. He's my boss. And... he's becoming a friend." If she'd known how much it would hurt to make a statement like that, Holly might have rehearsed it a time or two, to assure herself that it would sound more convincing. "There's absolutely nothing romantic between us." She half ran up the stairs, stopping on the landing to say, "Come on. Let me show you where you're staying, and then I'll put out the snacks I've made."

She pulled out all the stops, explaining that Maude's grandparents had raised her after her parents were killed in an accident and then willed the house to her. A single mother by that time, Holly added, Maude turned it into a B&B to provide for herself and Parker, naming the rooms after the characters in her favorite movie, *The Ghost and Mrs. Muir.*

"She sounds delightful," Laura said. "I can't wait to meet her."

"She's still in rehab?" Bob asked.

"Yes, but she's making steady progress, so I expect her doctors to let her come home any day now."

"I hope so," Laura said. "We'll all help out any way we can."

"It's the least we can do," Bob agreed, "since she refused to let us pay for the rooms."

When Holly had told Maude that her family was considering a visit, she'd insisted that they stay at Coastal Cottage free of charge.

But the poor woman had enough on her mind without worrying about how she'd pay the bills associated with her hospitalization, so once the decision about the trip was final, Holly took matters into her own hands. And because Hank had been keeping Maude's books for the past few years, Holly was able to deposit a check that protected Maude's ego while adding to her bank balance.

The tour ended in the kitchen. "So, are you hungry? I know it's too late for a real meal, so I made some light snacks."

"That's a rhetorical question, I presume," Frank said.

Adam patted his flat belly. "Lead us to it...then stand back."

As they gathered around Maude's kitchen table, talking and laughing, Holly was reminded of Sunday dinners at her parents' house, with all her cousins and their wives and kids gathered around the long dining room table. Only one thing could make this scene better: Parker.

A quiet knock at the back door interrupted the happy banter.

"Is there room for one more?"

* * * * *

Her family was everything Parker thought they'd be, and the hours spent in their company before contagious yawns sent them upstairs were far more agreeable than he could have imagined. Would he have enjoyed the visit as much if he hadn't so recently been welcomed into a family of his own?

Parker didn't think so.

He hung around under the pretense of helping Holly clean up the kitchen. But the real reason he'd stayed was to test the waters.

Hank had raised some excellent points during their prior conversations, and each had prompted additional questions in Parker's mind.

"So what did you think of them?"

Parker dumped ice from the tumblers into the sink as Holly covered the snack plates with plastic wrap. "They seem like good people. I like 'em."

"And they like you too."

They seemed like the type of people who'd treat anyone well, especially during a first meeting. "Really. And you know that because..."

"Because," she said, opening the fridge, "my family has made an art form of grilling my—"

Parker looked up from the dishwasher to see what had silenced her so abruptly. One glance at her blushing face told him that if she had ended the sentence, it would have been with a word like *boy-friends*. Is that how she saw him?

"So did you get a chance to visit your mom today?"

"I did," he said. "But not for long. They took her down for X-rays, and she told me not to hang around for the results." And he'd been only too happy to take her up on the offer.

Holly's silence spoke volumes: in his shoes, she would have stayed. Well, he hated to disappoint her, but Maude had opened that can of worms, not him.

She fired up the teapot and pulled two mugs from the cabinet. "Are things any better between you two?"

If he could figure out how she always seemed to know what he was thinking, maybe Parker would have half a chance at keeping her out of his head. "They're going as well as can be expected, I expect."

She sent him a tiny smile. "Well, at least you're trying. That's more than most people would do in your shoes."

"In my shoes?"

She put the mugs on the table, with napkins and spoons and the wooden box containing Maude's collection of herbal teas. "I know it seems silly, sipping hot tea on the first of July, but the whole process, from brewing to pouring to sipping, has always soothed me."

She shrugged, and he took it to mean that Holly hoped it would soothe him too.

"What I meant," she said, filling both mugs with hot water, "was that under similar circumstances, most people would take the easy way out. Storm off in a huff, telling themselves they had a perfect right to feel betrayed and hurt, and then get busy settling scores."

The teapot hit the burner with a tinny *clank*, and then Holly sat at the table and plucked a tea bag from the box. "I think I'm in the mood for something spicy tonight." She read the label aloud. "'CINNAMON DREAMS.' I wonder who comes up with these names."

He knew her well enough to understand that she'd get to the point in her own good time. And since he couldn't think of a place he'd rather be—or a person he'd rather be with—Parker said, "Same people who choose street names, I reckon."

She shoved the box closer so he could choose a tea bag too. "What're you in the mood for tonight?"

Parker chuckled.

"What's that smirk all about?"

What he was in the mood for was a hug. A big long one. And a kiss. Maybe even a couple of them. He grabbed a random tea bag. He unwrapped it and tossed it into the hot water. "If you ever tell anybody I willingly drank something called 'Orange Mist,' I might just have to punish you."

Her quiet laughter echoed throughout the room. Echoed in his heart too, telling him that she didn't believe for a minute that he'd ever hurt her.

"But you," she said, picking up where she'd left off, "instead of behaving like a caveman, you exercised restraint. *Serious* restraint." Holly covered his hand with hers and gave it a squeeze. "I know it isn't easy, treating her with respect and kindness right now, considering that what she told you effectively turned your whole world upside down, but you're doing it." She gave his hand another squeeze then let go and stared into her mug. "That inspires a lot of respect," she said quietly.

It felt good hearing that, especially from this woman who'd come to mean so much to him. "In a weird way, she did me a favor."

He didn't expect her to understand that and had started to explain, when she said, "Just one more reason to admire you."

Parker didn't get it and said so.

"You've chosen to dwell on the positives. All the good things she did before 'the big confession,'" she said, drawing quote marks in the air. "That and the fact that if she hadn't turned your world upside down, you'd never have found your father and, in the process, a whole big loving family."

There were tears in her eyes. Tears of joy. For him. Seeing that touched a place inside him that Parker never even knew existed. To this point, he'd kept a safe distance from her, mostly for her sake. But the memory of holding her—especially that night on the beach—put him on his feet.

He scooted her chair away from the table then turned it around so that he could kneel in front of it. For a long moment he stayed that way, hands gripping the chair back on either side of her graceful neck, content to look into her eyes, at the way her brows lifted as she smiled nervously under his scrutiny and wondered what he was doing. He might have given more thought to what he'd done differently this time, to keep her from reading his mind…if she hadn't lifted both dainty shoulders as she loosed a sweet sigh.

"If you know what's good for you, you'll tell me to hit the road."

Her head tilted, one corner of her mouth lifting in a teasing grin. "Now why would telling you to do a crazy thing like that be good for me?"

"Because if you don't," he grated, "I'm gonna kiss you."

Holly blinked and then linked her fingers behind his neck. "If that's your idea of a threat, you're sadly mistaken."

He'd never been much of a praying man, but when she pressed her lips to his, Parker prayed. First, that Holly was the one he'd spend the rest of his life with, and second—that if she wasn't, for the strength to live without her.

"Wow," Holly said.

His sentiments exactly. If he'd known it would feel that good, that right, he might have summoned the courage to do this weeks ago. The book probably wouldn't be almost finished if he had, but—

There you go again, he thought, *putting the cart before the horse.* What if her breathy "wow" meant something entirely different from what he hoped it meant?

But Holly had kissed him, not the other way around.

Right?

Hardly proof that his hopes—that she cared for him too—had any connection to reality, but it was something to look forward to.

For the first time in as long as he could remember, Parker *was* looking forward. And everything he saw out there on life's horizon had a direct link to this amazing woman in his arms.

Chapter Twenty-One

....

The cookout had been more pleasant than he'd expected it to be, due in no small part to Holly, who'd flitted around like a little bird, making sure everyone had what they needed. While she and her mom cleaned up, Parker and Hank sat on the deck with Bob, Adam, and Frank. His guests had such an easy, friendly way about them that the time passed quickly, and before he knew it, Parker found himself side by side with Holly on the only available seat on the deck: a fifties-style metal glider.

Hank and the Leonards were no different than others he'd viewed fireworks with, oohing and ahhing as each colorful burst lit up the sky. Holly's reaction? That was a first, and something told him that even as a boy he hadn't reacted to the noisy displays with half her enthusiasm. If she enjoyed them this much as a full-grown woman, how had she behaved as a little girl?

The question made him smile and inspired a picture in his mind: Blond ponytails bobbing, tiny white sneakers skipping, as she clapped and squealed happily. It made him wonder what a child of their union might look like. Hopefully the spitting image of their beautiful mother, because—

"Oh, these are my favorites!" she said, pointing as big white dots flashed overhead, each accompanied by a rib-wracking *boom*. "Reminds me of parade drums. I love those too." In the lull between explosions, Holly added, "Do you have a favorite?"

She'd asked a similar question before shopping for cookout supplies, and though he hadn't told her that, given a choice, he'd choose thick pork chops to just about any other grilled meat, she'd bought a package...and made the best finger-lickin' sauce to go with them that he'd ever tasted. How did she *know* these things about him?

"Well?"

"Well, what?"

She shoulder-butted him and, laughing, said, "Earth to Parker, Earth to Parker."

"Oh. Right. Favorite firework. I guess—"

"Doesn't that sound goofy, though? Referring to them in the singular, I mean?"

She laughed again, making Parker long for a way to guarantee that he could start and end every day hearing it.

"Yeah. Goofy." You're *goofy*, he thought, grinning, *goofy about her*.... "I like 'em all," he said.

"Equally?"

"Sure. Why not?"

In place of an answer, Holly launched into an abbreviated lesson of the time and materials that went into the creation of pyrotechnics. "So the least you could do," she said, "is choose at least one that's—"

Adam moaned. "See what we grew up with?"

"And lest you think college made her that way," Frank agreed, "think again. She's *always* been this way."

Parker was tempted to ask "What way?" when Adam said, "Keep that in mind, for, ah, for future reference."

Her dad's laughter echoed into the night. "Just a friendly little tip from the Leonard boys."

Groaning, Holly hid behind her hands.

"What're you doing?" Frank asked.

"Hoping that when I open my eyes, you'll be upstairs sleeping." She peeked between two fingers. "*Quietly.*"

Laughing, her mom chimed in with, "Here's a friendly little tip from the Leonard family matriarch: they're *all* this way and always have been. Keep *that* in mind for, ah, future reference."

They all enjoyed a good laugh, including Parker. *Especially* Parker, because he'd taken their "for future reference" to mean that they approved…if things between him and Holly took a more serious turn.

Serious. The concept nearly induced another chuckle. Because he couldn't get much more serious about her. And when he got back from Germany, he intended to tell her just that.

The reminder of his upcoming trip prompted him to lean close to her ear and whisper, "When they leave for the cottage, I need to tell you something."

She leaned forward to get a better look at his face. "Ooh, sounds ominous."

Laughing, he said, "No. It's good news, actually."

Then why, her wide-eyed expression said, couldn't he share it in front of Hank and her family?

"It's got to do with Ben," he explained.

That stymied further questions but didn't stop her from shooting

"I don't get it" and "What about Ben" looks his way for the remainder of the fireworks display.

It was nearly eleven by the time everyone left, and she wasted no time backing him into the deck rail. "I'll only be a few minutes," she called as they headed up the beach. "Just going to help Parker clean up a bit." Waving, she added, "Don't wait up...I know you're tired."

Once they were out of sight, she whirled to face him. "All right, mister, out with it. What's this top-secret Ben-related news of yours?"

"He's in Germany. All the paperwork has been approved, and he's even got his very own passport. At least, that's what Hank's pal at the State Department tells me."

Holly gasped. "That's fantastic, Parker! Does it mean... Are you... When can... Oh my goodness, that's just about the best news I've heard in—in—in I don't know when!"

"I'm leaving tomorrow to go get him."

Her smile wavered, but only slightly.

"And Dan—er, my dad—is flying overseas with me."

She gasped again. "He is? That's terrific!"

"It was his wife's idea."

"Wow." She winked. "When you get absorbed into a family, you don't fool around, do you?" And then she laughed. "I can hardly wait to meet him. Them. Ben. Your dad and his family. *All* of them," she said.

"They already think the world of you."

She'd leaned over the rail and looked down at the sand but straightened in response to his last comment. "They do? But—"

"I told them how you pitched in, from Maude's heart attack right straight through to the news about Ben. They're grateful." He squeezed her shoulder. "Not as grateful as I am, but then, they don't know you. Yet."

When she blinked up at him, Parker wished he had a little of her talent for mind reading.

"So I'm guessing you'll leave tomorrow evening?"

He nodded.

"How long will you be gone?"

"Ten days."

He could be wrong, but he didn't think they'd been apart for longer than ten *hours* since she arrived in Folly Beach. Parker could see that she was struggling now, between joy at the reason he'd be gone that long and the *fact* that he'd be gone that long. "I'm planning to buy a SIM card over there, so I'll be able to call every day to update you."

She hadn't asked why *ten* days, instead of seven or a full two weeks. A good thing, since he wasn't sure himself. "Near as I can figure, red tape snarls things up on the other side of the Atlantic too."

At the mention of it, Holly glanced across the water and sighed. "Can I give you a lift to the airport? I'm sure Hank won't mind loaning me his truck."

"Dan, I mean my dad, has some sort of parking pass, so we'll take his car." Gently, he chucked her chin. "But thanks for asking."

"Wow. Ten days. It's going to seem like three times that long."

He figured she must be wondering what she'd do with all that time all by herself. Her family would leave at first light the day after tomorrow, and with Maude still in rehab... "Maybe you can ride back to Baltimore with your folks, spend a few days with them, then catch a one-way flight back."

She frowned. "For one thing, I'd never fit in the car with those big-as-gorillas cousins of mine hogging the backseat." She looked out to sea again. "Ten days without seeing that gorgeous beach? I don't think so."

When she met his gaze, Parker thought his heart might stop.

"Besides, how cool will it be when you call every day—you know, to make your daily reports—if I'm standing here, looking out *there*, pretending that if I stand on my toes, I might be able to look over the waves and see you?" She giggled. "No way I could do that from Baltimore!"

Those daily calls would accomplish so much more than bringing her up to speed on what was happening in Germany. They'd fill his ears with the music of her voice and fill his heart with reminders of why he'd gone ape over her. But he'd wait to tell her all that. When he got back and introduced her to Ben and had a chance to see how well they got along, well, there'd be plenty of time to tell her that she was the sole reason he'd racked up so many romancing minutes on his cell phone.

"Will you join us for lunch tomorrow, so that I'll know you got one last healthy meal before jetting off for Europe?"

He hadn't yet packed. Hadn't talked to the rehab staff to let them know why he wouldn't be coming around to see his mother for a few days. "Maybe while I'm gone, you can look in on Maude once in a while?"

"Of course."

"And walk through the house every couple of days. You know, to make sure the water heater didn't spring a leak or anything?"

"No problem."

"Keep an eye on Hank too, will ya? 'Cause he's been lookin' a little green around the gills lately."

"You know, I've been thinking the same thing, so you can count on that too."

"So what time is lunch?"

Both eyebrows went up as she snickered. "Um, maybe at *lunchtime*?"

Laughing, he shook his head. "Does that mean noon, straight up? Half past? What?"

"Sorry. Don't mean to be a smart aleck. Guess I'm just not very good at good-byes."

Was that a tear he saw, glittering in the corner of her eye? He couldn't be sure...until it rolled down and left a shiny streak on her cheek. "Aw, Holly," he said, gathering her close. "This isn't good-bye." He held her at arm's length. "It's just ten days, and they'll pass," he snapped his fingers, "just like that. And think of it: when I get back, I'll have a big-eyed kid in tow, who I know will fall head over heels in love with you." *Just like I did.*

Holly rested her head on his shoulder and sighed. "I know. Sorry."

"Sorry? For what?"

In place of an answer, she said, "I'm sure gonna miss you."

He held her face in his hands. *Nowhere near as much as I'm gonna miss you,* he thought. If things turned out the way he hoped they would, once Ben was—

"Say!" She broke free of his embrace and started pacing the length of the deck. "I have a super idea...."

Parker leaned back against the rail and, with arms folded over his chest, waited for her to tell him all about it.

"Ten days…that gives me plenty of time to redo one of your upstairs rooms for Ben. Have you decided which will be his? I mean, I could paint and hang boy-type curtains." She stopped walking to ask, "Does he have a favorite superhero? Is he a race-car fan?"

"He loves airplanes. Doesn't matter what kind. Single prop, double engine, passenger jets, fighter planes, helicopters…"

"Perfect!" she said—and went right back to pacing. A second, maybe two passed before she stopped again. "But wait. Did you… did you have plans to wait, you know, until he got here, so that the two of you could fix up his room?"

He held out his arms, and Holly unquestioningly fell into them. "To tell you the truth, I never gave any of that a thought. My primary focus was getting things set up and getting him *here*. But knowing the way the poor kid has been living these past three years, well, trust me, anything will be an improvement over that."

"Remind me, how old is Ben?"

"Nine."

Her hands clasped under her chin, she echoed, "Nine. As soon as I see the folks off the day after tomorrow, I'll get started." She crinkled her nose. "Did you tell me which room?"

"No, I didn't. Mine's the one at the top of the stairs, the first door on your right."

"Yes. I remember from the tour you gave me."

Parker remembered too, because the whole time he showed her around, he pictured her in every room. "I'll let you decide which of the other three Ben might like best."

He could feel her trembling like a racehorse at the starting gate, just waiting for the start buzzer to sound. "So…lunch is at noon, then?"

"Sure. Noon. I'll make spaghetti and meatballs. And garlic bread. No, no, that won't do. Too heavy for a long flight over the Atlantic."

"I'm sure you'll think of something. And it'll be perfect." *Just like you are.*

She heaved an enormous sigh then bracketed his face with both strong, sure hands. "We'll have five pairs of eyes on us tomorrow, watching, so I won't be able to do this."

"Do wha—"

His question was muffled by her lips, which pressed to his in a long and heartfelt kiss.

"You be careful over there, you hear? The pickpockets are everywhere, and you'll be preoccupied, watching over Ben."

She kissed him again, longer this time, with even more feeling.

And then she raced down the deck steps, each footstep kicking up little arcs of sand as she raced over the beach.

Only the wide-eyed kid, waiting for him to make good on a promise given years earlier, could make him leave her.

Chapter Twenty-Two
....

Parker slid open the portal curtain and blinked into the blackness on the other side of the window. It was hard to tell where the night sky ended and the dark ocean began. The dim cabin lighting reflected the silhouette of a flight attendant whispering up the aisle, to make sure those passengers who wanted to watch the movie had headsets. The drone of the engines all but dissolved the rumbling snores that rippled over the seatback behind them.

"Never have been able to sleep like that on a transcontinental flight," Dan said, jerking his thumb over one shoulder. He chuckled. "Part of me envies him. The other part wants to shake him awake."

Parker had always been the same way. In fact, the one and only time he'd slept on an airplane had been the trip from Afghanistan to the hospital in Germany, and he'd only slept then because his attendants had shot him full of mind-numbing painkillers.

"Your grandmother wants to meet you as soon as we get back."

He pictured the stylish elderly woman who'd pointed him out in the restaurant. "I'm looking forward to it."

"Just a word to the wise," Dan said, "she'll have none of that *Isabel* nonsense. You'll call her *Grandmom,* same as my kids do, or pay the price."

"What price?"

Laughing, Dan said, "Don't know. None of us has ever been brave enough to find out."

"How long has she been in the wheelchair?"

"Going on three years now, and she'll never let on, but she hates that contraption."

Parker imagined all sorts of scenarios that might explain why she couldn't walk. "What's the reason for it?"

"Congestive heart failure. Doctors give her a year, maybe two."

"Sorry to hear it." And he was too, for the loss his father and family would experience when she passed, and for himself, because he'd have so little time to get to know her.

"Dad died of colon cancer last year," Dan said. "That pretty much took the fight out of her."

"How long were they married?"

"Sixty-four years."

Parker couldn't imagine sharing that much life with someone and then losing them. *Might be easier,* he thought, *to go through it alone.* Then he pictured Holly and knew that not even the prospect of losing her could make him go it alone.

"So this woman you're seeing," Dan was saying, "when will we meet her?"

"When we get back and Ben has a couple of days to settle in. If I know Holly, she'll want to have everybody over so he can meet his new family."

"Right in line with everything else you've told me about her." Dan nodded. "She sounds lovely."

"Understatement," Parker said, grinning.

"So what's the holdup, if you don't mind my asking?"

"Holdup?"

"Why haven't you asked her to marry you?"

Parker only shrugged, because he could think of a dozen reasons without even trying.

"It's obvious you're crazy about her. What else matters?"

"Well, there's Ben, for one thing. I'm not sure how she'll feel about having a war orphan thrust into her life. And the whole sudden family thing…" Parker sighed. "The truth is out, and I'm as thankful as all get-out about it. But it doesn't change what I am."

"What you are? I'm not following."

Several terms floated in his head, none of them pleasant.

"If you're referring to the fact that Maudie and I weren't married when you were conceived, you can just put that right out of your mind. No one—especially not God—considers you illegitimate."

No one but me, Parker thought. And what if Holly, whose faith and beliefs in the Almighty were so easy to see, agreed with Parker?

"If she's everything you say she is, that'll never even enter her head." Dan nudged him with an elbow. "And don't you be a hot-headed young fool and put it *into* her head."

"She has a right to know."

"How much have you told her?"

"She was there when Maude told *me*. Didn't seem like there was much to tell after that."

Dan pursed his lips and then said, "She treats you differently now, is that what you're saying, than she did before she knew?"

"No. If anything, she's even sweeter now than…"

"And you're wondering if all that affection is inspired by pity."

"Something like that." Parker harrumphed to himself. Not *something* like that. *Exactly* like that.

"Ann and I will celebrate our thirtieth anniversary in a couple of months. Add to that the fact that I've been a son for sixty-odd years and the father of a daughter for twenty-eight, and I can tell you with reasonable certainty that women hate it when men presume to know what they're thinking." He laughed quietly before adding, "The truth is, we poor slobs don't have a clue anyway and couldn't get one if they sold 'em at Sears." He elbowed Parker again. "So why torture yourself, second-guessing Holly?"

"Just spill the beans, eh?"

"Might as well. What have you got to lose?"

Holly, that's what.

"If she's everything you say she is," Dan repeated, "she'll welcome the truth. You're the living, breathing example of what happens when people lie and withhold things. A little fatherly advice?"

Parker nodded.

"Tell her everything. All of it. If we're wrong, and she isn't the great girl I think she is, isn't it better to know it sooner rather than later?"

"Yeah. I suppose."

"Trust me. Father knows best."

Yawning, Dan stuffed a little white pillow behind his neck and reclined his seat back. "Try to get some shut-eye, son. That's what I'm gonna do." Then he turned off the little overhead light, crossed his arms over his chest, and closed his eyes.

And left Parker with so much to think about that he wondered if he'd sleep, even once he'd tucked Ben safely into bed at the hotel in Germany.

* * * * *

"How'd you figure that out so fast, you little monkey?"

Ben grinned, exposing two brand-new incisors and a gap on either side of them. "It was easy," he said. He spent the next two minutes explaining to Parker how he'd pulled Holly's name up on the Internet.

Parker stared at the image of her beside her academic credentials. Ben had asked Parker about his book project, and about his coauthor too. But who knew a nine-year-old could pay such close attention and retain that much information? Grinning, Parker realized that he'd better be a lot more careful about what he told the boy from now on.

"She is quite beautiful, isn't she?"

"Yeah, she sure is."

"Very easy on the eyes," Dan agreed.

"What, exactly, is her most pronounced flaw, then?"

Parker didn't know which struck him hardest—that Ben had become so proficient at English since their time together in Afghanistan, or that Holly was anything short of perfect.

Dan asked the question swimming in Parker's head: "What makes you think there's something wrong with her?"

"Well, Granddad, according to her biography, she is thirty years old." He stared at Holly's image on the screen. "It would appear that she is ideal." Meeting Parker's eyes, he added, "But if that were true, would she not be married?"

Parker nearly blurted out how grateful he was that she *hadn't* married. If flaws were the reason, well, Parker was thankful for those too. He spent the next few minutes explaining how Holly had dedicated many years to pursuing a doctorate and many more to securing a position of respect among her peers. With a kid as savvy as this, it probably wasn't smart to tell Ben about her fiancé's death. "I'm glad she didn't find her Prince Charming. If she had, she wouldn't have been available when I needed help on my book."

And with my life.

"It seems to me," Ben said, shutting down the hotel's computer, "that you and she would both do well to consider marriage now." He shrugged. "While waiting for you to arrive, I happened to see an episode of Dr. Phil." He tapped his temple. "He is a very wise man."

Dan chuckled and Parker grinned.

"According to this man, this Dr. Phil, all children fare better in a two-parent household, but for a boy in my situation, two parents are even more important."

"A boy in your situation?"

"Yes, Granddad, coming from a country that is riddled with war and losing my own mother and father to—"

Parker wrapped him in a fierce hug and ruffled his thick, dark hair. The action accomplished three things. First, he just loved the boy to pieces and didn't want him dwelling on that awful part of his past. Second, he figured it couldn't hurt to show how much he cared, every chance he got. Last, in this position, Ben couldn't see his face. A kid that savvy would no doubt read his emotions as easily as he'd read Holly's bio…

…and know without a doubt that not only did Parker agree with every word, but that he intended to take his advice just as soon as possible.

* * * * *

Holly knew that the main reason it hadn't been even harder to say good-bye to her family was because she had plenty of work to keep her occupied. She'd spent days trolling the shops and malls for just the right things to decorate Ben's room. Finally, in a big-box department store, she found everything she'd been looking for.

She'd chosen the room farthest from Parker's for Ben, partly because it overlooked the ocean, and partly because, in a very few years, Ben would appreciate the added privacy provided by the room at the end of the hall. It took one day to paint the walls and another to give the baseboards and moldings a coat of bright white. At sunset on the eighth day, Holly stood in the doorway to admire striped curtains and plaid bed linens that exactly matched the blue-gray hue of the walls. She'd suspended a dozen model airplanes from fishing line tacked to the ceiling. On the dresser sat a replica of Apollo 13, while pedestal lamps—with shades that would glow with solar-system formations when turned on—stood on the night tables. She'd scoured the house for books that had anything to do with aeronautics and lined them up on the desk, where a Kitty Hawk–shaped lamp would illuminate Ben's homework. Then, the pièce de résistance, a shelf unit she'd found in the basement, where she'd tidily arranged board games, a yo-yo, a baseball and catcher's mitt, a small stereo and CDs, and a thirteen-inch color TV.

Maybe it was just as well that she hadn't thought to ask Ben's size, because filling the closet and dresser with jeans and shirts and sneakers was something Parker and his newly adopted son should do together.

When she finished Ben's room, Holly scrubbed the entire house. Stocked the fridge and pantry too. Having grown up with a bunch of burly boy cousins, she thought she knew what sort of meals and snacks a young boy would enjoy. It occurred to her that, having lived so long in a war zone, Ben's stomach might need time to adjust to mac and cheese, burgers and fries, and ice-cream sandwiches. But she bought them anyway...and hid them behind healthier, easier-to-digest foods so that Parker could introduce them into Ben's diet a little at a time.

With the house finished, Holly headed outside, where she weeded the flower beds—or what would have been flower beds, if Parker had planted things that bloomed. Three flats of easy-care plantings, purchased from the nearest nursery, brightened the walk and the foundation. Six hanging baskets, each glowing with bright blooms, hung from spinning hooks above the white picket porch rail. She dragged a few of the deck chairs around front and found that, with a coat of white paint, they looked very warm and welcoming, positioned on either side of the door that way. Then she unfurled Old Glory from where it had stood in a corner in the foyer and displayed it from the flag holder attached to a support post.

One more day and he'd be home. And one look at his handsome face would tell her if he understood she'd only tried to make the place warm and welcoming for Ben.

It was twilight when she locked up and started for the cottage. "Please God," she whispered, standing at the end of his walk, "let him like it."

It would cut her to the quick to have him think of her as some pushy, aggressive woman who was trying to invade his house, when all she really wanted was to capture his heart.

* * * * *

The moment he walked through the door, Holly could see the changes in him. As he introduced Ben to Hank, she remembered that first phone call from Germany, when he'd described the myriad questions and the stacks of papers he'd signed before taking custody of Ben. "What, they think he's a *spy*?" she'd joked. The moment of eerie silence told her what he couldn't: the authorities weren't taking any chances, even with a boy that young. She'd expected such worrisome things to have taken their toll, so her heart swelled with relief when, despite faint dark circles—evidence of the long flight and jet lag—his tense "looking into the sun" expression had been replaced by a calm, self-possessed smile. He stood taller too, as if he'd left the burdens of a lifetime on the other side of the Atlantic.

As for Ben, Holly had prepared herself to greet a shy, hollow-cheeked waif who'd cling fiercely to his new father. So it caught her completely off guard when he grinned the instant they made eye contact and then raced across the room to hug her with an intensity that belied his size. "How happy am I," he said, "to meet the beautiful Holly at last."

A sob choked off her voice. *Just as well*, Holly thought, since she wouldn't have known how to respond to his sweet greeting anyway. Over his head, her gaze met Parker's, and it surprised her to see tears in his eyes too. When he crossed the room to join them, she cringed inwardly, half expecting that all those hours in a cramped airline seat would exaggerate his limp. Instead, it was barely noticeable, and as he slid an arm around her shoulders, she said a silent prayer of thanks.

Parker ruffled Ben's thick, dark hair. "So, you gonna stand there all day, hugging the beautiful Holly, or would you like to see the rest of your home?"

"Oh, yes, it would be a delight to see it all." Halfway up the stairs, he stopped. "You will come too, yes?"

"Absolutely," Parker answered in her stead. And when she caught up to them, he mouthed, "Which room?"

"Up front," she said, her heart hammering—because in moments, she'd see for herself whether Ben thought she had a lick of interior-design talent.

Grinning, Parker announced, "First stop, Ben Brant's bedroom."

His big inky-brown eyes widened as they darted from the hanging planes to the bedside lamps and the toys and games lining the shelves. "I will sleep well here," he said, nodding.

As they moved from room to room, he asked questions about the furnishings and the people pictured in the framed photographs, about the purpose of each kitchen appliance, and why there were so many buttons on the TV's remote control. He gasped at the sight of Parker's extensive collection of DVDs, CDs, and books, and gasped again when Holly opened the refrigerator to fix them a light snack. "I hope you drew a map," he said once she joined them at the table.

Sadly, she knew exactly what he'd meant. "Half the fun of a new place is getting lost in it," she said, winking as she gave his hand a reassuring squeeze. "Tomorrow, when you wake up, you can pretend you're an explorer!"

"And if I *do* get lost," he said, grinning, "I will call out in a very loud voice, 'Dad, where am I?'"

While Ben aimed a few more questions at Parker about the microwave and the coffeemaker, Holly tried to memorize his charming accent. With television, school, everyday conversation…in very little time, he'd no longer over-pronounce every vowel, wouldn't accent every *T* or enunciate every syllable. The change would ensure his quick adjustment to the town where Southern hospitality echoed in every word that drawled from the mouths of the locals, but Holly missed his unique phraseology even before it was gone.

Now, with a full belly and the excitement of travel and seeing his new home behind him, Ben yawned and rubbed sleepy eyes. "Guess I'd better tuck him in," Parker said as they headed for the stairs.

"Good idea," she agreed.

"I hope you can stay, but if you have to go before I get back, I'll call you first thing in the morning."

"Yes," Ben said around a yawn, "unless I want to smell like the camels, I will need a change of clothing, and as my dad has said many times, we are in serious need of the woman's touch."

His invitation touched *Holly*. Laughing, she said, "I'll clean up in here. You guys just take your time."

An hour later, she quietly let herself out and locked the door behind her, and an hour after that, she was almost asleep when her cell phone rang.

"How will I ever thank you?"

Parker…

"I can't believe how much you accomplished in just ten days."

"I enjoyed it." *Every minute of it.*

He told her how Ben sat up in bed, pointing out all the little touches of welcome she'd given his room, before dropping off to sleep. She heard the weary edge in his voice, and although Holly needed to hear about their last day in Germany and the flight home, Parker needed his rest *more*. "I hate to be a party pooper," she said, faking a yawn, "but all your excitement has completely worn me out!"

"Yeah, I'm bushed too."

"Should I come over there in the morning to fix breakfast? Or would you two rather come here?"

"Here. Definitely. But let me call you when we're up and at 'em. I'm hoping Ben sleeps in a little."

"I'm hoping *you* sleep in a little."

"Yeah. That'd be nice."

"Sweet dreams, Parker."

"That's a given. Especially now."

Then he said good night, promised to call her in the morning, and hung up, leaving Holly to wonder if that last comment meant what she hoped it did.

* * * * *

It took each of them two trips to get everything from Parker's truck to Ben's room, and as he and Holly worked side by side, putting it all away, Ben gathered his school supplies and slid them into his new backpack, chattering about what his first day at school might be like. And then, suddenly, the prattle stopped.

Ben had fallen asleep on his bed.

"Poor kid," Holly said. "I can't even imagine what's going on in that adorable head of his."

Parker closed the closet door and walked out of the room, signaling Holly to follow. "I can't imagine what's going on in *your* head," he said in the kitchen. "You shopped and painted and baked casseroles and cleaned this place from stem to stern. What would possess you to ─ ?"

"Oh, there wasn't all that much to clean, really. I think your drill sergeant would be proud. Although…"

Parker sipped the lemonade she'd made yesterday. "Go ahead. Let me have it. I was a soldier. I can take it."

"Was?" She waved the retort away. "I thought it was just the marines who said 'Once a soldier, always a soldier.'"

"But you found an area of the house that wasn't shipshape."

Nodding, she said, "Tried to bounce a quarter off your bed." She shrugged and added, "*Thud.*"

"Well, there you have it," he said, laughing, "proof that I'm not—"

The phone rang, interrupting him. "—perfect," he finished, grabbing the handset. It was Maude's doctor, giving him a heads-up that she'd be released in a week. Sooner, if she passed her stair-climbing test tomorrow. *No time like the present,* Parker thought. He'd been wondering when it was safe to tell her that he'd met his dad…and his dad's family. That he'd gone to Germany and brought back the little Afghan boy he'd told her so much about.

"I see no reason why she can't handle all of that," the doctor said. "Her heart's in better shape now than it was ten years ago. If you want to err on the side of caution, tell her things on a need-to-know basis, a little at a time, and see how she reacts. But I'm confident she'll handle things well, at least physically."

"Will she need an in-home nurse?"

"A housekeeper, maybe, to help with the laundry, vacuuming, floor scrubbing—but she's actually better off getting back into her old routine as quickly as possible. She'll even be able to drive short distances, since she spent the first weeks of her recovery in the rehab center. Getting out and on her own will do wonders for her spirit. "

"What do you mean?"

"Depression is fairly common after heart surgery, and your mother has exhibited a few of the symptoms: lack of appetite, insomnia, very little interest in what's going on around her.... All perfectly normal, and in ninety-nine out of a hundred cases, it corrects itself once a person is home and surrounded by friends and family."

Unfortunately, I'm all Maude's got.

Parker thanked Dr. Williams then hung up and relayed the information to Holly.

"I'm right there if she needs anything," Holly assured him, "so you can focus on getting Ben settled in and adjusted to his new life."

She was here at least through August. But would she stay...if he asked her to? Parker's heart ached, just considering the possibility that she might not. "I know that, and I appreciate it."

Hours later, after she'd gone to the cottage with her typical "I need to make sure everything will be just so, when Maude gets home" statement, Parker checked his e-mail. It seemed rather anticlimactic, now that he had Ben with him and the adoption was final. But there were bound to be a pileup of turtle and lighthouse project messages that had gone unanswered while he was in Germany. So while Ben napped, Parker scrolled through the posts, deleting spam, replying, and saving those requiring research or additional information.

And then he spied one from a sender whose screen name he didn't recognize, and it said HOLLY in the subject line. The cursor hovered over the tiny cartoon envelope before he clicked the mouse and opened the file. Instantly, he knew who the sender had been. Sometime during the night Ben had awoken and decided that, rather than wake Parker, he'd fire up the laptop Holly had installed on his desk…and set himself up with an e-mail account. "IMProud-2BBrant" hadn't made a single typo or spelling error when he wrote:

"To the beautiful and kind doctor Holly, I ask you to consider marriage to my father. He needs a wife and I would appreciate a mother, and from this arrangement you would get two strong men to take care of you. I can see that my father cares for you, and I am fond of you as well. I hope you will consent." And it was signed, "Respectfully, Behnam H. Brant, aka Ben."

Chuckling, Parker read the P.S.: "The *H* is for *Hakim*, but in my heart, it stands for *Happy*."

His first instinct was to delete it. He put the message into his Drafts folder instead. Obviously he needed to have a talk with the boy even more than he needed a wife. After powering down the computer, he headed outside to get a better look at all the gardening Holly had done in his absence. When he'd left for Germany, the place had been reasonably orderly and organized, but she'd put her shine on everything. "From the mouths of babes," he muttered, his hands pocketed as he admired the homey touches she'd given the front porch.

Ben had thanked him for teaching him to speak English, for training that helped him survive the war-torn Afghan streets. But in this case, the boy had taught Parker a valuable lesson: because overthinking things often muddied the waters, it was sometimes better to speak from the heart.

And he'd do just that...all in good time.

Another wise saying came to mind as he returned to the kitchen: "Never put off until tomorrow what you can do today." He'd be wise to heed it, because the list of things he needed to tell the people he loved was growing longer by the minute.

Chapter Twenty-Three
....

Holly carried an empty box into the rehab center, thinking it might make things easier for Parker to get his mom home tomorrow if the cards, flowers, and plants were already packed up and gone. She'd just rounded the corner to Maude's room when Hank's angry voice stopped her.

"I've spent nearly six years walking on eggshells," he said, "and I can't do it a day longer. You need to make up your mind, Maudie, whether or not you want me in your life."

Holly held her breath. *Tell him you love him, Maude, before you lose him forever!*

"Seems I have a whole lot to be sorry for." Maude sighed. "Remember that old song...'You Always Hurt the One You Love'? Well, it seems that I've hurt a lot of people."

"Maybe that's because you *have* hurt a lot of people."

After a moment of silence, Maude said, "I'm sorry, Henry."

"Didn't come here for an apology. I just need to know where I stand."

She sighed again. "I can't believe what a mess I've made of my life."

"And Parker's. And Daniel's. And mine too, to some degree. But self-pity is what got you into this mess in the first place. I hate to be so hard on you, but it needs to be said."

"I won't argue with you."

"See? You're doing it again," he said roughly. Hank groaned. "You're a strong, capable woman, and that's just one of the reasons I love you, the way I've loved you almost from the day we met. You built up that B & B business single-handedly, and it kept the wolf from the door for you and your son. You're the last person who should need to resort to self-pity."

"But you know the truth about me, Henry. You've always known the truth."

"Is that it? Is that why you refuse to believe that I love you?"

"Yes," she said, her voice barely more than a whisper.

Holly heard a quiet rustling and suspected that it was Hank taking Maude in his arms.

"You've doubted yourself for so long, I guess it's only natural that you doubt me."

"It isn't your fault, Henry, that I built my life on a foundation of lies."

"Not your whole life, only the 'you were young and stupid' part."

Holly heard Maude's one-of-a-kind chuckle. "I guess God knew what He was doing, putting a hitch in this old ticker. It was scary, but if the heart attack hadn't happened, I don't know if I ever would have worked up the courage to tell Parker the truth."

"You know what your biggest problem is?"

Holly heard the smile in Maude's voice. "No, but I'm sure you're going to tell me."

"You bet I am. You're stubborn. And pigheaded. Obstinate and inflexible."

"Please don't make me sorry I gave you that thesaurus for your birthday last year...."

Laughing, Hank said, "Don't interrupt me when I'm on a roll, woman! What I'm trying to say is, you're a good woman, and if you *hadn't* been all those things, you would have 'fessed up decades ago. But knowing you, you told yourself to wait for the right time, a better time, and kept telling yourself that so often and for so long that eventually you told yourself that time would never come."

"It's true. All of it. I don't deserve a good man like you, loving me, but it seems you do, and—"

"There's no *seems* about it."

Another sigh, and then, "I love you too. And I always have."

"Then you'll marry me?"

"Goodness, Henry, I—I… When?"

"Neither of us is getting any younger, Maudie."

"That's true too. But I have a big mess to clean up, still, with Parker. Will you give me some time to make things right with him?"

"I've waited this long. Guess I can wait a little longer."

Holly heard rustling again, and then Hank said, "Well, I'd better get a move-on. I'm supposed to meet Parker on the dock."

"Good, he's sticking to his charter-boat routine. At least that didn't change after I upended his life."

Would Hank tell Maude that Parker and Ben were meeting Dan and his sons for an afternoon sail on the *Sea Stallion*?

"I think I'm gonna beg off. I have a little shopping to do."

For an engagement ring? Holly wondered. And then she realized that any minute now, Hank would step into the hall. What would he think when he saw her standing there outside Maude's door? *That you're an eavesdropper, that's what!*

She hurried toward the elevators, intent on going back down to the lobby until Hank left. As it was, he got the impression that she'd just arrived on Maude's floor. He gave her a sideways hug and then relieved her of the box. "If you brought this to pack up all Maudie's cares and woes, you can leave it for the maintenance crew."

It took some doing, but Holly managed to pretend she hadn't heard most, if not all, of their conversation. "Oh?"

He tossed the carton aside and gave her a big bear hug. "I asked her to marry me, and she said yes."

"That's wonderful, Hank, for both of you!"

He held her at arm's length. "I'm headed into town for a ring," he said as the elevator doors opened, "before she has a chance to change her mind." He stepped into the car and thumbed the DOWN button. "But don't you let on, you hear? Not even to Parker."

"Don't worry," she said, grabbing the box, "my lips are sealed."

"I'm betting that by month's end, you're gonna have a ring of your own."

Holly gasped. "A—a...*what*?"

"Can't think of a better way for him to convince you to stay," Hank said as the doors slid shut. "Can you?"

* * * * *

Parker spent the night tossing and turning and pacing the downstairs. He stood on the deck looking out to sea, trying to put together the conversation that had to take place between him and Maude—soon. The golden line signaling sunup had just started to glow on the horizon when he remembered Holly telling him that she'd always been an early riser but it wasn't until coming to Folly

Beach that sunrise became her favorite time of day. "I make a point now," she'd said, "to get up. Rain or shine, I want to be there, watching the new day dawn."

He grabbed the portable phone from the kitchen and dialed her number. "Hey," he said when she picked up, "are you out on the deck, watching the new day dawn?"

"Wow, what a memory," she said, the sound of her laughter making his heart race.

"I'm picking Maude up today, so I was wondering if you'd mind keeping an eye on Ben. Over here. Just until I get her settled in."

"I'd love to."

He heard the hesitation in her voice, and he knew what it meant. "You're probably wondering why I don't bring Ben to the cottage, so I can introduce him to his grandmother."

"I'll admit, that did cross my mind."

"I haven't told her about Ben yet. Well, not the part about the final adoption, anyway."

"But she knew why you went to Germany, right?"

"Yeah, but I haven't seen much of her since we got back." That sounded weird, even to himself, considering they'd come home more than a week ago. "I figure once she's back on familiar turf, I'll take Williams's advice and hit her with one thing at a time."

"Starting with Daniel and his family."

"Exactly. So maybe you could join Ben and me for breakfast, and afterward, I'll head for the rehab center. No rush. Long as I get her out of there by noon, they won't charge her for an additional day."

"No rush on your end, either. Getting back to your place, I mean. I'll take Ben for a nice long walk, maybe introduce him to the volunteers. He'd probably love pitching in to clear the beach for the turtles. Maybe I'll even pack us a lunch and we can eat it on—"

"I'm not planning on being over there anywhere near that long, so pack an extra sandwich. I'll find you, and we can eat together."

"So Ben's still asleep?"

"Yeah. He seems to be getting onto a pretty regular schedule."

"That'll be helpful once school starts."

Small talk. He hated it. Always had, always would. But since he had no idea how to broach the subject of how to break it to Maude that he'd met Daniel and the whole Brant clan, he didn't have much choice but to participate.

"So, okay, enough chitchat. You didn't just call to ask me to babysit, did you?"

If he married her, would she have more access to his thoughts, or less? Grinning, Parker said, "I just figured that since I'm socially inept, maybe you'd have some advice. You know, for how I might jump into the subject without causing another heart attack."

Holly laughed. "She isn't going to have another heart attack. Dr. Williams said so, right?"

"Right."

"Then relax."

"Easy for you to say."

"Actually, it *was*." She gave another giggle, and then she cleared her throat. "But seriously? My advice is, thank her for telling you the truth. She'll be shocked, because I'm sure it's the last thing she expects to hear. And that's when you can admit that if she hadn't spilled the beans, you never would have met Daniel. Or his mother and wife and kids."

Leave it to Holly to help him see that things really could be just that uncomplicated. "So what's your preference? Pancakes and sausage gravy, or bacon and eggs?"

"You're the chef. I'll leave that choice up to you."

"French toast it is, then."

"I'm touched—and tickled pink that you remembered!"

Without even thinking, he blurted out, "If I had half a brain, I'd marry you, before some other guy figures out how easy you are to please."

Holly didn't respond right away, and when she did, it was with, "Then I guess you should thank God."

"For what?"

"For giving you half a brain. See you in a half hour."

Thankfully, the phone's steady "Hang up the phone, stupid!" buzz sounded in his ear, or he might still have been staring at that same spot on the wall when she arrived.

* * * * *

"So when are we going to talk about it, son?"

"I haven't even pulled out of the parking lot yet. It can wait until I get you home."

"Will Holly be there?"

"No, she, ah, she had a few things to do. Down on the beach. With the turtle-project volunteers."

"The way she took to this place, you'd think that girl was born and raised here. Why, did you notice how she's picking up a bit of a Southern accent?"

Yes, Parker had noticed that.

"Did she tell you she stopped by yesterday with a big box?"

"What for?"

"To carry home all the plants and balloons people sent. Obviously, she overestimated the number of friends I have." She sighed. "All I've gotten are the things you brought six weeks ago and the book and spider plant from Opal. Thank God for her visits or I'd have had no company at all. Well, except for you and Henry. And Holly, of course."

Parker cringed inwardly. Every time he'd passed the hospital gift shop, he'd told himself to go in and grab another bouquet of flowers or a box of candy. Something to brighten her room and say what he'd been too angry to say: "Get well, because I love you."

"Thank God for Hank, eh?"

"Yes. Thank God."

He would have sworn she'd sighed like a love-struck schoolgirl. "At least you have one thoughtful man in your life."

No response, unless he counted that second giddy sigh.

"He isn't my boyfriend."

"You can say that until you're blue in the face, but it won't change the fact that he's crazy about you." *Not that I'll ever understand it, the way you run him around...*

"He's my fiancé."

Parker braked for the red light and looked over at her. "Your *what*?"

"Yesterday. He asked me yesterday."

"And you said yes."

The light turned green, and he thanked God for peripheral

vision. Without it, who knows how long he might have sat there gap-mouthed and gawking.

"And I said yes."

Well, wonders never ceased. Parker didn't know what he'd do when next he saw Hank, congratulate him…or console him. "Did you two set a date?"

"Not yet. I want to make sure things are okay between us first."

Good grief. She reminded him of a sappy teenage girl sometimes. "Why'd you say yes if things aren't okay between you?"

"Not between Henry and me. Between *you* and me."

"We're okay."

"Parker…"

"What can I say? You're my mother. Nothing will ever change that."

"'You can say that until you're blue in the face,'" she quoted, "but it won't change the fact that I hurt you."

You hurt Daniel too, he said. And without even intending to, she'd hurt his dad's entire family. And Hank, Holly, and Ben too. "Look, we'll be at the cottage in a minute. Holly made a surprise for you. Once you've seen it and gushed appropriately, then we can hammer at this some more." He glanced at her. "Okay?"

"Okay."

"Aren't you curious to know what Holly did?"

"Oh, knowing her, she baked me a cheesecake. Or made a pan of lasagna. She has a way of finding out what a person's favorite things are, all without ever giving a hint that's what she's doing."

He hadn't thought to ask if Holly had prepared a meal or a dessert. He wouldn't put it past her. But Parker didn't think anything edible could compare with all the work she'd put in to moving Maude's room to the first floor of the cottage.

"I'll bet whatever it is, it's delicious," Maude said. "She's amazing, that Holly."

Yeah. She was amazing, all right. "I don't know as I'd call it delicious, exactly, but then, you women have a strange way of describing things sometimes."

When Maude finally saw the room, it took ten minutes for her crying jag to end. And when it did, she was in such an upbeat mood that Parker hated to darken it by dredging up the past.

Maude took care of that for him, and for the next half hour, she talked and cried and cried and talked, vowing to spend the rest of her days making things up to him. Parker remembered Holly's advice and realized he couldn't have asked for a better opening.

And so he took it. He told Maude about his first meeting with Dan and how, right from the get-go, he'd accepted Parker as his own and then introduced him to the rest of the Brants. Maude took it well. Far better than he could have imagined, so Parker went for broke and told her about Ben too.

"So I'm a grandmother?"

Her voice rang with awe and gratitude, and for a minute there, Parker worried that the waterworks might start up again. Instead, she said the word a half dozen times. "What fits me better—Gran? Grams? Gramma?"

"You could always let Ben choose."

"When do I get to meet him?"

"Right now, if you like. He's on the beach with Holly, working with the turtle volunteers. She packed a lunch, but I can whip up an extra sandwich."

Maude loved the idea and said so.

It seemed they'd buried the hatchet...except for one irksome detail. "Can I ask you one question, before putting this ugly business behind us?" At least if he had anything to say about it. He took her silence to mean that it was all right to ask the question. "What's my last name?"

She looked startled. Sounded surprised too, when she said, "Why it's Brant, of course."

"But if you and Dan never married—"

"I don't know what the laws are about such things these days, but back then, all I had to do was spell my name for a nice lady with a clipboard and tell her who your father was. That's all she wanted, so I didn't see much point in answering questions she hadn't asked."

He felt a huge weight begin to lift from his heart. "So the name on my birth certificate—and my driver's license and passport—it's legal."

"Completely."

It never occurred to him before to ask why she'd chosen his first name. "So why Parker, of all the names in the baby book?"

A strange, whimsical smile lit her face. "There I was, young and naive and...I mean, really, if I had any brains at all, would I have let myself get into a fix like that?" She waved the question away. "I'd lived with my grandparents for years by then, but they were barely making ends meet themselves. So I knew I'd have to get a second job, maybe a third. But I was about as dumb as a box of rocks, and that scared me."

Her voice trailed off, and tears shimmered in her eyes as she said, "Then, about a month before you were born, Gran and Gramps died in that awful pileup on Route 30, and I felt like a babe in the woods, lost and alone, wondering how I'd keep a roof over your head and food in your belly. And then you were born and looked up at me with those big brown eyes, and I felt like I'd found my way out of those scary woods. You saved me. So I named you Parker, because it means Keeper of the Woods."

She smiled across the table at him, erasing any doubt Parker might have had about her love for him. "I know I shouldn't have kept the truth from you. I was just so ashamed, bringing you into the world that way. I promised myself to tell you when you were old enough. And that day, when you were about eight, and you marched up to me and announced that you weren't a baby..." A sob choked off her words.

He remembered that day only too well. She'd never given him a straight answer where his father was concerned, and in his little-boy head, he figured that was because she thought he couldn't handle knowing that his father had died. He'd been ripe for the picking when he saw the news broadcast honoring an Air Force pilot, who was killed when the fighter jet he'd been testing ran into a flock of geese. His wife and daughter had looked straight into the camera and said that yes, they'd miss him, but they were proud to know he'd given his life for his country. He'd gone straight to Maude with the story, and when he followed it with, "I'm not a baby. You can tell me the truth," she'd shut herself up in her room. Hours later she came out, red-eyed and sniffling, and he took it to mean that Daniel really had died a similar death. He'd never forget that she'd let him go a lifetime, telling schoolmates and army buddies that his father had died a hero. Would never forget the succession of lies—the ones she'd told outright and those of omission—but if he ever hoped to take a deep breath again, Parker had to put it behind him.

And the only way to do that was to forgive her.

He got to his feet and walked around to her side of the table. "Call Hank," he said, kissing her cheek, "and set the date. You and I are okay."

Would he ever trust her again?

Possibly. But that didn't matter. What mattered were the two people in the house down the beach, where colorful flowers now bloomed and Old Glory snapped from its new home on the front porch.

Chapter Twenty-Four
....

Sunday dinner at his grandmother's house was like nothing Parker had ever experienced. He'd seen more food in one place at one time...but only at restaurant buffets. From one end of the long table to the other, big bowls of steaming side dishes surrounded a platter of juicy roast beef. Isabel insisted that Parker sit on one side of her, with Ben on the other, and despite their protests at displacing his dad and Parker's eldest brother, that's precisely where they ended up.

"Better enjoy it while you can," joked Bob Jr. "I'm not normally this generous."

Every Brand seemed genuinely interested in tightening Parker's ties to the family. They took turns asking questions about his military service, his charter-boat business, his house on the Folly Beach coast. They wanted to know about Ben's trip to Germany and how he liked his new room. They asked if he enjoyed working with the turtle and lighthouse projects...and how he felt about the marine biologist from Baltimore who was helping Parker write a book about it all. Ben summed it up in one sentence: "The only way I could be happier here in America with my new father is if Holly could become my new mother."

297

Good-natured taunts and dares rose up from just about every-one at Isabel's table. Bets were made on when Parker would voice the question, and each was countered with the hope that Holly would say yes when he did.

All that took place in this wonderful and welcoming family atmosphere, yet no one seemed the least bit interested in Maude. Parker chalked that up to good manners and respect for his step-mother. As the child who'd been the result of the brief, long-ago relationship, his very existence would tie Dan to the past—and to Maude—forever. Ann and Dan had built a beautiful life, and their reward had been three kids and three grandchildren. In a few months, when his sister's baby girl was born, the total number of lives impacted by Maude's lies would number thirteen. Remark-ably, not one held Parker accountable for her harmful secrets and deceptions.

Already, he felt that he fit right in, and surrounded by such loving acceptance made him feel sorry for Maude, who had never known anything like this, not before her parents died, and not after she was sent to live with her grandparents. All things considered, she'd done pretty well by him, and for some reason, that realiza-tion sparked an idea: with Holly as his life partner, *they* could build something like this and give Maude and Ben—and Hank—the gift of belonging to a big, happy family too.

The concept began to take shape as the Brants laughed and talked over coffee and his sister's famous cheesecake, and it became even clearer as the men and boys boarded the *Sea Stallion* for an afternoon sail off Charleston's coast. He'd never seen Ben happier or more animated. He'd thank his dad and brothers for that later. For now, Parker simply enjoyed watching the boy behave like a child who knows he's loved and free—and *safe*—ought to.

He overheard Ben telling Dan about the little message boat that had washed ashore during Hurricane Hugo. "I would like to write on it too," Ben said, nodding enthusiastically. "I would use the reddest red and the bluest blue paint."

"Is that so?" Dan said, slinging an arm over the boy's slender shoulders. "And what would you paint?"

Ben demonstrated his painting technique, hands and arms gesturing enthusiastically. "'Ben Brant is a proud American!'"

Parker had felt "my heart is bursting with pride" emotions every time he saluted Old Glory or watched fellow soldiers standing at attention as medals were pinned to their chests. But until now, he'd never experienced it for completely personal reasons, and it made him gladder than ever that he hadn't given up on his promise to bring Ben home. His "build a family" idea took on an additional facet as he pictured the boat.

"Make sure to protect your toes when you do it," Parker's youngest brother advised, "because I hear that old tub has been decorated so much that thick layers of paint fall off in big chunks."

Ben stared at his sneakered feet. "Okay, Joe," he said, grinning when he looked up, "I will watch out for my toes."

Only one thing could have made these moments more special: Holly, standing beside him. Because Ben needed her almost as much as Parker did.

Almost.

* * * * *

A soft August wind riffled Holly's hair as she faced the Atlantic. It was still warm enough to walk barefoot on the beach, and she was determined to do it as often as possible before the sad and inevitable happened and she had to aim her little convertible north to Baltimore.

She'd thought of little else besides Parker's kiss—or, more accurately, the way he'd returned *her* kiss—because it roused so many conflicting emotions and questions.

Her reaction was all the proof she needed that she'd finally reached a place of peaceful acceptance of Jimmy's death, and it stirred newfound joy, because that kiss was the closest Parker had come to admitting his feelings for her. But how deep did those feelings *go*? He'd never been one to beat around the bush, so if he loved her, wouldn't he have said so straight-out?

She'd given him the benefit of the doubt, blaming his on again–off again displays of affection on bad romantic experiences of his past…getting Ben to America safe and sound… and on his mother's worrisome health and the shocking confession it inspired. But Ben had blended into Parker's world as if he'd been born to it, just as Parker had melded with the Brants, and Maude was out of danger and contentedly planning her wedding.

Flustered, Holly kicked the sand. She was a grown-up, so why was she behaving like a silly teenager who was too shy to admit that she'd developed a crush on a cute boy in study hall? She'd been on her own for years, making big-girl decisions that earned the respect of scientists and educators, friends and family. She'd earned her own respect too, working her way through school and securing a position that allowed her to live on her own and come and go as she pleased. So where was it written that the decision about her future with Parker was his and his alone?

The answer, unfortunately, was all wrapped up in fear and uncertainty. Because what if she laid her cards on the table and admitted that she loved him...

...and he didn't feel the same way?

That would hurt almost as much as losing Jimmy had, that's what.

Bending, Holly picked up a stone rounded by the unrelenting surf. She identified with it just a little bit, because the ebb and flow of life itself had smoothed her rough edges too. If she left here next week never knowing whether or not Parker loved her too...? She'd be hurt—and disappointed. And she'd probably always wonder *what if....* "But you aren't going to *die,* for heaven's sake."

She had a wonderful family—and because of Maude's confession, a new appreciation for every single one of them—and a fulfilling job. Before leaving for Folly Beach, she'd finished decorating her Ellicott-City town house exactly the way she liked it. She loved her sporty little convertible, even if, as her cousins pointed out, it was impractical in the wintertime. And she'd been blessed with good health. Every woman, she supposed, needed a "one who got away" story. Holly tossed the stone back into the Atlantic. "And now you've got yours."

She'd completed her final edits on the book he'd titled *Folly Beach: The Edge of America,* and once Parker gave the manuscript his stamp of approval, they'd type "The End" on the last page and send it off to his New York editor. With a final tally of nearly forty nests producing nearly four thousand hatchlings, the turtles' migration was over. Holly's work here was mere days from ending, and when it did, so would her reasons for staying in Folly Beach.

Baltimore was where she'd been born and raised, so why did this quaint little town feel so much like home to her?

Holly could answer that one with one word: Parker.

She *could* lay it all out there—confess her love and force him to say yea or nay to a future together. But with all he'd been through, with all he'd continue going through in the next weeks and months, Holly loved him too much to add to his burdens. Besides, if God had intended for the two of them to be together, wouldn't He have shown them a sign by now?

Instead, she'd rely on Him to provide her with all the strength she'd need to remember this summer—and the very special man who'd touched her heart—with warmth and fondness. It wouldn't be easy, getting through these next few days, but with God to guide her, she'd do it. And Holly knew exactly how she'd start—once she secured Parker's permission to borrow his kitchen and dining room. If everything went well, maybe she'd give *him* something to remember about her summer in Folly Beach too.

Chapter Twenty-Five

....

Holly figured the Brants had a right to some private moments, considering the newness of it all, but that didn't stop her from wondering why, in one minute, Parker seemed off in a world of his own, and in the next, he and one of his siblings were off in a corner, whispering. And why did they all look so…so *odd* when she caught them at it?

They gathered around Parker's dining room table, eating and chatting and laughing like they'd been doing it all their lives. It felt good, seeing them together this way, and it would be another beautiful scene she could remember once she returned to her life in Baltimore.

She'd baked a ham and made all the trimmings, using generations-old recipes handed down from both sides of her family. Holly knew the meal was a success when Parker's stepmother, sister, and sisters-in-law all asked if she'd share the instructions for each dish.

It seemed odd, celebrating without Maude and Hank, but Holly had a feeling that, in time, even they'd be included in this warm family circle. It was definitely something she intended to pray for—not only for Maude's sake, but for Parker's as well.

Hours after the table had been cleared and the dishes were done, Daniel suggested going to the beach for coffee and a second round of dessert. While the adults carried things down from the deck, Dan and his grandchildren combed the sand for driftwood and produced a bright, hand-warming fire.

Holly had just handed a toasted marshmallow to Ben when Parker said to her, "How about taking a boat ride with me?"

"Just me?"

"Just you."

She glanced around at the smirking faces of his family. Why didn't they seem to be surprised that he'd asked her to go off with him and leave them without a host or hostess? "But what about—"

"Don't worry about us," his dad said. "We aren't shy. If we need anything, we'll help ourselves."

Every Brant, from the eldest to the youngest, snickered and chorused their agreement.

"Why do I get the feeling there's a conspiracy afoot?" she teased as Parker led her toward the pier.

A smattering of giggles was her only answer.

"I have to admit, it's a lovely night for a cruise, but it just seems odd…and a little rude, if you don't mind my saying—"

He handed her a life jacket then fired up the boat's motor. "I don't mind a bit."

"Where are we going?"

"Not far. I have something to show you." He winked over at her. "Trust me."

They motored for a few minutes, and then Parker eased the *Sea Maverick* alongside a weathered old wharf and tied off. He jumped onto the dock and held out one hand to her, and Holly gladly took it. *One more scene for the memory book...*

Behind him, the dim glow of lantern light created a tiny, sunny halo above a small table. On one side of it was a sheet-covered easel, and on the other, a white Adirondack chair.

"So that's where the missing chair went!" One hand on her hip, Holly said, "But I don't get it. Why did you—"

He slid a shiny silver package from under the table and handed it to her. "Sit," he said, gesturing toward the chair, "and open it."

"Parker, I don't understa—"

"Humor me," he said, holding up a hand, traffic-cop style. Then he slid a cooler from under the table and withdrew two long-stemmed goblets and a bottle of sparkling water. He filled the first glass and, holding the bottle aloft, said, "Well, what are you waiting for?"

Heaving a huge sigh, Holly sat down. Holding the bread box–sized package, she gave it a little shake. "Animal, vegetable, or mineral?"

"No hints," he said, filling the second goblet. "Just get busy."

She loosed another sigh then untied the enormous white-satin bow. "This is goofy, Parker. It isn't my birthday or—"

Eyes narrowed, he raised one brow, and the silent warning made her giggle and get back to work. Inside the outer box she found a smaller one, wrapped exactly the same way, and in it, a third. Then a fourth, until she found one the size of a paperback novel. *Well,* she thought, lifting it from its tissue-paper bed, *it isn't an engagement ring. Those always come in little square boxes.*

Right?

The admission shouldn't have disappointed her, but it did. Maybe he'd bought her a gift certificate, a thank-you for all the work she'd done on the book. And then as she removed the lid, she remembered their agreement: he'd pay her at the end of summer, using advance monies paid by his publisher. The box was the perfect size and shape to hold a check.

Swallowing another bit of disappointment, she started digging through the tissue paper inside. But Parker grabbed her hands and stopped her.

"That's far enough. For now." He put the boxes onto the table, one at a time, and pulled her to her feet. "This," he said, turning her to face the easel, "is for you." And then he whipped off the sheet and exposed a portrait of them, side by side aboard his boat, with the bright June sunset behind them.

She stepped closer to get a better look. Had he enlarged the photograph the Davises had taken of them that day during the comical three-hour tour? No, she discovered as her finger slid down the canvas, this was a painting. And upon closer inspection, she saw his signature in the lower right-hand corner.

Straightening, she looked into his eyes. "Parker, when did you have time to paint this? Your life has been pure chaos lately—"

"I worked on it nights when I couldn't sleep...."

No doubt there had been plenty of those, what with Maude's emergency surgeries, all he'd gone through to get Ben to America, and then finding out he had a father and a whole big loving family.

"...for thinking about you."

Then he produced a flashlight from inside the cooler and led her farther up the beach.

"Oh, wow, it's that cute little boat," she said, grinning. "I've never been this close to it before." She grabbed the flashlight and started reading out loud: "CLASS OF '92 ROCKS! JULIE AND TIMMY 4-EVER. MARTY 'HEARTS' VALERIE." She giggled. "And look at this one." She stepped closer. "Why, it's so fresh, you can still smell the paint!"

"Really. What's it say?"

"It just says 'MARRY ME.' Aw, that's so sad."

"Sad?"

She nodded. "The writer didn't even have the confidence to add the person's name." Holly thought she knew how the message-writer felt *exactly.* "I sure hope whomever wrote it gets the answer she wants. Or he. Whichever…"

"Yeah. Me too." Then he took her hand and guided her back to the chair.

And like an obedient and very confused child, Holly sat, her heart pounding like a parade drum as he got onto one knee in front of her. The last time—the only other time he'd done this— Parker had kissed her like she'd never been kissed. Holly didn't know if she could survive a second one, knowing that, day after tomorrow, there wouldn't be a third.

But instead of kissing her, Parker rummaged through the tissue in the box and withdrew a ring. "I know it'll fit," he said, "because I took the liberty of poking through your jewelry box one afternoon while you were visiting Maude at the rehab center. I borrowed one of your rings so I'd be sure to get the right size."

Gently, he took her left hand in his and held the ring between his right thumb and forefinger. "Put this on," he said, turning it right and left so that it reflected the silvery beams of the moon, before giving a nod toward the painting, "and you can have that for a wedding gift."

"This? I—I..." She couldn't decide what to look at, the boat with its semi-cryptic message, the beautiful painting, the glittering ring, or Parker's handsome, loving face. "You're...are you? Is this a—"

Tears filled her eyes as her lower lip began to tremble. She'd already packed her suitcases and made up her mind to go home. Gassed up the car and everything, so she'd be ready to hit the road running, back to her job at the university and her humble town house, where she'd try her level best to keep a rational perspective on every magical moment that made up this, the best summer of her life.

"I know it's asking a lot. I'm a mess. My life is a mess. This whole 'surprise, you have a big family' thing, and Maude, and Ben..."

He'd completely misunderstood the reason for her hesitation. For her tears too. If she could only find her voice, she'd explain that none of those things mattered, that—

"...but I promise you, Holly," he continued, "it's temporary. All of it. I'll get a handle on all that. But I'll have a lot more incentive to do it faster with you at my side."

She thought of all the endings so recently crossed off her to-do list and, still unable to speak past the sob in her throat, Holly nodded and smiled and threw herself into his arms...

...and knocked him flat on his back in the sand.

Laughing and crying at the same time, she tried to apologize, but Parker stopped her with one finger pressed over her lips. "I couldn't have orchestrated a more fitting beginning to 'us,'" he said. Taking her in his arms, he added, "Holly Folly, will you do me the honor of becoming my wife?"

"Parker Brant, you are the answer to my prayers. Of *course* I'll marry you!"

She dotted his face with kisses, pausing only to ask, "What took you so long?"

About the Author

....

With more than 3 million of her books in circulation, Loree has 82 books (three optioned for movies), 67 short stories, and more than 2,500 articles in print. Dubbed by reviewers "a writer whose stories touch hearts and change lives," she has earned hundreds of Readers' Choice and industry awards. Loree will add five more titles to her list before the fall of 2012.

When she isn't writing, you can find her in the kitchen (cooking up things that explain her lifetime Weight Watchers membership), the garden (killing any bug that crosses her path), painting/sketching (one of her pen-and-ink drawings hangs in the home of actress Lea Thompson), and reading *other* authors' books. You can read her "writerly rantings" at www.theloughdown.blogspot.com and in her monthly column, "Loree's Lough Down" (*Christian Fiction Online Magazine*).

Loree and her husband split their time between a little house in the Baltimore suburbs and a *really* little cabin in the Allegheny Mountains. She loves to hear from her readers and personally answers every letter sent to www.loreelough.com.

Love Finds You in Sisters, Oregon
by Melody Carlson
ISBN: 978-1-935416-18-0

Love Finds You in Charm, Ohio
by Annalisa Daughety
ISBN: 978-1-935416-17-3

*Love Finds You in
Bethlehem, New Hampshire*
by Lauralee Bliss
ISBN: 978-1-935416-20-3

Love Finds You in North Pole, Alaska
by Loree Lough
ISBN: 978-1-935416-19-7

Love Finds You in Holiday, Florida
by Sandra D. Bricker
ISBN: 978-1-935416-25-8

*Love Finds You in
Lonesome Prairie, Montana*
by Tricia Goyer and Ocieanna Fleiss
ISBN: 978-1-935416-29-6

Love Finds You in Bridal Veil, Oregon
by Miralee Ferrell
ISBN: 978-1-935416-63-0

*Love Finds You in Hershey,
Pennsylvania*
by Cerella D. Sechrist
ISBN: 978-1-935416-64-7

Love Finds You in Homestead, Iowa
by Melanie Dobson
ISBN: 978-1-935416-66-1

Love Finds You in Pendleton, Oregon
by Melody Carlson
ISBN: 978-1-935416-84-5

*Love Finds You in
Golden, New Mexico*
by Lena Nelson Dooley
ISBN: 978-1-935416-74-6

Love Finds You in Lahaina, Hawaii
by Bodie Thoene
ISBN: 978-1-935416-78-4

*Love Finds You in
Victory Heights, Washington*
by Tricia Goyer and Ocieanna Fleiss
ISBN: 978-1-60936-000-9

Love Finds You in Calico, California
by Elizabeth Ludwig
ISBN: 978-1-60936-001-6

Love Finds You in Sugarcreek, Ohio
by Serena B. Miller
ISBN: 978-1-60936-002-3

*Love Finds You in
Deadwood, South Dakota*
by Tracey Cross
ISBN: 978-1-60936-003-0

*Love Finds You in
Silver City, Idaho*
by Janelle Mowery
ISBN: 978-1-60936-005-4

*Love Finds You in
Carmel-by-the-Sea, California*
by Sandra D. Bricker
ISBN: 978-1-60936-027-6

*Love Finds You
Under the Mistletoe* by Irene
Brand and Anita Higman
ISBN: 978-1-60936-004-7

Love Finds You in Hope, Kansas
by Pamela Griffin
ISBN: 978-1-60936-007-8

Love Finds You in Sun Valley, Idaho
by Angela Ruth
ISBN: 978-1-60936-008-5

*Love Finds You in
Camelot, Tennessee*
by Janice Hanna
ISBN: 978-1-935416-65-4

*Love Finds You in
Tombstone, Arizona*
by Miralee Ferrell
ISBN: 978-1-60936-104-4

Love Finds You in
Martha's Vineyard, Massachusetts
by Melody Carlson
ISBN: 978-1-60936-110-5

Love Finds You in
Prince Edward Island, Canada
by Susan Page Davis
ISBN: 978-1-60936-109-9

Love Finds You in Groom, Texas
by Janice Hanna
ISBN: 978-1-60936-006-1

Love Finds You in Amana, Iowa
by Melanie Dobson
ISBN: 978-1-60936-135-8

Love Finds You in
Lancaster County, Pennsylvania
by Annalisa Daughety
ISBN: 978-1-60936-212-6

Love Finds You in Branson, Missouri
by Gwen Ford Faulkenberry
ISBN: 978-1-60936-191-4

Love Finds You
in Sundance, Wyoming
by Miralee Ferrell
ISBN: 978-1-60936-277-5

Love Finds You on
Christmas Morning
by Debby Mayne and Trish Perry
ISBN: 978-1-60936-193-8

Love Finds You in
Sunset Beach, Hawaii
by Robin Jones Gunn
ISBN: 978-1-60936-028-3

Love Finds You in
Nazareth, Pennsylvania
by Melanie Dobson
ISBN: 97-8-160936-194-5

Love Finds You in
Annapolis, Maryland
by Roseanna M. White
ISBN: 978-1-60936-313-0

COMING SOON

Love Finds You in
New Orleans, Louisiana
by Christa Allan
ISBN: 978-1-60936-591-2

Love Finds You in
Wildrose, North Dakota
by Tracey Cross
ISBN: 978-1-60936-592-9

Love Finds You in Daisy, Oklahoma
by Janice Hanna
ISBN: 978-1-60936-593-6

Love Finds You in Sunflower, Kansas
by Pamela Tracy
ISBN: 978-1-60936-594-3

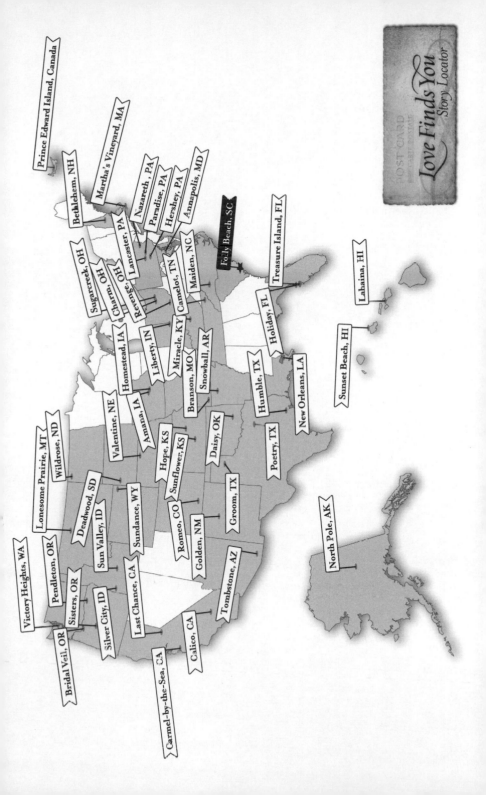

Love Finds You
Story Locator

POST CARD

Prince Edward Island, Canada
Bethlehem, NH
Martha's Vineyard, MA
Nazareth, PA
Paradise, PA
Hershey, PA
Annapolis, MD
Lancaster, PA
Sugarcreek, OH
Charm, OH
Revenge, OH
Folly Beach, SC
Camelot, TN
Maiden, NC
Treasure Island, FL
Homestead, IA
Liberty, IN
Miracle, KY
Holiday, FL
Lahaina, HI
Branson, MO
Snowball, AR
Sunset Beach, HI
Valentine, NE
Amana, IA
Humble, TX
New Orleans, LA
Lonesome Prairie, MT
Wildrose, ND
Hope, KS
Poetry, TX
Daisy, OK
Deadwood, SD
Sunflower, KS
Sun Valley, ID
Sundance, WY
Romeo, CO
Groom, TX
North Pole, AK
Victory Heights, WA
Pendleton, OR
Silver City, ID
Last Chance, CA
Golden, NM
Sisters, OR
Bridal Veil, OR
Carmel-by-the-Sea, CA
Calico, CA
Tombstone, AZ